"These children have been through so much. I wish I could track down the father and get things sorted out for them. They deserve to know where they belong."

"And feel safe," Sadie added.

"Agreed." Logan's gaze caught hers and held it so firmly she couldn't look away. At the way he regarded her, the strength and goodness she saw in him and knew existed, her heart lifted. He lifted a hand to her cheek and brushed his fingers along the side of her face. "We will work together to make sure these children are safe."

She leaned into his hand. Beth's words reverberated inside her head. *Too soon.* Slowly she turned her head, forcing him to pull his hand back even though it was the hardest thing she had done in some time.

Not only was it too soon to think about opening up her heart to him.

It would always be too soon.

Linda Ford lives on a ranch in Alberta, Canada, near enough to the Rocky Mountains that she can enjoy them on a daily basis. She and her husband raised fourteen children—four homemade, ten adopted. She currently shares her home and life with her husband, a grown son, a live-in paraplegic client and a continual (and welcome) stream of kids, kids-in-law, grandkids, and assorted friends and relatives.

Books by Linda Ford

Love Inspired Historical

Big Sky Country

Montana Cowboy Daddy
Montana Cowboy Family

Montana Cowboys

The Cowboy's Ready-Made Family
The Cowboy's Baby Bond
The Cowboy's City Girl

Christmas in Eden Valley

A Daddy for Christmas
A Baby for Christmas
A Home for Christmas

Journey West

Wagon Train Reunion

Montana Marriages

Big Sky Cowboy
Big Sky Daddy
Big Sky Homecoming

Visit the Author Profile page at Harlequin.com for more titles.

LINDA FORD

Montana Cowboy Family

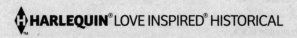

HARLEQUIN® LOVE INSPIRED® HISTORICAL

Recycling programs
for this product may
not exist in your area.

LOVE INSPIRED BOOKS

ISBN-13: 978-0-373-42506-8

Montana Cowboy Family

www.Harlequin.com

Printed in U.S.A.

For the Lord gives wisdom; from his mouth come knowledge and understanding.
—*Proverbs* 2:6 (NIV)

I dedicate this book to my dear friend Brenda, who daily faces difficult things but does so with unfailing dignity and grace. She'd be the first one to say it's because of God's sufficiency and her dependence on Him.

Chapter One

Bella Creek, Montana, 1890

Logan Marshall stared at the place where he'd left his lunch. The sack was gone. The second day in a row. Stolen. The muscles in his jaw bunched. Nothing bothered him worse than any form of dishonesty. His stomach rumbled. How could he work without food to fuel his strength? And Grandfather would expect Logan to be working. The school wasn't finished. As a Marshall and grandson of the founder of Bella Creek, Logan had to do his share and had been assigned the task of rebuilding the schoolhouse. It, along with all the buildings in that block, had burned to the ground during the winter.

Following the fire, the doctor and teacher had left, requiring the town and the Marshalls to find replacements. The doctor's residence and office had been rebuilt already and Logan glanced at the new building next door where Dr. Baker and his daughter, Kate, lived and worked. Kate had brought her friend, Isabelle Redfield, with her, and Isabelle had since married Logan's brother, Dawson.

He shifted his attention across the street to his uncle's mercantile store. The new teacher, Sadie Young, presently held classes in the back room of the store, but every day she crossed to her living quarters in the rear of the schoolhouse. Grandfather had decided her rooms should be finished before completing the classroom, saying it wasn't suitable for her to continue living in the hotel.

Daily, as she made her way from the store, she stopped to see how much progress had been made on the rebuilding. He understood she was in a hurry to have her students moved into the school, but he couldn't rush the work if he wanted it done right.

Besides those daily visits, he'd met her several times since she had come to Bella Creek with the others. Sadie Young was about his age with brown hair, a perfect oval face, hazel eyes like late-summer leaves, and healthy-looking skin. Not a bad-looking woman, but she was so shy he wondered how she managed to teach. Something about her shyness triggered a protective note in him, which he managed to quell.

He wasn't interested in her for any reason. He might be only twenty-two, but he had learned enough lessons about women to last a lifetime and to make him completely wary of them. He rocked his head back and forth. Once he'd been enamored of a woman he considered to be ideal. She'd seemed so sweet and innocent. He'd been shocked to learn she had questionable morals. She'd teased him into following her to the nearby rough town of Wolf Hollow, where he'd thought he could protect her, but he ended up trapped by his shame and her continued deceit. Learning that his ma lay on her deathbed had brought him home, and he'd promised Ma he'd never fall into such a trap again. Later, after Ma's death, when Logan was what he considered to be a mature eighteen-year-old, he met a woman and her daughter when they moved into the boardinghouse. The girl seemed like a gentle young lady. She went to church with him and attended the family dinners. But it turned out she was part of a gang and was setting up a robbery. Worse, even, she was married to one of the robbers.

He figured it would take a lot for him to ever again trust a woman. Even more for him to trust his own judgment.

His experience was enough to make him look at Miss Young with a certain guardedness. But never mind Miss Young. Logan had to find his lunch before the thief ate it all. He eased around the schoolhouse, eyes sweeping the area for clues. A flash of material behind the stack of lumber at the back of the lot caught his attention. He eased forward. What kind of robber stopped so close to the scene of his crime?

He edged around the corner of the lumber pile, his muscles tensed to spring forward, but at the sight of a little boy opening up Logan's lunch sack, he ground to a halt, his anger completely gone. This was one of Miss Young's students. What was the child doing over here when he should be in the classroom with the other children?

The boy looked up, saw that he was discovered and stuffed the sack behind his back. He considered Logan with wide brown eyes, doing his best to look innocent.

Logan took a moment studying the boy. He had on overalls so thin you could spit through them. There was a button missing on his shirt. His dark blond hair was in sore need of a cut. Logan didn't recognize the child. There must be a new family in the area he hadn't heard of.

"I think you have my lunch," he said in a slow, lazy drawl.

The boy's thin shoulders came forward. He twisted his hands palms upward as if to prove he had nothing.

Was there anything sadder than a hungry boy? His own hunger gnawed at his stomach. He lowered himself to the ground, his back to the lumber. The boy drew his legs closer to his body and watched Logan.

Logan saw how tense the boy was. "What's your name?"

"Sammy."

"Got a last name?"

"Sammy Weiss."

"Howdy. I'm Logan Marshall." He stretched his legs out. "Guess you're as hungry as me. Think we could share the lunch?"

Sammy waited, and when he realized Logan wasn't giving up, he pulled the sack from behind him and handed it to Logan, his eyes never leaving the promise of food.

Logan carefully divided the lunch into two portions. The boy's eyes followed every move of Logan's fingers. He passed one half of the food to Sammy.

"I like to thank God for my food before I eat."

Sammy bowed his head, loudly swallowing saliva.

"Thanks for food and sunshine and fresh air and good work. Amen."

Before Logan could lift his sandwich to his mouth, young Sammy had taken a large bite. He ate like a boy who wondered where he'd find his next meal. "You're new around here, aren't you?" Logan knew everyone within a forty-mile radius.

Sammy nodded. He pushed his mouthful of food to one cheek. "Been here more'n a week."

"Where'd you come from afore that?"

"Wolf Hollow."

That explained his grubby clothes and hunger. The rough mining town to the west had its share of men and women whose dreams of making it rich had been shattered by reality.

"Where are you living?"

Sammy jerked his thumb over his shoulder as if that provided all the information needed.

They ate in silence, Sammy's full attention on his food while Logan contemplated what to do about the boy.

Sammy finished before Logan, so Logan stuffed what was left back in the sack to eat later and pushed to his feet. "I expect the teacher will have noticed your absence by now."

They could hear someone approaching. A woman called, "Sammy? Where are you?" The schoolmarm must have realized she was missing one of her students.

Sammy jerked to his feet and flung about, seeking escape.

Logan caught him by the collar, a little disconcerted when the boy shrank back, his eyes blinking at a galloping rate. "I'm not going to hurt you, but you need to face up to your sins like a man."

Sammy straightened but his jaw quivered.

Miss Young held up her skirts as she ran around the school building in search of Sammy. She wore a dark gray skirt as plain as unbuttered bread and a white shirtwaist fitted so tightly around her neck it must surely choke her.

At the sight of Sammy in Logan's grasp, she dropped her skirt and ran her hands over her head to make sure every hair was in place. Logan was pretty sure not one single strand would dare escape.

She spared Logan the briefest of glances and turned her attention to Sammy. "I was concerned about you."

"I's okay."

"Except you're supposed to be at school with the others."

"I don't like school." Sammy sighed mightily. "But I promised my ma I would go."

She held a hand out to him. "Then let's return."

Sammy ducked away from her offered hand and sauntered across the yard in the general direction of the store.

Miss Young paused to speak to Logan. "Thank you for taking care of him." She was too shy to even meet his gaze.

"I know you have students to look after at the moment, but when classes are over, you and I need to talk about this." Like he'd said to Sammy, the boy must take responsibility for his actions. If left unchecked, stealing lunches might escalate into stealing bigger things. Things that would get him jailed or hanged. Best to nip the tendency in the bud.

Miss Young's gaze jolted to his at those words. "I'll deal with the boy in school."

"He stole from me. That makes it my business."

Her demanding look had likely been perfected with her wayward students, but he'd lived with Pa and

Grandfather long enough to endure the most challenging of looks without flinching. Not to mention two older brothers, Dawson and Conner. They were only four and two years older respectively, but not above bossing Logan around. Even his little sister, Annie, who at nineteen ran the house ever since Ma died four years ago, felt she had the right to expect Logan to do as she asked.

Nope. No mousy little schoolmarm had a hope of making him quake in his shoes. He touched the brim of his hat. "Until school is out," he said, and sauntered away.

Sadie would have welcomed more time crossing the street and rejoining the classroom. Something about Logan Marshall left her heart fluttering and her breathing so rapid she might have run around the block three times. But she'd left one of the older girls in charge long enough. She'd have to deal with her turmoil of emotions later. She rang the bell and called the children in from their play behind the store. The area was little more than the back alley, but until they moved into the schoolhouse, it sufficed. Lunch time had precipitated Sammy running away. For the fourth day in a row he had forgotten his lunch. She began to think no one prepared one for him. The children made the same conclusion and teased Sammy. Before she could intervene, the boy had gone outside saying he wasn't hungry. When she'd checked on him, he was gone. The same thing had happened yesterday but, before she could search for him, he had returned, swaggering a little, looking slightly smug. Her warning bells had sounded. This little boy of seven brought out all

the protective instincts she possessed, but she wasn't
lulled into believing he wasn't capable of mischief.

And she was right. He'd stolen from Logan Marshall! What had he taken? And why had he stolen
from a Marshall? They ruled the town with unwa-
vering firmness. Sammy's family had recently moved
to Bella Creek, so Sammy might not know that yet.
She spared a tight smile, wondering if knowing would
make any difference to the boy. He had a certain brash-
ness to him that made her think he often did things
he shouldn't.

The children filed in. She read to them. She assigned
lessons and checked answers. She replied when spoken
to though, from the questioning looks on several faces,
she guessed they had asked their questions more than
once. Finally the afternoon classes ended and she dismissed the children with a wave and a wooden smile.
Only then did she sink to her chair, plant her elbows on
the desktop and bury her face in her hands. She made
certain to have a book open in front of her, should anyone step in unannounced. Hopefully, they would think
she pored over lesson preparation.

Shudder after shudder raced up and down her spine.
She was no longer a naive sixteen-year-old but a wiser,
stronger, more careful woman. Still, the thought of facing one of the Marshall men with their broad shoulders
and piercing blue eyes filled her with dread.

Big or little, powerful or weak, she simply did not
trust men. Not after her father's business partner had
cornered her in her bedroom, tossed her on her bed
and done unspeakable things to her.

After he was done, he smiled at her. "That was fun,
wasn't it?"

To this day she didn't know if he'd meant the words seriously or simply mocked her pain. After he'd left she'd curled into a little ball, her pillow clutched to her chest and cried. Her tears were spent, her insides hollow, when her mother came in some time later. She'd confessed it all, hoping for, longing for, comfort. But she'd been instructed to wash her face and come down to dinner even though that man—Walter—would be at the same table.

She'd been told to never mention what had happened. It would ruin her father, would put the family out of business and lastly, as if it mattered least, it would ruin Sadie.

Every time she had to face the man brought a repeat of her pain and fear. After a few weeks she had persuaded Mother to let her go stay with Aunt Sarah, her mother's younger sister. Sadie had found a degree of comfort there, but her insides remained raw that her family—the very people who should protect her—had turned their backs on her pain and fear.

Time was supposed to heal all wounds and she tried to believe it. She had even allowed herself to be courted by shy, gentle Ronald Wilson. She'd gone so far as to agree to marry him, but as the time for the wedding approached she couldn't go through with it. She had never told Ronald her reason for breaking it off. Could hardly explain it to herself. Yes, she was afraid of the intimacy of marriage, but it was more than that.

She was soiled. Ruined. Unworthy.

She drew in a long breath and lifted her head. That was in the past. Time healed all wounds, she repeated to herself. Or perhaps time simply allowed a scab to form.

All that mattered now was being a good teacher, showing the children how to succeed in life and protecting them from dangers.

She rose. Her knees shook and she sat down again. She needed some inner strength and knew where to go for it. Since her own Bible was in her new living quarters—two little rooms on the end of the schoolhouse—she reached for the bigger Bible that she kept in the classroom.

She pulled it to her and opened to a verse that had become her strength in the four years since that fateful day. 1 Samuel 30:6 "David was greatly distressed… but David encouraged himself in the Lord his God."

Her finger trailed along the verse as she offered a silent prayer for help. *God, strengthen me and uphold me with Your righteous right hand. Help me be able to speak boldly to Logan.* Like she'd said to Isabelle Redfield the first day they arrived, the Marshall men frightened her with their size and self-assurance.

To be honest, she felt something more than guardedness around them. Something more than stiff awkwardness. The Marshalls were the kind of men who held strict standards. She feared that if any of them learned her secret she would be run out of town as a fallen woman. They must never know.

She closed the Bible, tucked in her chin and waited for Logan Marshall to appear.

She didn't have long to wait. He rapped on the door frame and stood, worn gray cowboy hat in hand, waiting for permission to enter.

Feeling at a disadvantage sitting, she stood and waved him to the nearest chair.

He drew it forward, parked it in front of her desk and plunked down, piercing her through with his blue eyes.

Her knees wobbled and she sat. She lowered her eyes, avoiding his unblinking look, but still managed to study him. He was clean shaven, wore a gray shirt that had a smattering of wood dust on the shoulder and blue jeans that showed wear at the creases at the knees. Her gaze settled on his scuffed cowboy boots. A working man comfortable in his clothing and—she knew as surely as she sucked in her next breath—equally comfortable in his own skin.

She wondered how such confidence felt.

"Sammy stole my lunch. Two days in a row," he said without any preamble.

Only a lunch? She'd feared something much bigger. "I'm not surprised. He's forgotten his lunch every day. I've begun to think no one prepares one for him." There were more signs that the boy was neglected and worse, but she didn't mention them. One thing at a time.

"Whether or not that is so, he can't go around thieving. It'll end him in a heap of trouble. He needs to learn a lesson on the evils of dishonesty." Logan leaned back, one leg propped at an angle over the other.

She tried not to let his posture of power affect her, but it made her spine prickle and made her think he meant for little Sammy to be punished. Exactly what did he have in mind? She imagined the Marshalls, with their strong personalities, wouldn't flinch at much of anything, but she couldn't bear the thought of him treating Sammy harshly. She decided to nip that idea in the bud. "He's seven years old. Rather than sentence him to jail, perhaps we should find out what is going on with his family."

Logan shook his head. "Wasn't thinking of jail, but correcting him now might keep him out of one in the future."

She felt her eyes narrow at the wisdom of his words. Not that she was willing to turn a small boy over to a big man. "You're right. The boy needs to be punished. Let me take care of it." She'd spare the rod, but make Sammy realize the dangers of his choices. Perhaps she'd have him write lines. She sat up straighter, putting a fierce look on her face to convince him she meant to handle this well.

He dropped his foot to the floor and leaned forward, his gaze so demanding she couldn't look away. "You think he should be whipped?" His voice was soft, so she couldn't judge his meaning. He looked about, perhaps searching for a strap.

She rose to her feet, gripping the edge of the desk to hold herself steady, and gave him her most challenging look. "Mr. Marshall, I will not tolerate physical punishment in my classroom."

He leaned back and crossed his ankle over his knee again, taking his time about answering, as if considering how to handle the noncompliant schoolteacher. "That's good to hear."

She'd misjudged him and she sat down again, relief leaving her weak.

He continued. "But that isn't what I had in mind. And it's Logan, if you don't mind. Wouldn't want to be confused with all those Marshalls older than me."

"What do you have in mind then?"

"He stole from me. He can work for me to pay off his debt."

She stared at the man. "He's seven."

"Old enough to run and fetch. Besides, what he does isn't important, but owning up to what he did is."

His suggestion was so totally unexpected that she didn't know what to say. Every time Logan opened his mouth, he surprised her. She'd been expecting harshness. Instead, he'd shown compassion and caring. She slowed her breathing as she realized she'd expected a lack of sympathy and understanding such as she'd experienced from her parents.

He nodded, taking her silence to mean agreement. "Tomorrow after school then? Or do you think he should come over at noon? Yes." He answered his own question. "Noon would be better. Wouldn't want to keep him from his chores at home."

She pursed her mouth. "I'd like to know why he comes to school without a lunch."

"Like you said, he's seven. I'm guessing he forgot it."

"Four days in a row?" Was now the time to mention the other things she'd noticed?

Logan chuckled. "Little boys can forget lots of times." He got to his feet.

He was about to leave, but she wasn't through. She wasn't believing that a hungry boy would forget his lunch four days in a row. She rose to better face him as she spoke. "I believe there's more to it than that." She'd seen bruises on his arms and in his eyes.

He studied her, a challenge and perhaps a warning in his sky-blue eyes. "Send the boy over at noon. If he forgets his lunch again he might like to share mine." He strode from the room.

Drained, Sadie sank to her chair. Her head fell to her cradled arms on the desktop.

How had she been railroaded into agreeing to send Sammy across the street at noon hour? But at least he'd get fed. She'd pray he'd also repent of stealing. But something else bothered her. Logan seemed upset at her suggestion there was more than forgetfulness to Sammy not having a lunch. But she knew there was something not right about Sammy's situation, and she would do her best to find out what it was. She wouldn't let the Marshalls' power stop her, but she would have to tread carefully—because if she angered them, she could lose her job.

Chapter Two

The next day Sadie called Sammy to her desk on the pretext of going over his work.

"Sammy, I'd like to meet your parents. Can you ask them when would be a good time for me to call?"

Sammy jerked back from leaning his elbows beside her on the desk. "No point you coming to visit."

She held his gaze steadily for several seconds, but his eyes revealed nothing. "Why is that?" she asked when it became clear the boy would offer no explanation on his own.

Sammy shuffled his feet and looked past her right shoulder. "My father—"

She couldn't help but notice how he stumbled on the word.

"He don't care for company."

"I see." Except she didn't. What reason could a man have for not wanting visitors? "Perhaps your mother would welcome a visit when your father is away."

Sammy ducked his head and scuffed the toe of his shoe along the floor. "I'll ask."

"I'll write a note." She took a piece of paper and

penned a request to visit, folded it and handed it to Sammy. "Give that to your mother."

Sammy stuffed the note into his pocket. "Can I go now?"

She thought of mentioning the plan for him to help Logan at noon but, not knowing how he would react, she decided to wait until it was too late for him to run off. "Yes, you may." Sadie watched him return to his seat. Would he give his mother the note or would it be forgotten in his pocket?

All too soon noon hour arrived. She told the children to eat their lunches. Sammy again had not brought one. "Sammy, would you please come to my desk?"

The boy stuck out his chin in a defiant gesture and swaggered toward her.

She might have found his bravado amusing if it wasn't so sad. Aware that the other children watched and listened intently, she nodded toward the door that opened into the store. "We'll talk out there."

She didn't touch him, yet she felt his trembling. The poor child. "You have nothing to be afraid of." Her words offered him no comfort. She would have put an arm around him and drawn him to her side, but every previous attempt at physical contact had caused him to shrink back and she must respect his wishes in the matter. In time, he would learn to trust her.

They stepped into the store. Thankfully, no one but George Marshall, the owner of the store, was in and, apart from sparing them a friendly nod, he was busy rearranging an assortment of tools. A rather noisy job that would enable her conversation to be private. She faced Sammy.

"Mr. Logan Marshall has offered to let you go over to the schoolhouse for the lunch break."

Sammy's eyes narrowed. "Why?"

The door to the street opened and Logan strode in. He called a greeting to his uncle as he crossed the floor.

Sadie told herself there was no cause for a case of jitters, and yet her heart fluttered madly and her blood pounded in her cheeks. Men always made her nervous, but this was a different reaction and it defied explanation…a fact she didn't appreciate.

Sammy pressed his back to the door and his fists curled, making Sadie forget her own reaction. The poor child feared he was in trouble.

Logan tipped his head toward her in greeting, then turned to Sammy. "Well, young man, did your teacher tell you of our arrangement?"

"She said I had to go with you." Defiance colored each word.

"I didn't get time to explain why." She would let Logan do it.

He flickered a look at her that carried a whole world of accusation.

She ignored it. Her reasons for not telling Sammy sooner were valid.

Logan gave Sammy his full attention. "You stole my lunch two times."

Sammy's only response was a stubborn look.

Logan continued. "You know that's wrong."

Still no response.

"I could call the sheriff."

Sadie opened her mouth to protest, but Logan held up a hand to signal silence and she decided to wait and see what he had in mind. Still, if he thought to have the boy arrested, well, she wouldn't stand idly by.

Logan leaned back on his heels. His stance did not fool Sadie. He was ready to catch little Sammy should he decide to run.

"The way I see it," Logan continued, slowly, as if thinking what to say, "is you owe me for the stolen food."

"I gots no money."

"Then you will work for me."

Sadie almost smiled at the eager light in Sammy's eye.

"I don't have to go to school?"

Logan chuckled. "You can work during the lunch hour. But first we'll eat."

"Okay, then, let's go." He eased between Sadie and Logan and headed for the door.

A grin widening his mouth, Logan spoke to Sadie. "I'll make sure he's back for classes."

Sammy waited impatiently at the door. Logan plunked his hat on his head and the two left the store.

Sadie watched as they crossed the street…the big man who cared about a little boy and the little boy doing his best to match Logan stride for stride.

Satisfied the boy was in good hands, she turned back to the classroom. If only she could be a little bird on the eaves of the schoolhouse and watch the two together.

Sammy returned just before the bell rang, a wide grin upon his face.

At recess, the other boys surrounded him, demanding to know where he'd gone. He refused to tell them and a couple of them looked angry. She'd have to make sure they didn't torment him.

At the end of the school day, she reminded Sammy of her note for his mother. He nodded and raced away.

The children all departed and she quickly tidied the classroom, then went in search of Logan. She was so anxious to learn how things had gone between him and Sammy that she would willingly seek out the very man who had the power to upset her carefully constructed world. One that had narrowed down to her students, a few friends and her books.

He saw her coming and hung his hammer on a nail to wait.

"Sammy seemed pleased with himself when he came back," she said.

"He's a good kid. He ate half my lunch. While we ate, I told him a man must live by certain standards or he couldn't call himself a man."

She swallowed hard. Just as she'd suspected, the Marshall men had high standards. A woman like her would not be accepted. Probably not even tolerated. She could imagine the look of horror she'd receive if they found out about her past.

Turning her attention to another matter, she asked, "What do you know about Sammy and his family?"

Logan leaned against the wall and faced her. "I've been asking about them."

She didn't wait for him to say what he'd learned. "His father doesn't like company. Don't you think that sounds ominous? I sent a note home asking to visit his mother."

"You might have a hard time doing that. From what Uncle George learned at the store, the mother died a short time ago. A man came by to ask about an empty place on the west edge of town. He assumed the man was Mr. Weiss though he didn't give his name. I guess the man hasn't been around again since."

"Sammy's mother's dead? Why wouldn't Sammy just say so? Why would he lie about such a thing?"

Logan shrugged. "Maybe he's afraid you might consider it unsuitable for a boy his age to stay with his father."

"He has no reason to think I would object. Why would he?" Her eyes were hot with denial and objection. "The poor child. Who comforts him?"

"I expect his father does."

Recalling the bruises she'd noted, she wondered if the father offered any sort of understanding to the child. "Being a father or mother does not necessarily mean a person knows how to comfort. Or even desires to."

"Sadie Young, you have a very jaded opinion of family life." He planted a big hand on her arm, an act so solicitous that her insides crackled. "What happened to make you that way?"

The trembling started deep in her soul and spread in ripples to her limbs. She must not let him know how his words affected her, and she stepped away, forcing him to lower his arm to his side. "This isn't about me. It's about Sammy. I'm convinced there's more to the story than we know, and I intend to investigate."

Logan watched her carefully. "Have a care how you deal with this hurting family. I recall how difficult it was when my mother died. I expect they're in need of a few kind words to get them through their loss."

"I would never be unkind, but neither would I hesitate to intervene if a child is being—" She sought for a word that would describe her concerns without demanding she provide more information because, apart from a few bruises that could be explained as normal boyhood bumps, and the hurt she saw in Sammy's eyes, her suspicions were based largely on recognizing something in the boy that echoed from her own wounded spirit. "If a child is being intentionally hurt."

He shoved his hat back on his head and looked heavenward, his eyes closed for a moment. He met her gaze, his piercing and demanding. "I see you're going to be stubborn about this. At least promise you'll let me know before you do anything."

She met his eyes, matching him hard look for hard look. She had no intention of backing down before his insistence.

"Miss Young, I can't let you visit a widower without an escort."

She swallowed hard. Was he really interested in protecting her reputation? Gall burned at the back of her throat. If only he knew how impossibly late such concern was. But she had two choices—agree or walk away. She guessed if she chose the latter, he wouldn't hesitate to bang on her door and demand her promise. Better to give it of her own volition. "I'll let you know." She wanted nothing more than to run to her quarters, but she walked away in what she hoped was a calm, controlled manner.

"Be sure you do," he called.

She closed the door, but the wooden barrier did nothing to quell the racing of her heart. He'd touched her in a comforting way. He'd shown genuine care for a hurting family. And he seemed concerned about her reputation. Comfort, understanding, consolation—all things she'd once yearned for—and now got from a man she was half-frightened of. It unsettled her through and through.

She pushed back her shoulders and lifted her head. She no longer needed any of those things. She'd found them with God, through reading the scriptures, and in standing on her own two feet. But an innocent touch from Logan and those supposedly dead feelings rushed through her like floodwaters. She did not thank him for bringing those emotions to the surface.

She must ignore those feelings, ignore the man who triggered them. She looked about her rooms for something with which to occupy herself. Her flowers. They always filled her with a sense of peace and beauty. Sitting at the little desk where she also prepared school lessons, she pulled out the thick book in which she pressed the flowers she gathered. Shortly after her arrival on the stagecoach a few weeks ago, Logan's sister, Annie, had taken her for a buggy ride out to the open fields, and she'd picked wild crocuses to add to her collection. They were dried and she chose a piece of heavy paper. With her tweezers, she gently lifted the crocuses from their place of preparation to glue them in an arrangement. At some point, she'd add other flowers and create a picture to frame and hang on the wall.

Her usual sense of peace eluded her as Logan hammered on the outside of the building.

All weekend, Sadie worried about Sammy. Was he getting fed? Did someone comfort him? Or did someone hurt him? She busied herself on Saturday by cleaning the classroom, preparing lessons and baking a cake.

But Logan and another man worked on the school-house, and their noise and—she allowed herself to admit—Logan's presence made it difficult to concentrate. She slipped next door to visit Kate.

"Did I see a small boy with Logan yesterday?" Kate asked.

Sadie had met Kate on the stagecoach earlier in the spring as they traveled to Bella Creek. Kate was as ordinary as could be, often wearing a big white apron to protect her clothing from the things she encountered as her father's assistant. Kate's father was the new doctor. Kate had brought her friend Isabelle with her to Bella Creek. Sadie smiled thinking of Isabelle. Imagine, an heiress in their midst, and none of them had realized it at first. Kate and her father had come in response to a plea for help from the townspeople of Bella Creek, the request for a doctor and a teacher after a devastating fire.

She turned her attention to Kate's question. "Little Sammy Weiss." She explained the situation. "Have you or your father had occasion to meet any of the Weisses?"

Kate said they hadn't and they turned the conversation to other matters.

On Sunday, Sadie glanced about the congregation. Sammy wasn't there. She told herself there might be a good reason the family didn't attend. Perhaps they weren't churchgoers, but she'd been hoping to see them.

Instead, she ended up meeting Logan's gaze across the aisle. The blue sky of outdoors echoed in his eyes, sending a jolt through her. She jerked her gaze away and stared hard at the preacher...another recent new-comer. She forced herself to listen carefully to each of

Preacher Arness's words and left the service strengthened and encouraged.

She might not be acceptable in the eyes of many people, should they learn her secret, but she was wholly accepted by God through the cleansing blood of Christ. Humming a hymn under her breath, she smiled at each who greeted her. Grandfather Marshall took her hand and asked after her well-being. Although his kind words brought a sting of tears to the back of her eyes, she managed to answer calmly and moved on before Logan could do more than nod. She had no need to avoid him, and yet she couldn't stand and make polite conversation with him, either.

Monday morning, Sammy handed her a note as he entered the classroom. "From my ma," he said. He walked away before she could think what to say.

Logan said Sammy's ma had died. Was he mistaken? How was she to find out?

She opened the note and read it: "I'm sick. Can you come some other time?"

She studied the writing. Many of the older children wrote better than this, but perhaps the woman had not been properly schooled, which would explain the promise she'd elicited from her son to attend classes. But why would someone say the mother was dead?

She set the children to work and checked on each of them. She paused at Sammy's desk and bent close to speak privately to him. "I'm sorry your mother is ill. Can I do anything?"

"No, ma'am," he whispered.

"If you think of something, don't be afraid to ask." She pressed her hand to his back.

He flinched so sharply that she jerked her hand away.

"Are you hurt?" Had this occurred over the week-end? It was the first time she'd touched him in that particular place but, in truth, he had shrunk back from every touch she offered. Pain and anger tore at her insides. There had been a time she'd thought family to be a place of shelter and protection. There were families who portrayed these ideals, and many others that did not.

He sidled away as far as his desk allowed. "No." His brown eyes were big and watchful.

She didn't need the details to know this child had been hurt and was afraid. She glanced about. Now was not the time or place to say anything.

She waited until recess and called him to her desk as the others went out to play. "Sammy, if you need someone to talk to, or if you need help of any sort, please let me know."

He shook his head hard, sending his overgrown dirty blond hair from side to side. "There's nothing to say and I don't need nothing." He scurried outdoors. It was plain as the nose on his face that he didn't want to talk to her.

She stared after him. *Oh, Father, this child is in need of help. I know it as clearly as I know someone should have helped me. Show me what to do.*

At noon, he hurried out to join Logan before Sadie reached the door.

By the time school let out, she knew what she must do. Her only regret was having given her promise to Logan to tell him before she did anything.

As soon as the children departed, she hurried across the street and confronted him. "Look at this." She handed him the note. "I thought you said Mrs. Weiss had passed away."

He read the few words. Logan shook his head, as puzzled by the message as she. "I've never known Uncle George to be wrong."

"Something isn't right and I'm going out there to find out what it is."

"But she asks you not to."

"I told you I would not hesitate to visit a family if I felt the need and, in this case, I do. I said I'd let you know and I'm doing that. I fear Sammy is in some sort of danger." She told him about the bruises she'd observed on Sammy's arms and the way Sammy had flinched at having his back touched. "I'm certain he's been whipped hard enough to leave him hurting."

"You're sure?"

"Not completely, but I won't let it go until I know the truth." Uncertainty filled his eyes as he studied her.

"Very well. If you're determined to do this, I'll take you."

"While I appreciate your offer of help..." Which it had not been. "I prefer to go alone."

"Why?"

She considered her reply. She could hardly say it was because she didn't want him hovering at her side making her aware of things she'd sooner not think of. Like the strength of him physically and in other ways. Not to mention that he made her think of how the Marshall family was a model of all the things she thought family should be, but was only a dream for many people. "If the woman is ill, she might not want a strange man showing up."

"Or the teacher, either, yet you are set on going."

Challenge upon challenge passed between them.

"Fine," she said finally, only because she knew he wouldn't give in.

"Very well. Let me get a buggy from the livery barn and I'll come back for you." He was on his way before she got her agreement out. While he did that, she hurried to her quarters and bundled up the cake she'd baked Saturday. At least she wouldn't arrive empty-handed.

She stood in front of her living quarters, ready and waiting, when Logan drove up with the rented buggy.

Logan jumped down and came around to help her up. He retained her hand even after she was safely seated.

She brought her gaze to his, knew hers revealed her determination and hopefully none of her quaking fear at what they might discover. She couldn't say what he thought, but his look gave her a jolt of courage...much-needed courage.

He released her hand and she took a deep breath, only to have it rush from her as he climbed into the buggy and sat beside her. They were on their way.

She tried to pretend Logan wasn't at her side and tried to pretend she didn't draw some strength from his presence. He wouldn't be there if he knew the sort of woman she was. Soiled, dirty, ruined.

She shivered at the thought he might somehow learn the truth about her.

Logan was silent as they made their way down the streets of Bella Creek. Was it just a few days ago he had thought the schoolmarm shy and retiring? Today she was a determined, headstrong woman, ready to walk into an unknown situation in order to protect a child. Was she truly so noble, or was there more to it than that? Or less? Grandfather had warned Logan to be careful not to judge every woman based on his experience with two of them, but how was he to know what lay hidden beneath the prim appearance of Miss Sadie Young? He would not believe anything but his own heart, which wore a permanent warning—a stay-away sign.

Nor would he let the teacher go alone to confront Mr. or Mrs. Weiss or whomever they'd discovered. After all, the family had come from Wolf Hollow, and that alone was reason to be cautious, though he couldn't help wondering at the mixed information he'd learned. There was something not right.

They drove past the tidy houses of Bella Creek and reached a slightly wooded area where squatters often used the ramshackle house standing there. "I believe this is the place." He pointed to the right. He hadn't been past in over a year and it had not improved one bit. The yard was littered with debris. Once it warmed up, the flies would be thick as syrup.

He pulled to a stop in front of the house. A window had been repaired with scraps of wood.

Logan helped Sadie down, "Careful where you step." Poverty always bothered him. Being careless about taking care of one's property bothered him even more, because the first couldn't be helped but the latter could. However, if they'd only recently moved they likely hadn't had time to clean up. Or if the parents were ill...or worse...there would be no one to do it apart from Sammy and, though the boy was a good little worker, he needed guidance and instruction.

Sadie grimaced. "I understand that some people are content to live like this. I'm not here to judge how Sammy lives, only to see if he's safe."

Logan nodded. "Let's go find out."

Someone must have surely heard their approach, but no one came to the door to welcome them.

Logan took Sadie's hand and guided her across the littered yard. She clung to him. He told himself it was only to keep her footing and there was no need to feel all protective toward her. After all, she'd been prepared to come here on her own and would surely have managed fine without his help.

He was grateful she didn't have to. They reached the door and he rapped his knuckles against the worn wood. From inside came a rustling and a muted voice, but no one came to the door or called out an invitation to enter.

Sadie gave him a questioning look and he shrugged. "Maybe they didn't hear." He knocked again, harder this time, and again they waited, knowing someone was inside. "We need to speak to you," Logan called. "May we come in?"

Silence and then a shuffle of feet, and the door opened enough to allow Sammy to peek through. "Teacher? Mr. Marshall? What're you doing here?"

Sadie squatted down to eye level with the boy. "I was worried about you and came to make sure you are okay."

Logan leaned closer to peer through the narrow opening of the door. The interior showed little sign of life—a bare table and an equally bare cupboard. He'd never seen a kitchen with nothing to indicate food preparation. "Can we come in?" he asked when it became apparent Sammy didn't mean to extend an invitation.

Sammy glanced behind him, then shook his head. "I don't think so."

Sadie straightened and turned to Logan. "This isn't right," she whispered.

He nodded.

"I'm okay," Sammy said. "You don't need to worry none about me."

"But, Sammy, we are worried." He knew he spoke for both of them. As he studied the boy, a pair of small feet entered his field of vision. "You have a little brother or sister? And a sick mother?"

Sadie gave him a look full of appeal, seeking his help, perhaps even his opinion. He tried not to let the notion make him feel that she might see him as a man worthy of her respect. Which, he thought with a degree of irony, he was. What he meant was he no longer cared if a woman thought so.

Nevertheless, he listened to her silent call for help and shouldered the door open, the squawk of its rusted hinges rending the silence.

Sammy stepped back. An older girl pulled him close while, in her other arm, she held a smaller girl. The older girl wore shoes with the toes cut out to accommodate her feet. Her dress had a tear in the skirt and was almost colorless from frequent washings. The little one was barefoot and her faded pink dress was equally worn, yet they were both surprisingly clean.

In a glance Logan took in the room—a bed with no mattress and only a scattering of blankets. A narrow wooden table sagged to one side, and nearby was a single chair with rungs missing in the back. Again he was struck by how empty the place was of belongings. Or any sign of domesticity. Not a curtain. Not a dish. Nothing.

"Where's your mother? Your father?" Sadie's words were surprisingly gentle considering the state of the place and the children.

Logan remained at her side, stifling an urge to put an arm about her shoulders and protect her from the glaring truth. "You kids are alone, aren't you?"

Sadie pressed a hand to her throat. "Alone? Is that possible?" She studied the silent trio. "I think you better explain what is going on."

Sammy looked up at his older sibling, a slender girl with hair lighter than Sammy's and the same dark eyes. She shook her head in answer to Sammy's unasked question.

"We got nothing to say," Sammy said.

Logan pulled forward the only chair, two rungs missing in its back, and indicated Sadie should sit. Her glance at Logan informed him that the misery of the children's situation brought her pain. Sadie placed a package on the table and unwrapped a cake. Three pairs of eyes lingered on it, then eased away. It didn't take more than a glance around the place to know they were likely hungry.

He wished he could erase the pain for Sadie and the children. But things like this couldn't be undone...only resolved, and he prayed for wisdom. *Lord, help us unravel this mystery.*

Slowly, softly, Sadie began to speak. "Sammy, are these your sisters?"

Sammy nodded.

The older girl tightened her arm about Sammy's

shoulders. If Sadie noticed the warning gesture, she ignored it. "What are their names?"

"She's Beth." Sammy indicated the older girl. "And this here is baby Jeannie."

Jeannie, the blondest of the three, with the same dark eyes, wasn't a baby anymore, but Logan understood that the youngest child often got called the baby for a long time.

"How old are your sisters?" Sadie continued in her gentle voice.

"I'm thirteen," Beth said. "And Jeannie is three. Why?"

Sadie managed a slight smile as she met Beth's eyes. "It's just something teachers ask children. Let me introduce ourselves. I'm Sammy's teacher, Miss Young, and this is Logan Marshall."

Beth nodded. "I know who you are. But why are you here? I—Sammy took a note asking you not to visit."

Logan noted the hesitation, as if Beth had been about to say she had sent the note. He glanced at Sadie, saw by the flash in her eyes that she had heard the same thing.

Her gaze returned to the older girl. "Yes, he did. But I couldn't help but be worried. Especially when I saw that his back hurt him."

Both Sammy and Beth adopted impassive expressions.

"Sammy, who has been hurting you?"

"Not Beth."

"I wasn't accusing Beth." She looked to Logan, seeking his opinion.

He gave her a slight nod to indicate she should continue questioning the children.

"Where's your mama?" she asked them.

"Mama?" Little Jeannie spoke for the first time.

"Hush, baby." Beth jostled the child.

"I want Mama." Jeannie looked ready to cry.

"Hush, hush. Remember what I told you."

Jeannie nodded. "Mama not coming back."

So Logan's uncle had been right.

"I'm sorry," Sadie said. "You must all be very sad."

Nothing but more unblinking stares from Sammy and Beth.

"Where is your father?" Logan asked. Though his deeper, more demanding voice jolted the pair, they quickly recovered and pressed their lips together.

"Where's your papa?" he asked again, softer this time.

Little Jeannie, her eyes full of fear, whimpered and clung to Beth. Beth's jaw muscles twitched as she clenched her teeth. Her eyes narrowed and she wrapped her arms about Jeannie in such a protective gesture that a shiver climbed Logan's spine.

Logan crossed the floor to the cupboards and threw open the only remaining door. Empty. He touched the stove. Cold. He confronted the children. Sadie was right, both in thinking things weren't as they should be and coming here to check on them.

He stilled his raging heart. "There is nothing in the house to eat."

No response from any of them.

He circled the room, hating every inch of it as a place for children to live. He stopped behind Sadie's chair and gripped the back. "When is your father returning?"

Jeannie whimpered and buried her face against her sister's shoulder.

Beth glowered.

Sammy trembled. What was he afraid of?

"He's gone, but he'll be back." Beth tried to look as if that was all that mattered.

"Where is he?" He'd find the man and make him look after these kids. And he'd make it clear that he must treat them kindly.

"Said he'd bring us something to eat," Sammy blurted out.

"Hush," Beth warned.

Sammy hung his head.

Logan assessed the little information the children had provided. One thing was clear—they couldn't stay here.

"I'll take you to the ranch, where you'll all be well taken care of."

At the same time, Sadie said, "Children, I am taking you home with me. I'll make sure you are well taken care of and that no one will hurt you."

Logan gave Sadie a hard look. "You live in tiny quarters."

"You live with a houseful of people who, apart from your grandfather, are all busy, and he can't take care of the children."

He rocked his head back and forth. Did she realize she would be absent as much as anyone at the ranch? Somehow, he knew that little truth wouldn't change her mind. "Who will look after Jeannie when you're teaching?"

The stubbornness slid from her face.

"I look after Jeannie," Beth said. "But we aren't going with either of you."

Logan and Sadie forgot their argument as they confronted the children.

"You can't stay here," Sadie said. "It's not…" She glanced about and seemed to struggle to find the appropriate word. "Safe." A heavy beat passed as everyone stood poised to argue. "It's only until we can locate your father," Sadie added.

A look passed between Sammy and Beth. Logan could not interpret it except to know it put him on edge.

Jeannie struggled to get down, and Beth could not hold the squirming child. The little girl went to the table and stared at the cake.

"Who would like some?" Sadie asked, her look including all the children.

Sammy surged forward, but Beth pulled him back.

Ignoring their response, Sadie took a knife from her bag and cut a piece. "Jeannie, would you like some cake?"

She nodded and took the offered morsel. "Thank you," she said before she devoured the treat.

Sadie cut two more pieces and indicated Sammy and Beth should each take one. Beth shook her head and gripped Sammy's shoulder, but the boy slipped away and took the cake, making short work of it.

"When did your father leave?" Logan demanded, his voice more sharp than he intended, but to see the way the children ate…

"He left Friday and good rid—" Sammy's words were cut short as Beth poked him.

Sammy jumped and gave his sister a glaring look. "What?"

"How many times do I have to tell you we keep our business to ourselves?"

"Lots, I guess," he mumbled. "Want your cake?"

"I'm not hungry," she said, although her eyes practically devoured the treat.

"Can I have some more?" Sammy asked Sadie.

"Certainly." She handed him another piece, then turned to Logan. "Can I speak to you outside?"

Three pairs of eyes followed them to the door. She went to the far side of the buggy and waited, her eyes flashing green shards. "These children cannot stay here."

"I agree."

Her fierce expression didn't falter. "Good. We agree on that point, at least. Now would you mind helping me get them to my place?"

"Your place? Where is everyone going to sleep? Do you even have enough bedding for four people?"

"I'm sure I can get what I need at your uncle's store."

"That's so." But still, it seemed just plain wrong for her to take them home. "At the ranch, they would be surrounded by many loving people."

"Is it fair to ask Annie to take on more?"

He almost gave up at that. "Annie can manage. After all, she doesn't have Dawson and Mattie to look after anymore."

Sadie sighed as if he missed the whole point.

"Shall we let the children make the choice?" he said. Of course, they would choose the ranch. What child doesn't want to live on a ranch with lots of adults to dote on them? "Besides, we know what it's like to lose a mother."

She looked past him, far past him. "Maybe I understand them better than you and your kin can."

"Now why would you say such a thing?"

"Because you come from a loving, supportive, forgiving family. How can you begin to understand what these kids are dealing with?"

He wished he could see what her past held that made her eyes seem lifeless as she brought her gaze back to his.

"Let's go ask the children." She took half a step and stopped. "What if they keep insisting they will stay here?"

He considered the possibility and suddenly chuckled. "Guess we could tell them there's a nice hot meal waiting for them with cake to follow."

The heaviness left her face and she grinned. "I heard the way to a man's heart is through his stomach. I suppose it applies equally to children."

He took her arm and led her back to the shack. "We'll soon find out."

The children stood lined up waiting for them to enter. He wondered how much of the conversation they'd been able to hear through the thin walls and barely-there window.

Side by side, he and Sadie stood before them. He and Sadie hadn't decided what to say to persuade the children they must leave, but while he mulled over possibilities, Sadie spoke.

"Children, I think you can see as plainly as we can that you can't remain here. I'd like you to come stay with me while we sort things out. You might enjoy sharing the stew I have planned for supper."

"Or you could come with me to the ranch." That

didn't sound very enticing. "We always have lots to eat."

"We'll go with the teacher," Beth said with finality.

Logan had agreed to let them make the choice. So that's how it would be. He glanced at Sadie, who didn't look like she was enjoying this victory. In fact, her eyes were dark. Was she regretting her offer?

She clapped her hands just like a schoolteacher should. "Very well. Let's get your things gathered up."

The children's belongings were pitifully few—three threadbare blankets, a change of clothes, well-worn jackets. Beth's and Sammy's were too small, while the arms of Jeannie's jacket hung past her hands.

Jeannie clutched a rag in her arms.

"What's that, honey?" Sadie asked.

"My comfie." She wrapped both arms about it, looking defensive.

"It's an old sweater of Ma's that she sleeps with." Beth looked ready to go to battle.

"Then, by all means, you must bring it."

Beth's shoulders dropped as she realized she wouldn't have to argue with Sadie about the rag.

They all headed for the door. Beth hesitated and turned about to look around the room.

"What is it?" Sadie asked.

"What will he do when he comes back and we're gone?" Her voice quivered.

"Why don't I leave a note explaining where you are?" Sadie had pencil and paper out of her bag before she finished speaking, then waited, allowing Beth to make up her mind.

"I guess that would be best."

Sadie wrote the note.

Logan glanced over her shoulder to read it: "The children are safe in Bella Creek."

She couldn't have given less information. He was about to protest when she turned to Sammy.

"Would you get me a rock?" The boy ran to do so.

Sadie took the rock, placed it over the paper in the middle of the table and stepped back. How long would the paper stay there before a mouse used it to build a nest?

They arrived at the schoolhouse and he helped them alight. "I'll ride out to the ranch and gather up some stuff for you and the children." He climbed back into the buggy and drove away before she could voice any arguments. He would assist with the children whether or not she welcomed it. In fact, he quite looked forward to doing so.

With a start he realized it would mean spending time with the schoolmarm. How had he managed to get himself tangled in a situation that had him helping a woman? Hadn't he learned his lesson? And why, in the back corner of his brain, had a little thought surfaced and left him wondering if this time things would be different?

He tightened the grip on the reins of his heart. He would not feel free to care about a woman until he knew everything about her—her present situation, her plans for the future and, especially, her past.

Chapter Three

Sadie stood in the doorway and faced three forlorn children huddled together in the middle of the floor. Her quarters had seemed roomy until now. As Logan had said, they would be crowded here. But they would be safe.

Without appearing to do so, she studied Beth. Was there a reason she'd chosen to come with Sadie? Was it because there were no men at the teacher's house?

With a shake of her head, she warned herself she too easily equated the children's situation with her own and she had no reason to do so. They wouldn't know the truth about things until they located the father. Perhaps he had been injured. But providing an excuse did not erase the way her nerves tingled with certainty there was more involved than a missing father and a deceased mother.

"Children, I will get beds arranged after Logan comes back." She'd ask him to help her bring cots she would purchase from his uncle's store. "In the meantime, let's put your things in the bedroom."

She led the way to the second room.

Beth looked around. "Where are we going to sleep?"

"We'll figure out something. After all, I'm the teacher." She wasn't sure why that should make the children trust her, but she smiled as Beth relaxed enough to set her squirming little sister down.

Jeannie hurried over to the bed and touched the bright quilt that Aunt Sarah had helped her make, insisting handwork was relaxing. If only her aunt knew how much pain had gone into every stitch as Sadie had made the quilt. She'd told herself that she would start a new life, she would be independent, she would help those in dire circumstances, she would be a teacher and find what she needed in that profession.

Jeannie patted the quilt. "Pretty, pretty."

"Don't touch," Beth warned.

"It's okay. You can certainly touch it. This is your home now." At least until the situation could be sorted out, though, if her intuition was correct, she'd make sure the children were never returned to a man who not only neglected the children but hurt them. "I made that quilt when I was eighteen. My aunt helped me."

"Where was your mother? Had she passed on?" Beth asked, her eyes full of sympathy.

"No, both my parents are alive, but I lived with my aunt for a few years. That's where I took my teacher's training."

"Oh," both Sammy and Beth said.

She cleared out a drawer in her dresser. "Beth, you can put the girls' things in here."

By shoving her books together on one shelf, she made room on another for Sammy's things. They had so little, but soon she hoped she could provide them with clothes and jackets that fit properly.

The enormity of the task she'd taken on weighed on her shoulders. A teacher's salary would not extend to feeding and clothing three children. *Dear Father God, please provide for us.* "I'm sure you're all hungry. Would you like a snack? Afterward you can help me prepare supper."

"Yes, please," Jeannie said. "I hungry."

"Me, too," Sammy said. "That cake was really good."

Beth hung back, not ready to admit she couldn't manage on her own.

"There's some cake left. Let's save it for dessert. But how does bread and jam sound?" Logan's aunt Mary baked bread and sold it through the store.

"Yes, please." Jeannie hurried into the kitchen and parked herself at the table. Her brother and sister followed.

Thankfully, those who had furnished Sadie's rooms had provided four chairs, so there was room for all of them. And no more. She wouldn't think that it meant she couldn't invite Logan to share their meals. Or simply come for tea. It was not like she longed for his company. But he had offered to help. Insisted on it.

She sliced bread, spread butter and jam, and placed some before each child. They thanked her and ate neatly. Almost too neatly, as if concerned she would scold them—or worse?—if they dropped a crumb.

Again she was overreacting. She had no reason to think they were being anything but polite, and if she cared to acknowledge what it really meant she would have to say the parents had trained them well. But her gut insisted there was more to the situation than either she or Logan understood.

The children finished and carried their dishes to the

dishpan. "I'll clean up," Beth said, handing Sammy a tea towel so he could dry.

"I appreciate that." She would not take away their independence. While the children did dishes, she got out vegetables and the leftover meat to make into stew.

"We can help with that, too," Beth said.

So she parked the children in a row beside her. Beth diced meat, Sammy peeled the carrots, and Sadie gave Jeannie a basin of water and let her wash the potatoes. Satisfaction filled her insides. This could be her family for a few days.

She stiffened at the pain that grabbed her insides. This might well be the only family she would ever have, and knowing it would be temporary filled her with stinging regret.

Once the vegetables and meat were prepared, she tossed it all into the biggest pot she had and set it to stew. In minutes a succulent aroma filled the room.

They cleaned up. Jeannie played happily with a handful of peelings she'd rescued. Beth and Sammy stood by the cupboard, looking about as if searching for something to do.

Sadie would have no trouble keeping them busy in the classroom, but what would she have them do in their new home?

Before she could come up with an answer, the rattle of a wagon pulling up to the door drew them to the window.

"It's Logan," Sammy announced.

"Indeed, it is."

"He's got stuff with him."

Logan jumped down, hurried around the back and lifted out a wooden box.

Sammy rushed to open the door.

Logan entered and looked about, giving each of them a smile. "Sure smells good in here."

"What's in the box?" Sammy asked.

"Sammy." Beth sounded horrified at her brother's question.

"Why don't you look and see." Logan set it down and waved them all forward.

Beth hesitated, which was enough impetus for Sadie to move closer and have a look.

Sammy lifted out a jar of canned meat. And then another of peaches. "It's food."

"Yup." Logan looked pleased with himself. "When I told my family about you children coming to live with Miss Young, they said they would help." He brought his gaze to Sadie, his eyes bright with pleasure.

She wasn't about to refuse the offering. "Thank you to you and your family." There were potatoes, carrots and turnips, canned goods and—she lifted out a cloth-wrapped bundle—two loaves of fresh bread.

"I have a few more things in the wagon. Sammy, give me a hand." He trotted back outside.

Grinning at being asked, Sammy joined Logan and they brought in a small cot. "There are two of them. Where do you want them set up?"

Her relief was palpable. "This will solve the sleeping situation. Put this one in the bedroom." They shuffled the furniture around to make room for the cot. "I'll sleep here and the girls can have the bigger bed."

"Oh no, miss." Beth blinked and fluttered her hands. "We wouldn't think of putting you out. Me and Jeannie can sleep on the cot."

"Nonsense." She draped an arm across the girl's

shoulders, feeling them tense. Did the father beat her, too? She would certainly be keeping an eye out for any evidence. "It only makes sense for the two of you to take the bigger bed."

"What about me?" Sammy demanded. "Where am I sleeping?"

"Ma always said you could sleep standing up, so we'll just prop you in a corner somewhere." The room silenced at Beth's comment.

Logan was the first to realize she was teasing her brother and chuckled. "Looks like that problem is solved."

Beth's pleased smile was fleeting but beautiful. Sadie and Logan glanced at each other. Seems he was as relieved as she to see this lighter side of the girl.

Sammy shuffled his feet. "Aw, I can't really sleep standing."

"No?" Logan grinned at the boy. "Then maybe you can help me bring in the other cot while Miss Sadie decides where she wants it."

Sammy followed Logan, trying his best to match the man's longer strides.

Beth watched with a thoughtful, guarded expression. She turned, caught Sadie watching her and blinked away any telltale emotion.

Logan and Sammy returned and stood in the room, holding the cot. "Where do you want it?" Logan asked.

Sadie sprang into action. "I'll shove this armchair to the side and the cot can go along this wall."

Logan and Sammy set it up and stood back to study it. "How does that look to you?" Logan asked Sammy.

"Looks better'n standing in the corner."

The boy earned a chuckle from both adults and a

fleeting smile from Beth. Jeannie climbed to the cot and sat down on the metal slats. "Sammy sleep here?"

"Seems he thinks it will do." Logan patted Sammy's back.

The boy flinched so sharply that Logan's hand fell away.

The boy's pain was obvious. Sadie's jaw tightened. Her nostrils flared as she fought back tears. Had Logan seen it? She widened her eyes to stop the threatening tears and looked at Logan.

His eyes had grown stormy. His expression had hardened. He'd noticed. Would he begin to share her suspicions regarding the father or would he blame it on the falls of an active boy?

He turned back to Sammy. "Shall we get the rest of the things?"

The pair went back out and returned with a mattress for each cot.

Then he brought in a box of clothing. "Annie thought you could use this. It's mostly stuff either she or Mattie have outgrown."

Logan couldn't miss the way Sammy had flinched when he'd touched his back. It was on the tip of his tongue to ask the boy how he got hurt, but he didn't want to make the children more defensive and guarded than they were already.

Annie had sent a stack of bedding, and he handed some to Sammy to carry in while he filled his arms with the rest.

"I'll make the beds." Beth hurried to do so. "Come on, Sammy. You can help."

"Aw, that's girls work."

"We do our share." Beth waited at the bedroom doorway. "I'm not doing it without you."

Sammy followed, taking his time.

Jeannie trotted after them. "I help, too."

Sadie let them handle the job on their own. She stood by Logan's side. "I appreciate all this, though I fully expected to buy what I need at the store."

"I'm prepared to help in any way I can." So was the rest of his family, but he wanted her to acknowledge his support.

"That's very generous, especially considering..."

Although she didn't finish her thought, he could feel a wave of resistance from her. He guessed she had already judged and condemned the children's father. Not that he could blame her. "I'm trying not to jump to conclusions about the missing Mr. Weiss. I know some fathers believe in spare the rod, spoil the child." He shook his head. "It's got to be difficult to lose one's wife and have three children to take care of. Might even drive a man to do things he shouldn't...to make mistakes in his judgment." Sadie continued to study him with a stubborn, unbelieving look on her face. He wanted her to understand that sometimes a man needed a second chance. He was grateful he'd been given a couple of them. "I know I've made enough mistakes in my life."

Her eyebrows rose at that confession. He hoped she wouldn't demand an explanation, because he didn't intend to tell her how faulty his judgment was concerning women.

"Every man deserves a chance to start over. I'm willing to give Mr. Weiss that much leeway."

She crossed her arms, a look of defiance on her face.

"Just because your family is perfect doesn't mean these children don't need someone to defend them."

He leaned closer and spoke firmly. "And I'm not suggesting they don't. I'd be hard-pressed to stand back and allow the children to be mistreated." He sat back on his heels. "Though the law is on the father's side."

The children finished in the bedroom, went to the cot in the living room and proceeded to work together to prepare it for Sammy. Any more conversation between Sadie and Logan would have to wait for another time and place.

The bed done, the three children sat on it, watching the adults.

He told himself he did not see wariness in every pair of eyes. Except he did, and it seemed out of proportion for young ones who had been offered a place of shelter and a warm, nourishing meal.

He sniffed. "Sure smells good in here."

"We made stew," Jeannie said, a shy smile brightening her brown eyes.

"You're welcome to join us," Sadie said. "After all, you've been busy taking care of our needs."

She managed to say thank you at the same time as she pushed him out of the picture, making him feel he had no part in this plan. He wasn't about to accept that. He faced her. "Miss Sadie Young, let's get something straight. The children have chosen to stay here, but, in essence, we are partners in this venture. Understand?"

Her eyes went from surprise to shock, and then she put up a barrier so he couldn't tell what she thought.

"Understand?" he repeated, wanting her to agree.

"If you insist."

He closed his eyes. Agreement, yes, but not the way

he wanted it. But what was he to do? He looked at the children. Jeannie had climbed onto Beth's lap and clung to her. Both Beth and Sammy had a tight, closed look about them. Of course they didn't know what to expect when the two adults who had whisked them away from their home seemed to be angry with each other. From now on, he would be careful to confine any sign of disagreement between himself and Sadie to private moments. "Thank you for inviting me to share supper with you. I accept."

Sammy looked toward the table. "Where you gonna sit? There's only four chairs."

Logan chuckled. "I'll be right back. Don't eat without me." He jogged out the door and across the street to Marshall's Mercantile. "Uncle George, can I borrow a stool?"

His uncle stared at him like he'd fallen through the roof and landed in the middle of the store. He recovered from his surprise. "Help yourself, but may I ask what you need it for?"

He told about the children moving in with Sadie. "I'm joining them for supper but we're shy one chair." He grabbed a stool from the corner. Normally, men gathered around the stove to visit, but none were present at the moment. "Say, have you heard anything more about Mr. Weiss?"

"Nothing. I've not seen hide nor hair of the man since he stopped by to inquire about the house, if you care to call it that. I thought he'd be in to stock up, but nope. Maybe he's got all the supplies he needs."

"No, they were out of food." He didn't say how little the children had. Somehow, he felt he needed to keep private the details of their situation.

"You could ask at the post office."

"I'll do that in the morning." He'd be asking at every business in town until he found the man or learned of his whereabouts. "Thanks for the stool."

"Keep it as long as you need."

He hurried back to the school. He sure wasn't getting much work done on the building. Grandfather would have something to say about that.

Sammy waited at the door and held it open for Logan. The table was set for five, a pot of stew in the middle and a pile of sliced bread on a plate beside it. Logan's mouth watered. He had left home with the wagon loaded for Sadie and the children just as Annie was serving supper. He could help himself to leftovers when he got back, but it wasn't the same as a warm meal.

He parked the stool by the table. "This is just like a real family." He meant for the children to feel at home and glanced about at the four people waiting for him. Their expressions varied from curious, on Sammy's part, to Jeannie's innocence, to guarded wariness in both Sadie and Beth. Sadie had made her jaded opinion of family clear. Someday he'd find out what had happened to cause that, but to see a similar expression on Beth's face, a sweet thirteen-year-old, twisted his gut.

He made up his mind at that moment to show them they could trust him and, by doing so, learn to believe in the goodness of family.

"Please, everyone sit down." Sadie motioned toward the chairs.

He perched on the stool. Sadie ended up kitty-corner to his right. Beth sat across from him, sliding her chair as far to his left as possible, likely so she could be close to Jeannie, who sat at the other end. That left Sammy to sit next to him.

Logan was relieved when the boy grinned at him as he took his place. "Us men got to stick together," Sammy said with a great show of expanding of his chest.

Beth ducked her head but not before Logan caught the smile on her face.

He only wished she'd looked at him long enough to see his answering smile. He turned to Sammy. "We sure do." He was about to pat the boy on the back when he remembered how he'd flinched and settled for squeezing his arm.

"'Course, I *am* the man of the family now," Sammy boasted.

Beth's head came up, her eyes wide with shock. The same sense of shock raced through Logan and he looked to Sadie. Her eyes narrowed, her lips tightened. She'd heard the boy and, like Logan, wondered what he meant. It was surely a slip of the tongue.

"While your father's away?" Logan prompted.

"Yeah. That's right." Sammy studied his plate, then gave the pot of stew a longing look. "Sure smells good. Makes my taste buds work really hard."

Sadie blinked away her shock and curiosity. "Shall we eat before it gets cold? Logan, would you say grace?"

Logan nodded and looked about the table for the children to bow their heads.

Sammy and Jeannie did so quickly. Beth, however, held his gaze for a moment. He couldn't read her expression. She was far too good at hiding her feelings.

But he sensed something challenging in her look before she clasped her hands and bowed her head.

He bowed his head and gathered his thoughts. "Lord God, thank You for family to share the plenty You have provided. Thank You for the food to bless our bodies and Your love to bless our souls. Amen."

He lifted his head and turned toward Sadie to help her serve the meal. His gaze brushed past Beth and then jerked back at the glisten of tears in her eyes. "Beth, is something wrong?"

What a silly question. There were so many things wrong. Her mother dead. Her father missing. And now being shuffled off to live with strangers. "I mean did I say something, do something, to upset you?"

She shook her head, blinking her eyes until all sign of tears disappeared. "No. I just remembered something. Nothing important."

Sammy handed his plate to Sadie to fill it with stew. "You remembered—ow. Why'd you kick me?"

"Sorry. It was an accident."

Logan looked from brother to sister and back again. It had been no accident. Beth meant to stop Sammy from saying something. But what? No point in asking. The children weren't about to tell them anything. He took Beth's plate and handed it to Sadie to fill, and then Jeannie's and Sammy's. Last, he handed his to Sadie.

Their gazes connected and held as a dozen thoughts blazed through his mind that he wished he could share with her. She lowered her eyelids enough for him to know she had the same questions he did. He gave a slight lift of one shoulder and she raised her brows in acknowledgment. They would do their best to discover the truth about this family, but if the way the children withdrew was any indication of how reluctantly they'd give answers, it wasn't going to be easy.

The children each took a slice of bread and turned their attention to the meal, eating quietly and neatly, their silence such a marked contrast to mealtimes at the ranch that Logan wasn't comfortable. He much preferred the noisy interaction of people talking.

Jeannie had stopped eating after one mouthful and Beth took Jeannie's spoon and offered her some stew. Jeannie opened her mouth, leaned forward and cleaned off the spoon.

"Beth?" Jeannie said, as soon as she could speak around the food.

"What?"

Jeannie leaned closer to whisper to Beth. "He's not like the man."

"Hush. Eat your supper."

This time Logan let his gaze roam from one child to another, then to Sadie. When he saw the uncertainty in her eyes, he turned back to Jeannie. "What man is that, little one?"

Beth pressed a restraining hand to Jeannie's arm. "Don't talk. Just eat your meal."

Jeannie studied her sister for a moment, then nodded and concentrated on her food. But every few seconds her gaze would jerk to Logan. As soon as she saw he watched her, she quickly ducked her head.

There were far too many mysteries surrounding this family. Logan would begin looking for their father tomorrow morning and allow the man to answer the questions racing through his mind.

They finished the stew and Sadie cut the remaining cake to give everyone a piece.

Jeannie had two mouthfuls left when she started to whimper.

"What's wrong, honey?" Sadie asked.

The child's whimpers turned to wails.

Beth rose. "I'm sorry. She's tired."

Logan rose, too. "Do you want me to carry you to the bedroom?" He reached for her. Her wails turned to screams and he backed away. "I'm sorry. I should have thought." Of course she was frightened. He was a stranger.

Beth scooped her up and took her away, closing the bedroom door behind them. She could be heard murmuring softly to the distraught child.

"She always does this," Sammy said. "Ma used to say she ran out of sweet before she ran out of day."

The crying moderated and, after a few minutes, ended. Beth sang a soothing song. Logan couldn't make out the words.

Sadie rose and began to clean up the kitchen.

Logan looked about. Should he go or should he stay? Was he welcome? Or was he part of the problem? He didn't know and wasn't about to ask. Instead, he followed his instincts and carried a stack of dishes to the dishpan and filled it with hot water.

"You don't have to do that," Sadie protested.

"I know I don't, but my ma taught me to do my share."

She put away the butter. "I can't see the men doing dishes on a busy ranch. Don't they rush in to eat and leave again as soon as the food is gone?"

Sammy carried the cups they'd used for water and stopped halfway to the cupboard to watch and listen.

Logan grinned at him. "Hey, us men can do dishes as well as we can rope a cow. Right, partner?"

Sammy gave Logan a look of disgust. "Dishes is women's work. And the sooner they learn that the better for 'em." He put the cups down and whacked one fist into the other palm.

A chill ran up Logan's spine. "That what your pa says?" He kept his voice gentle in the hopes of getting some information from the boy.

Sammy shrugged. "Nah. Not my pa. Someone else."

"Well, let me tell you. That someone else is wrong. Very, very wrong. There is nothing wrong with men helping with dishes or sweeping the floor or anything like that. It's true what Miss Sadie says. Sometimes the men are too busy to take time for household chores, but when my little sister was born, my pa did all those things for my ma. He said she deserved a rest. And my grandfather took care of my grandmother and did all those things when she was ill. You ever see my pa and grandfather?" He didn't wait for Sammy to answer. "They are big men." He flexed his muscles to indicate both size and strength. "No one would call them sissies." He gave Sammy a mock scowl meant to make the boy realize men could be men and still do dishes.

Sammy looked him up and down twice. "Are they as big as you?"

Logan would not expand his chest as Sammy had earlier, but he couldn't keep from glancing at Sadie to see her reaction and barely managed not to stare as she grinned at him.

"All the Marshall men are big and blond," she told Sammy.

"And they do dishes?"

"I'll tell you a secret." Logan leaned over and crooked his finger to bring Sammy closer so he could whisper in his ear, though he didn't speak too softly for Sadie to hear. "My brother Dawson just got married and he said doing dishes with his new wife is the best part of the day."

"No!" Sammy's look dared him to say it was the truth.

"Yup. He says it makes his wife so grateful she kisses him right then and there."

"Yuck. Sure hope nobody's going to kiss me if I help with dishes."

Logan and Sadie looked at each other and laughed. He couldn't help but notice the twinkle in her eyes. Was she thinking doing dishes together would be special?

He slammed a fist into his thoughts. Of course she didn't, and neither did he.

Again remembering Sammy's sore back, Logan squeezed the boy's arm. "I can't promise someone won't want to kiss you but probably not until you're a lot older and then you won't mind."

He backed away. "Ain't no one gonna kiss me."

Logan grinned, knowing Sammy's attitude would change soon enough. "Come on. Let's be brave men. I'll wash. You dry." He handed Sammy a towel.

"What's Miss Sadie going to do?"

"I'll put things away and wash the table."

"Okay."

At the reluctance dragging the word out, Logan glanced again at Sadie and, when their eyes met, he saw a reflection of his amusement and they grinned at each other. Her smile slowly disappeared but their look held. The moment was fragile with possibility. His heart lurched sideways.

She blinked rapidly and spun away to scrub the table until it could well bleed if it had any life in it.

He brought his attention back to the basin of hot water and the dirty dishes, telling himself he had imagined the sensation that she'd seen deep into his soul. But something had happened and he was at a loss to understand what.

Beth tiptoed from the bedroom just as Sammy dried the last pot. "I'm so sorry, but Jeannie wouldn't let me go until she fell asleep."

Sadie gave the girl a sideways squeeze. "I'm glad you were there to comfort her. It must be scary to have your father disappear and then be moved."

Beth didn't say anything but slipped from under Sadie's arm.

Logan couldn't miss the disappointment in Sadie's face. He'd have to reassure her that it would take time to win their trust.

"Sammy, let's fill the wood box." Sammy trotted after him. As Logan chopped wood, Sammy gathered it up and carried it inside.

Logan returned indoors and looked around. Everything was in order. The children fit into these rooms with ease, and Sadie appeared to have everything under control.

His sense of peace exploded as screams came from the bedroom. He rushed to the door, as did everyone else. They crowded through. He looked around and saw nothing amiss except Jeannie sitting in the middle of the bed, her mouth open as she wailed, tears washing her face.

"Mama. Mama," she gasped.

Beth sank to the edge of the bed and pulled her little sister onto her lap. "Hush, baby, hush."

Jeannie clung to Beth's neck. The high-pitched crying softened to shuddering sobs. Finally, Jeannie sniffed. She wiped her eyes and stared at Logan. "Papa?"

Beth shifted the youngster to her other shoulder. "It's not Papa."

Jeannie leaned around Beth to stare at Logan. Even in the dim light of the room darkened by heavy drapes, Logan could see how her eyes widened. His heart went out to this poor child. He lifted a hand, thinking to brush it over her hair, then, remembering how wary the children were of being touched, he lowered his arm to his side, at a loss to know what to say or do.

Jeannie struggled free of Beth's grasp and made her way around the bed to stand in front of Logan. "Papa." She said the word with such conviction that Logan knew her sleep-drowsy mind had convinced her that her papa had returned. He could not disappoint the child even though she would soon realize he wasn't their father.

He picked up Jeannie.

With a deep sigh, Jeannie rested her head against his neck, her comfort rag clutched in one hand. Her warm breath tickled his skin and he breathed in the scent of little girl. Something that he would have denied if asked stirred within him. Would he ever have a child of his own? He pushed aside the question and, following his earlier instincts, brushed his hand over her head, her hair soft as a downy chick. His eyes grew surprisingly hot.

Beth and Sadie stood before him. Beth's hands curled into fists. Her lips drew into a thin line and her eyes were hard as river rock.

Sadie's eyes revealed little in the low light, but her lips curved upward.

He met her gaze and felt a jolt in the pit of his stomach that he was at a loss to understand. Except it seemed she approved. Of what? The way Jeannie had come to him thinking he was her pa? Or did she like seeing him hold a little girl?

"She's asleep again. I'll take her." Beth's tone made it clear she didn't approve of this contact between Logan and her little sister.

He slipped the child into her sister's arms and stood by as Beth put her back to bed. He was ready to take Jeannie again, should she want it. But Jeannie curled on her side, her rag pulled to her chest, and slept.

They tiptoed from the room.

In the evening light coming through the windows, Logan could see Sadie's expression better.

She scrubbed her lips together and looked thoughtful. "Does she waken often like that?" she asked Beth.

Beth shrugged. "She'll be okay once I'm beside her."

That didn't really answer Sadie's question and Sadie shifted her gaze to Logan, seeking guidance.

He gave what he hoped she'd see as an encouraging smile. "Everything is strange to her right now."

"I guess that's so." Sadie sounded relieved.

"I could stay a little longer if you like." Would she welcome his offer or see it as interference?

He didn't have to guess Beth's feelings. She glowered at him.

"I said she'll be fine," she said. "I could go to bed with her right now, if you're worried."

Sammy laughed. "I'm not going to bed so early."

"We'll be fine," Sadie's words were firm, full of conviction.

Logan looked about. He could find no reason to delay his departure. "I best get home."

Sammy, who had crawled up to sit beside Beth on the cot, jumped to his feet. "You're leaving? Who will protect us?"

Logan's insides twisted. Why did the boy think he needed protection? He'd certainly had none out in that awful shack. "You're safe here. No one will bother you."

Sammy looked at the windows and the doors, his mouth working. "But what if they do?"

"I'll ask my uncle to watch out for you. Will that help?"

Sammy gave Logan some serious study. His chest rose and fell more rapidly than normal. "He can't see us all the time."

Logan looked at Sadie, saw her surprise and concern…and something more—a slight narrowing of her eyes as if she read something sinister in Sammy's fears.

He looked at Beth. She watched with an impassive expression, not willing to trust anyone to share Sammy's concerns.

"Why can't you stay?" Sammy asked.

"My family will be worried if I don't go home. Besides, I promised my grandfather to help him find some books." No one else was available to take care of the old man's needs. Besides, Grandfather asked only Logan for such favors. He hated to ask at all, but Logan went out of his way to see that Grandfather had everything he needed. This morning he had bemoaned the fact he couldn't reach the books on the upper shelves and said he was getting short of reading material.

Logan had promised that as soon as he finished in town, he would arrange the shelves so Grandfather could reach his books.

"I tell you what. I'll go get Miss Sadie's school bell. If you need help, you ring it really hard and Uncle George will come running." He'd alert a few close neighbors, as well. "How's that?" And first thing tomorrow he would construct a drop bar to secure the door.

Sammy seemed to slip a mask over his feelings. "Yeah, sure. You're right. We'll be fine."

Which, Logan understood, meant Sammy wouldn't be expecting any help from Logan. "I'll be back tomorrow and make sure you are all safe and sound." He was more than half tempted to move into the schoolroom so he could keep an eye on them day and night, but he could just hear all the ladies in town whispering that Logan Marshall was back to his wayward ways, though he failed to see how he was to blame for the actions of the girls he'd courted. No, for both his sake and Sadie's, he wouldn't set up quarters in the classroom.

He trotted across the street, retrieved the school bell from the back room of the store and took it to Sadie.

Still, he hesitated about leaving them. Three frightened children were a big responsibility.

"Walk me to the wagon," he said to Sadie.

Her resistance was so fleeting he might have persuaded himself he hadn't seen it. Then she nodded and followed him outside.

"Are you going to be okay with them?"

She bristled. "Of course I am."

"I expect the first night will be the worst."

"To be honest, I'm more concerned about tomorrow when I have to leave the girls to teach." She looked back at her living quarters. "They are all so afraid."

He heard the hard note in her voice and knew she blamed the father for the children's fears. "They have lots of reasons to be frightened. The death of their mother, their father missing, being alone out there, and now being here with people who are strangers to them."

"Not to mention the bruises on Sammy's back."

It wasn't something he could deny, given the evidence, but neither was he about to blame a missing father. But then who did he blame? "I'll be back before you have to leave, so the girls won't be alone and defenseless." He didn't know why he'd added the final word and wished he hadn't when Sadie spun about to face him. He'd only been thinking of Sammy's concerns—be they real or the fears of children who had experienced too many losses.

"You think they might have need of protection?"

"Don't all children?"

Her eyes darkened to the color of old pines. Her lips trembled and then she pressed them together and wrapped her arms across her chest in a move so self-protective that he instinctively reached for her, but at the look on her face, he lowered his arms, instead.

She shuddered.

From the thought of him touching her or because of something she remembered? He couldn't say, but neither could he leave her without knowing she was okay. Ignoring the idea that she might object to his forwardness, wanting only to make sure she knew he was concerned about her and the children, he cupped one hand to her shoulder. He knew he'd done the right thing when she leaned into his palm. "Sadie, I'll stay if you need me to. I can sleep in the schoolroom, or over at Uncle George's. Or even under the stars."

She glanced past him to the pile of lumber at the back of the yard. For the space of a heartbeat, he thought she'd ask him to stay, then she drew in a long breath.

"We'll be fine, though I would feel better leaving them in the morning if I knew you were here."

He squeezed her shoulder. "I'll be here." He hesitated, still not wanting to leave.

She stepped away from him, forcing him to lower his arm to his side. "Goodbye, then. And thank you for your help."

"Don't forget we're partners in this." He waited for her to acknowledge his statement.

"Very well."

"Goodbye for now. I'll see you in the morning." He forced himself to climb into the wagon and flick the reins. He turned for one last look before he rode out of sight.

Chapter Four

$\sim$

Sadie waved as Logan drove away. With the school bell clutched to her chest she felt a little like Sammy. Who was going to keep them all safe? Not that she feared an intruder. The danger that concerned her would come in the form of a man who thought he had the right to walk in like he belonged. No one would be suspicious of him until it was too late. And then many would still see him as a friend or partner. She shook her head, realizing she was thinking of her past, not her present.

Logan had said they were partners in caring for the children. She wished he'd used any other word than the one that made her feel dirty inside and out, her heart clenching with a sense of abandonment.

God, help me forget my past and focus on my future. Help me know what these children need. She went back inside and set the bell in the middle of the table.

"Miss Sadie?" Beth's voice carried a note of caution that Sadie wished she could erase. "I'm sorry I wasn't here to help clean up the kitchen. Next time leave the dishes, and I'll do them after Jeannie has settled."

Oh, Sadie ached at such an overdeveloped sense of responsibility, and it deepened her suspicions regarding the family. Could it be that Beth strove to avoid outbursts by taking care of every detail? "Beth, my dear, what you did was far more important than dishes."

Beth's eyes widened. "What do you mean?"

"You comforted and calmed a little girl. To my way of thinking that should always take precedence over dishes. Don't you agree?"

Beth nodded. "Yes, miss."

"Besides, there was plenty of help."

"I dried," Sammy said with some disgust. "Logan made me."

"That's good." The worried furrow in Beth's forehead disappeared.

Sadie felt the muscles in her own forehead relax. "I need to prepare lessons for tomorrow."

Sammy looked about the small room. "What're we gonna do?"

"You could work on your sums. You need the practice."

"Aw. No fair having to live with the teacher."

Sadie laughed. "I expect it has advantages as well as disadvantages."

Sammy's look demanded to know what the advantages would be but, before he could speak, Beth intercepted.

"I'll help him." She sat at the table and tipped her head at Sammy to indicate he should join her.

As slowly as possible, Sammy shuffled the three feet to the chair beside Beth.

Sadie handed them a work sheet. It would give her

a chance to observe Beth and assess what level of education she had received.

It was soon apparent that Beth had the basic skills necessary for math. Tomorrow, Sadie would give a reading assignment so she could judge her reading ability.

Sammy finished and grew restless. Beth shushed him several times even though he made little noise. Again, Sadie wondered if the girl wasn't overly cautious.

"Can I go out and play?" Sammy asked.

"Certainly. Don't go far. It will soon be bedtime." She looked to Beth. "What time do both of you go to bed?"

Beth glanced at the clock. It showed eight. "It's about time."

Sammy was out the door before either of them could inform him he must stay.

Again, Sadie looked to Beth for direction.

Beth watched her, seeking a clue as to Sadie's response. Again, that guarded cautiousness.

"Should I call him back?" Sadie asked.

Beth shrugged. "It wouldn't hurt him to run off some energy so he'll sleep better."

"What about you? Would you like to go out and play?"

Beth blinked, and blinked again. "Play?"

"Perhaps go for a walk? Enjoy some fresh air?"

Beth's gaze darted to the window. Her chest rose and fell rapidly. She jerked her attention from the window to the bedroom door. Her fingers bunched into tight fists. "I better stay in case Jeannie wakes up."

"That's fine. You do whatever you think is best."

Beth looked at her hands, seemed to realize how tightly she squeezed her fingers and hid them under the table.

Sadie could not let the moment pass without saying something. "Beth, I can tell you're afraid—" At the way Beth's eyes flared, Sadie moderated her speech. "Or worried. But I promise you, you are safe here. I'll make sure of it. So will Logan."

Beth watched Sadie steadily, giving no hint as to how she felt about Sadie's words.

Sadie waited.

Finally Beth spoke. "He isn't even here."

Sadie nodded. "But he did bring us the bell." She wondered if Beth would understand it was a little joke and was pleased when the girl grinned.

"Could you throw it hard enough to knock out an intruder?"

Sadie chuckled. "I might be better off to outrun one."

Beth's hands rested on the table and she picked at a thumbnail, then she bolted from the table. "I should call Sammy in." She went to the door and called her brother.

Sammy came, though he made it clear that he'd had other plans. "Tomorrow I am going to make a fort."

"Please ask Logan before you take any of his wood," Sadie said. "Wash up and get ready for bed." She dug a little shirt from the box of clothes. "You can wear this for the night." Changing clothes would give her a chance to get a good look at his back.

He washed at the basin of water she'd prepared then sat on the edge of his cot. "I'm a boy and you're a girl. I'm not getting undressed in front of you."

How was she to see his back if he refused to take his shirt off in front of her?

Beth sighed. "Sometimes he gets like this. Sammy, go to bed. I'm going now." She headed for the bedroom door.

Sadie hesitated, then took the lamp and followed her. She paused at the doorway. "Sammy, have a good night. Call if you need anything. Good night."

"'Night, teacher."

Beth slipped under the covers beside her sleeping little sister as Sadie set the lamp of the small table between the beds. Conscious of a pair of eyes watching, she turned her back and slipped from her clothes, hanging them on the nearby hooks. She pulled a simple cotton nightdress over her head, loosened her hair and began to brush it slowly and methodically. Should she hurry her bedtime routine or adjust it? Something Aunt Sarah said, came to mind.

Begin as you wish to continue.

Good advice. She finished brushing her hair and braided it. She took her Bible and sat on the edge of her bed. "I always read a few verses before I go to sleep. I hope it doesn't disturb you."

"Not at all."

Sadie knew Beth watched her, but she could not make out her expression in the low light. She opened her Bible and read a Psalm. "'Wait on the Lord: be of good courage, and he shall strengthen thy heart.'"

Thank You, Lord, for this word of encouragement. I trust You to guide and strengthen me on this unfamiliar journey.

"Miss, can I ask you a question?"

"Yes, of course. Anything you want."

"How do you know if he's a good guy?"

Sadie knew the girl meant Logan, and also a whole lot more. Like how would she know when, or if, it was safe to trust a man. The question reverberated through Sadie's insides. She'd trusted Father's partner. The whole family had. Learning he was not what she believed had shattered her ability to trust easily, and yet she trusted Logan. Why? She had to understand so she could answer Beth. "I wasn't sure at first that I could, but there's something about him. Perhaps it's his dedication to what he believes in."

"Like what?" Beth's voice ached with the need to know.

"Like family. He strongly believes in the value of family and does everything in his power to protect it." She might disagree with his stance but, as she said to Beth, his loyalty to his belief made it easier to trust him. "Plus, he's willing to help others and he admits his mistakes."

"Is that enough?"

"Beth, my dear, I understand your caution, and it isn't a bad thing so long as you don't allow it to shut you off from other people."

The lamplight allowed Sadie to see the girl watching her, searching for understanding and perhaps a whole lot more. It made Sadie feel so inadequate. She knew children only in the classroom setting. Not in a family setting. That was Logan's field of expertise.

And Logan had gone out to the ranch...to his family. They would always come first in his mind, and she supposed that was how it should be even if it had been quite different for her.

Their experiences with family would always be a

barrier between them. She could deal with that. Her first concern was protecting these children. She could manage on her own. Let Logan concern himself with those at the ranch.

The words she'd so recently spoken to Beth echoed in her head. *Don't allow your caution to cause you to shut other people out.*

Sadie did that. She knew she did. And she wasn't sure she could change.

Though, she admitted with a little smile as she climbed into bed and turned off the lamp, Logan had succeeded in breaking down some of her barriers without even trying. Perhaps without even caring if he did or not.

She turned on her side and tried to ignore the ache that sucked at her heart.

Logan was anxious to head for town first thing after breakfast, but as he was about to leave, a crash came from the sitting room He rushed in to see if Grandfather was okay. The older man had fallen trying to rearrange the chairs in the sitting room to better suit him. The other Marshall men had already left and Annie had gone out to get the eggs, so Logan stayed to help the old man to his feet and then moved the chairs to Grandfather's liking.

"Don't be doing anything foolish while I'm gone," he'd warned the old man.

"Pshaw. You don't need to worry about me. Better you think about that little schoolteacher and those kids. She'll be needing all the help you can give. If there's anything she needs, you just let us know."

"I'll do that, though the whole works of them are

mighty independent." It was more like *guarded*, but he wasn't going to get into that discussion with his grandfather.

"I like that little Miss Sadie. Have since they came out here that first day they arrived in town."

Logan knew he meant the doctor and his daughter and Isabelle, as well as Sadie. He and Conner had not been in attendance. "I found her a little shy." He didn't add that he no longer saw her as shy. Stubborn, yes, and wounded. He hadn't planned to use that word, but it fit her. He wondered who had hurt her.

"She's a sweet gal and don't you be overlooking that fact."

Logan tilted his head and considered his grandfather. "What are you saying?"

"Boy, you know what I mean."

Logan figured he probably did, but he wasn't going to admit it. His grandfather had a reputation as a matchmaker. "She's devoted to her teaching."

"Not so devoted she hasn't taken on a family, and I see her fitting the role perfectly. But—" Grandfather shook his gnarly finger at Logan. "You're as gun-shy around women as a green colt."

"With good reason."

"A few bad apples don't mean you can't ever enjoy apple pie again."

Logan snorted. "I like apple pie just fine." He finished adjusting Grandfather's things so they were within easy reach. "Now I have to get to town."

"I wasn't talking about pies." Grandfather's words followed him out the door.

Logan knew that but dismissed the old man's words as he settled into the saddle. He didn't normally gallop the four miles from the ranch to Bella Creek, but he wanted to get to town in time to talk to Sadie before she left for school.

His night had been restless, filled with fleeting images of dark eyes filled with fright, screams that jerked him fully awake, his heart pounding.

He didn't like being so far away from the school. What if they needed him? Partners shared responsibilities—yet he'd ridden away, leaving her to deal with the situation on her own.

The presence of a lumbering wagon on the street ahead made him slow his horse to a walk as he reached town. Never had the street seemed so long and so busy. What were all these people doing out and about so early in the day? His jaw muscles bunched. Because it wasn't early.

He rode into the school yard.

Sammy perched on the stack of lumber looking like all was right with the world.

A bit of tension drained from Logan's body. "Howdy," he called. He led the horse to the corner of the yard, tossed out some hay and oats he'd brought along. He'd fill a bucket with water once he had checked on Sadie and the girls.

Sammy sauntered over. "You leaving the horse here?"

"Yup."

"Can I ride him?"

"How'd it be if I let you ride after school so long as you do all your lessons?"

"Maybe I don't want to ride that bad."

Logan chuckled. "Sure you do. You just don't want to do your schoolwork."

Sammy scuffed the toe of his well-worn boots in the dirt. "What good is book learnin'?"

"I find it comes in pretty handy when I want to read the newspaper or fill out papers at the bank or figure out how much it will cost to buy a handful of candy."

"Yeah, I suppose."

Logan looked toward the back door. Was everything okay?

As if called by his silent question, Sadie stepped out.

His insides twisted at the dark shadows under her eyes, signs of a restless night. For a half a second he let himself think it was because she wished he'd stayed and helped, but then common sense reared its head and he acknowledged things might not have gone well with the children.

He went to her side. "You look like you could use a little walk." He offered his elbow.

"I don't have time." She tucked her hand about his arm. "But I do need to let you know about last night."

They left the school yard and went to one of the benches in the town square. They were far enough away the children couldn't hear them yet close enough they could see them.

He waited for her to sit and arrange her skirts about her. The same dark gray skirt, the same neck-choking shirtwaist. Her hair seemed a mite untidy, as if she hadn't had time to brush it into submission. He kind of liked what he saw though wisely he kept his opinion to himself. "You have a rough night?"

"We all did. Jeannie called out for her mama and papa every hour or so. Mostly Beth soothed and got her back to sleep, but twice she squirmed away from Beth and went out to the kitchen calling for her papa."

Sadie looked at Logan, her mouth working and her eyes about to run over with tears. "I think she was looking for you. That poor child. How confusing it is for her."

With his fingertips, Logan captured the one silvery tear that escaped and pressed it between his finger and thumb. "I'll be here all day. I'll spend time with her if she'll let me. Last night when she came to me, it was dark and she was half-asleep. I hope she isn't upset when she realizes I'm not her father."

Sadie watched his fingers as he circled the tips round and round on her tear until it disappeared into his skin. Then, with a slight shiver, she brought her sorrow-filled gaze back to his.

It was all he could do to stop himself from pulling her to his chest and comforting her. But he knew she'd object even if they hadn't been in public where a schoolteacher's behavior would be open to scrutiny. He felt her wariness. Knew the fact she'd allowed him to touch her signaled how weary she was.

"Sammy had a bad night, too. He woke up yelling and flailing around as if he fought someone off. Both Beth and I tried to wake him. Eventually he turned over and went back to sleep. I asked Beth if he did that often. She said only sometimes and he never remembers in the morning. Logan, if you could have seen him, you would know he's deathly afraid of something or someone. I know you would."

"Dawson told me of the nightmares Mattie had after her mother died. Perhaps it's normal considering their loss."

She stiffened. He knew she would present her argument about a missing and violent father. He didn't know what she expected him to do about it, so he spoke before she could voice her concerns.

"Sadie, I regret leaving you alone to deal with all this."

Her smile trembled. "You can hardly move in with us."

He wanted to say he could. But he knew it wasn't possible. He had no desire to ruin her reputation. "I know, but I'll stay around all day and do what I can to help."

She smacked her hands on her knees. "Good. I'll find it easier to go to work knowing you're with the girls. And I better get over there before my students arrive."

They returned to her rooms and she gathered up her lesson material and the bell. She studied Beth and Jeannie, who stood hand in hand against the wall, then brought her gaze to Logan.

He understood how difficult it was for her to leave the girls.

"They'll be fine with me," he assured her.

She nodded. "Sammy, make sure you're there on time." She left the room.

Beth crowded to the window and watched until she was out of sight. Then she withdrew into the farthest corner of the room, Jeannie held fast at her side.

Logan flinched before her fearful, accusing stare. He could not miss the fact that she was uncomfortable in his presence. "I'll be outside working if you need anything." He strode from the room. The sooner he got this family sorted out, the better for the children, but his promise to stay nearby while Sadie was at school meant he couldn't begin searching for the father.

However, he could work on the schoolhouse and get it finished.

Sammy hovered at Logan's side, watching Logan measure a board for the front step.

Across the street, the school bell clanged.

Logan jerked to his full height. "Sammy, you better not be late or we'll both hear from the schoolteacher."

Sammy took off like a shot, racing across the street without even checking to see if it was safe. He stopped long enough on the step to wave to Logan, then disappeared inside.

Logan nailed the board in place, then decided to work on the side of the building closest to the door to Sadie's living quarters so he could better see what went on there.

Beth came out and filled a pail with water, then dashed back in.

He knew she watched him without really looking at him.

From inside came the voices of the girls—Jeannie's thin, demanding tone and Beth's softer, calming one.

The conversation went on and on, Jeannie growing louder, more insistent. He figured they were having an argument and grinned. Would Beth prevail against her little sister?

And then the sound of voices ended. He heard the clatter of a pot on the stove. His grin deepened as he recalled some of the arguments he'd had with his brothers and with Annie. His ma had said family was the place to learn to give and take, to negotiate and to meet halfway.

Sadie had told Anne she didn't have any siblings. How did she learn those skills? Or had she? Maybe living with the Weiss children would help to make up for the unhappy experience of her family life. Again he vowed he would learn what had happened to her.

Then he informed himself he didn't care. All that mattered was taking care of the children. He had no intention of letting himself think about the schoolmarm as anything more than someone to help with them.

He bent to pick up another piece of wood and caught a flash of pale pink out of the corner of his eyes. Straightening, he looked that direction. Whatever— whoever—it was, they had disappeared around the corner of the building.

Shifting to the right, he watched the corner while he worked.

His attention was soon rewarded. First, Jeannie peeked around and drew back. She did it a second time and a third. Then she slowly edged into full view and watched him, her hands clasped behind her as she rocked back and forth.

Logan stopped working, his hands still up at the window and he waited to see what she would do.

She studied him, her eyes wide and hopeful.

He didn't move for fear of sending her into retreat.

Her hands came to her front. She stopped rocking. Her study of him went on and on.

He waited. Would she retreat or come closer?

"You aren't my papa." She said it with a good deal of resignation, as if not wanting to admit the truth.

"No, I'm not. I'm sorry."

Another spell of waiting as the child considered him.

His arms grew weary and he lowered them to his side. Other than that, he did not move.

"My papa's not coming back."

His gut kicked a protest. "Why do you say that?"

She glanced over her shoulder and when she saw no one, she leaned toward him and whispered, "I'm not supposed to tell anyone."

Logan stilled his reaction and quelled his questions. Had the father abandoned them with instruction not to tell? His teeth creaked as he clamped down on his jaw. He'd track down the man and make him come back and look after his family.

"Where do you live?" Jeannie asked.

"On a ranch four miles from town that way." He pointed in the general direction.

"You got a mama and papa?"

"My mama died, but I have my papa."

She nodded. "My mama died. My papa—" Again she glanced over her shoulder and didn't finish, even though Beth did not come into sight.

He wanted to assure her he would find her father and bring him back, but he didn't want to get her hopes up too soon. Something awful might have happened to the man. Then what would become of the children?

He provided his own answer. Sadie would keep them. And he'd help her. Or they could move to the ranch, where they would be surrounded by his large family.

The door behind Jeannie opened and shut with a bang. "Jeannie, where are you?"

"Oh-oh. Beth's mad at me." Jeannie darted past Logan and out of sight around the front of the school.

Beth stalked around the corner. "You seen Jeannie?" Each word carried the sharpness of a honed knife blade, as if she blamed him for any mischief Jeannie had gotten into.

"She went thataway." He jerked his thumb over his shoulder. "Don't be too hard on her."

Beth skidded to a stop and gave him a look fit to set a forest ablaze. "You got no right to stick your nose into our business. We can manage fine without help from you or anyone else. We only agreed to come because we were out of food." She stomped away.

His mouth agape, he stared after her. Was she this rude to Sadie? Or was it only him?

The door to the living quarters opened and closed and the murmur of the girls' voices reached him. At least they sounded kind enough, so Beth had only been angry with him and not her little sister.

He wished she understood that both he and Sadie were simply trying to help them. A little voice in the back of his mind echoed that he wanted to help Sadie, too. But would she let him?

Chapter Five

Noon hour rolled around and Sadie forced herself to sit at her desk, eat her lunch and watch the children eat theirs. Then she went out to the back and watched them play. All the while her thoughts were across the street wondering how Beth and Jeannie were managing and, against her better judgment, remembering how Logan had wiped tears from her eyes. *Partners*, he'd said. But his kindness felt gentler than anything the word *partner* meant to her. Did she trust him?

She'd tried to convince Beth she did.

Trust could only go so far. It sometimes couldn't stand being tested. If he learned how she'd been ruined by a man, he'd see her for who…what…she really was.

But for now they were together in looking after the children though, even there, they had very different goals. She had very little doubt that the children feared their father. Logan, on the other hand, thought the man only needed to be found and given some help in dealing with the loss of his wife.

He saw family as the salvation for these children.

And why wouldn't he. His family was strong and supportive.

She knew family did not always come to the rescue of the children.

But, for now, she welcomed his help. He was at the school making sure the girls were safe while she taught the town's children and kept an eye on Sammy.

She looked around. Sammy was in the far corner surrounded by a group of the boys. She knew immediately that they were teasing him and she headed that direction.

One of the boys looked over his shoulder and saw her approaching. The circle of boys dispersed.

Sammy fled before she could stop him.

She groaned. Not again. Turning, she trudged back to the temporary schoolroom. "Kitty, I'm leaving you in charge while I run across the street." Kitty was the eldest of the girls but, sadly, not the best of students.

"Yes, Miss Young. Is it Sammy again?"

She didn't answer. Kitty had been called on several times because of Sammy's habit of running away. "I'll be right back." Sadie went out through the store and headed across the street.

Logan sat with his back against the wall, enjoying the warm sunshine. He sprang to his feet as soon as he saw her. "What's wrong?"

"Sammy is gone again." Her voice thinned with worry.

Logan stepped away from the building and looked around. He crooked his finger and pointed toward the back of the lot.

Sadie eased forward until she could see Sammy sitting on the lumber pile. Logan's horse stood close enough that the boy could rub his hand up and down his head.

Sadie nodded, but she didn't go to the boy. "Maybe talking to the horse will calm him."

"What happened?" Logan asked softly.

"Some boys were teasing him."

"I suppose they were calling him teacher's pet. It's to be expected but not accepted."

"I've not shown him any special favors, so why should they say that?"

"Because he lives with you. All you can do is try not to draw attention to the fact. Come on, let's have a talk with him."

Side by side, they walked to the pile of lumber.

Only Sammy's darted gaze acknowledged their presence.

Sadie didn't say anything. Perhaps he only saw her as the teacher. She'd let Logan handle this if he could.

Logan propped one booted foot against a board and leaned his elbow on his knee. "I expect the noon break is almost over."

Sammy shrugged.

"Why don't you and I walk Miss Sadie back to the classroom?"

Sammy didn't respond for a moment, then he bowed his head. "You're gonna make me one way or 'nother, aren't you?"

Logan grinned at Sadie, then grew serious as he turned back to Sammy. "It's easier for everyone if you go agreeably."

Sadie's respect for Logan grew as she witnessed his patience with the child.

Sighing heavily, Sammy scrambled from the wood and dragged himself toward the street.

Sadie glanced at her living quarters, hoping for a glimpse of the girls, but there was no sign of them. Kate carried something from the doctor's house next door, saw Sadie and Logan, and waved. Sadie would have loved to explain about the children, but Sammy was halfway across the street and she followed him.

Logan unwound from his casual stance and fell into step beside her.

It crossed her mind to tell him she could manage on her own, but the words never got further than a fleeting thought.

They entered the store. Logan greeted his uncle and crossed to the schoolroom. He went right out the back door to the alley where the children played.

"Thank you, Kitty." Sadie stood in the doorway, watching Logan.

He went to the far corner, to the huddle of boys, who stood to attention at his approach.

She grinned. His size alone earned him respect, and his bearing even more so. He moved with the ease of one who knew who he was, and something about his carriage spoke of authority.

He stopped before the boys, crossed his arms and leaned back on his heels.

She couldn't hear what he said, but the boys all nodded.

He waved to the boys, returned to the doorway and smiled down at her with such sweet kindness that her heart stalled halfway through a beat. "We have an understanding. If you need anything more, I'm just across the street." With that he was gone.

She stood stock-still, staring at the play area without seeing anything though her head flooded with a kaleidoscope of dancing colors.

A clatter in the store jerked her back to her responsibilities as the teacher. She turned to get her bell from the desk and met the wide-eyed stare of three girls who had seen the whole thing and likely read all sorts of romantic meaning to her reaction.

"Time to resume classes," she said with as much aplomb as she could manage, and rang the bell outside to bring the children in.

The boys were subdued and their glances in Sammy's direction guarded.

What had Logan said to them to have such a profound effect? She'd ask as soon as classes ended. She glanced at the clock. Only two more hours to go until she saw him again.

Only to ask what he'd said, she told herself. Only to inquire as to how the girls had been all day. Nothing more. Certainly not the hope he would look at her again the same way he had in the doorway and trigger again that unfamiliar reaction.

She ducked her head to hide the smile that tugged at her lips.

As quickly as it came, the smile fled. She must never let the allure of a few special moments make her forget who she was.

Logan returned to work. Poor Sammy. It certainly wasn't ideal to be living with the teacher. Logan needed to locate the missing father as soon as possible, but he'd promised to stay with the girls and would have to wait until Sadie returned before he could leave.

Jeannie had gathered up some things she'd found in the yard and sat at the corner of the house with the assorted bits of wood in her lap. She arranged them and talked to them like they were her children.

The door opened and closed.

He edged away from the building in the pretense of looking for something and saw Beth sitting where she could watch Jeannie but not be seen by Logan as he worked. She held a book and bent her head over it, in a pose of deep concentration.

It jarred his thoughts to realize she was guarding her little sister against him.

Sadie had started out being just as cautious, but he'd seen a change in her. When he'd passed her in the doorway of the schoolroom, their gazes had connected with such force he'd almost stumbled. Telling himself it was only gratitude for helping with Sammy did not erase the way he felt. Not that he could even explain how that was. Only that something inside him seemed touched by honey.

To divert his wayward thoughts he began to talk to the girls, knowing Beth could hear even if he couldn't see her.

He talked about his brothers, his sister, Annie, and his niece, Mattie. He talked about the horses, and about the calves that were being born.

Jeannie listened raptly and said nothing, though once or twice she opened her mouth to speak, glanced at Beth and closed it again with a deep sigh.

Logan paused to cut a board. From his position he caught a glimpse of Beth. Her book lay unopened on her lap and he smiled to himself. She might not care to admit it, but she was listening to his ramblings, too.

He knew school was out when Sammy raced into the yard.

The afternoon had passed more quickly than he'd expected. Only three or four times did he look up and wish he could share the moment with Sadie. What would she think of his stories about family life? Would she listen if he tried to tell her, or would she grow silent and stubborn?

Jeannie bounded to her feet as her brother stopped to look around. "I play with you?"

Poor little girl had barely moved since lunch. Once or twice, when she had started to get up, Beth had murmured something and she'd sat again.

The children needed to run and jump. Constructing playground equipment had been at the bottom of his list, but he now moved it to the top. Swings first then a teeter-totter. Maybe he'd play catch with Sammy. The boy could stand something to do.

Sammy and Jeannie went around the far side of the lumber pile, and their murmured voices indicated they were playing contentedly.

Beth scurried inside and closed the door.

Logan looked toward the store. Where was Sadie? He stood, waiting. When she didn't appear, he dropped his hammer, jogged across the street and through the store. He jerked to a halt in the doorway and stared at Sadie. She sat with her head bowed.

"Sadie, are you okay?" He crossed to her side in hurried strides.

She glanced up, her eyes wide with surprise. "I didn't hear you enter. Yes, I'm fine. But I'm curious what you said to those boys at noon. Whatever it was, they behaved like model citizens all afternoon."

"I didn't say anything much. Told them I was working on the schoolhouse and it would soon be ready. Said wouldn't they be happy to be in a proper classroom with a proper play yard?"

"That's it?"

"That's about it."

"They must have read more into it. Likely they were impressed by your size." Her gaze went from one of his shoulders to the other, and a faint color stung her cheeks. "Maybe just knowing you're that close seemed like a threat to them."

It seemed she admired his size. He kind of liked that. "I might have mentioned that they should make things easy for Miss Young." He stumbled on the words. Her statement and her looks made him feel like expanding his chest.

Something dark and—dare he hope?—welcoming warmed her hazel eyes and then she blinked away all emotion. "I was fortifying myself by reading a few Bible verses and praying."

He shifted his gaze, saw the open Bible before her. "Are you fortifying yourself against me?" He closed his eyes. What had possessed him to speak such foolish words?

"Why would you suggest such a thing?" She kept her attention on the desktop.

"I'm sorry, but all afternoon Beth has been treating me like she wished I'd disappear." He explained how Beth had acted.

Sadie pushed to her feet. "Don't take it personally— I think she is afraid of men."

"Why…" The implication of her words made him

draw back. "You think her father has hurt her, too. Like Sammy?"

Sadie shrugged. "I'm only telling you what I suspect based on the behavior I've observed."

He rocked his head back and forth. It hardly seemed possible a man would hurt his own children, and he refused to judge without giving the man a chance to defend himself. "Their father could be hurt or in trouble." And if his reason for being absent was different than that, Logan would not accept any excuses for neglecting the children. "I'm going to track him down and bring him back to his family. I came to tell you I will start looking as soon as you come home to look after the children."

Her eyes had that brittle look to them again, the one that he'd come to recognize as signaling her distrust of family. A shock ran through his veins. Or did it signal a distrust of fathers? One day, he vowed, he would get her to tell him what had gone wrong to make her so suspicious.

She ducked her head without saying all the things he'd seen building behind her eyes. Perhaps she'd read his defensiveness and decided it was pointless to argue with him.

"I'll get on home so you can start looking." She gathered up some books and papers.

He stood, hat in hand, watching her. When he saw she meant to leave, he sprang forward and held the door for her. As he stepped back to let her go ahead of him, he remembered he had come racing over here to make sure she was okay. He'd hoped for a special look, like the one they'd shared at noon hour.

Instead, she marched ahead of him, her head high.

He knew if he looked into her eyes, he would not see warmth or even welcome.

His sigh, barely audible, drew her defensive gaze his way.

"What's wrong?"

He couldn't begin to find the words to explain his frustration. "It's been a long day." Let her read into that what she wanted.

They crossed the street together. Likely anyone watching would assume they were enjoying each other's company, though his mood was far from amicable. They parted ways in the school yard and he headed for his horse.

As he rounded the pile of lumber he saw that Sammy had gathered up broken branches and dried bushes and created an enclosure. He and Jeannie sat inside like pioneers trying to survive the roughest of conditions. Likely that's how it felt to them. Surviving harsh conditions not of their own choosing.

Logan grabbed the saddle blanket and put it on his horse's back.

Sammy scrambled from the pile of debris. "You gonna let me ride?"

"I've got an errand to take care of."

"Aw. You said if I did my lessons and I did..."

Logan had indeed promised. "Tell you what. I'll be back before dark and let you ride him. Okay?"

Sammy nodded, but Logan saw the doubt in his eyes. "I promise and when I promise, I do it." He thought of the missing father. "Unless something happens that I have no control over."

Sammy grew interested. "Like what?"

Logan gave it a moment's thought. "Like maybe my

horse breaks a leg." He patted his black horse. "Sorry, Brewster, I was only talking about what happens to other horses." He turned back to Sammy. "Or I fall and knock myself out."

Sammy pretended to fall on his head and rose, laughing. "You ever done that?"

"Nope. And I'd like to keep it that way."

He threw his saddle on the horse, cinched it and swung up. "I'll be back," he told Sammy, then lifted his gaze toward the door. Sadie watched him. He was too far away to be able to read her eyes or be certain of her expression, but if he had to guess he would say she looked just a little like she might miss him when he was gone. He bit back a groan. He was dreaming impossible things. Likely, she was anxious to have him leave. "I'll come back." He spoke directly to her, then waved to all of them, though Beth remained out of sight in the kitchen.

Logan meant to ask at every business in town if they'd seen the man or heard of him. He went from one place to the next, each time posing the same question.

"Has Mr. Weiss been here of late?"

The answer was consistently no—they had never even met the man—until he reached the blacksmith shop. At Logan's question, the blacksmith rubbed his whiskery chin. "He was here once. But that was weeks ago."

That didn't go along with what Uncle George had said or the children claiming they'd only moved here a week or so ago. Of course, the man might have been looking for a place for his family to live.

The blacksmith continued. "I only recall him because I once had a neighbor with the same last name and asked if they happened to be related. Mr. Weiss didn't think so."

He thanked the man and moved on. Not one other person could recall seeing the man.

"What's he look like?" the livery man asked.

"I've never seen him." Why hadn't he thought to ask his uncle or the smithy? Logan backtracked to the blacksmith shop and asked for a description.

"Far as I recall, he was medium build, light brown hair and brown eyes. Can't tell you much else. I do remember noticing he had a slight limp."

Armed with the description, Logan again made his rounds. Still no one could recall the man.

He went back to the store. "Did you notice that Mr. Weiss had a limp?"

"Can't say as I did. But the man wasn't wanting to chat. In and out. Anyone else seen him?"

Logan told of his futile questioning.

"Doesn't sound like the same man, but then I saw so little of him and I was busy with other customers," Uncle George said. "Have you asked out at Wolf Hollow?"

"I'll do that." For now, though, he wanted to get back to the school and share his disappointment with Sadie.

He rode across the street.

"You're back," Sammy shouted, holding his little sister's hand in a protective way that made Logan admire the boy. "Now can I have a ride?"

The boy's noise brought Sadie and Beth to the door.

Logan rode a little closer. Sadie's eyes asked a dozen questions. He gave a slight twist of his head to indicate his failure. She pulled her mouth down in what he hoped was disappointment and not resignation. He wanted to tell her he would find the man if he had to ride clear to Great Falls and ask at every farm or ranch on his way. Or back into the mountains and boldly go to every mine. "Is there time before supper to let him have a ride?"

She nodded, her eyes never leaving his. "There's plenty of time."

He didn't immediately turn to Sammy as he and Sadie continued to study each other. Did she mean more than Sammy riding the horse when she said there was plenty of time? His eyes narrowed, uncertain of what he thought he saw. Was she glad he hadn't located the man?

Sammy tugged on his arm and Logan set aside his questions. He pulled Sammy up behind him and reined down the alley. He kept Brewster to a walk until they left the town behind. At that point he let him gallop, Sammy clinging to Logan's back.

"Yahoo," Sammy yelled, and Logan grinned. He well remembered riding this way with either his pa or grandfather.

A mile later, he reined around and at a slower pace returned to the school yard.

Sammy swung down. "That was great. Thanks a lot."

Jeannie stood on the pile of lumber, watching and waiting.

"You want a ride, too?" Logan asked.

An eager light flashed in her brown eyes. She nodded, then glanced past him. Without looking, he knew Beth was observing them. Jeannie's lips pursed as she turned back to Logan. "Yes, please."

He pulled her up and put her in front of him and

rode sedately down the alley. He turned up the street and circled the block, returning a few minutes later to the school yard. He reined up at the door where Beth stood, her expression forbidding. He lowered Jeannie to the ground.

"She's back safe and sound."

Beth's look went on and on, silently challenging and warning.

Sadie came to the door and stood beside her, looking from Beth to Logan, no doubt wondering at how the air hung heavy with challenge.

Logan had nothing to prove, nothing to hide, and he broke away first. "Beth, do you want to ride?"

She scowled.

"You can ride on your own if you like." He dismounted and offered her the reins.

"No, thanks." She spun on her heel and retreated to the bedroom.

"What was that all about?" Sadie asked.

"I can't say, except she is very protective of her brother and sister, especially around me." At the way Sadie's eyebrows reached for her hairline, he wished he hadn't worded his answer that way. "Don't go reading more into that than simply normal cautiousness around strangers."

Her eyebrows lowered and she smiled without humor. "I wonder if you believe what you say or do you feel you have to defend your belief in family against all odds?"

"Yes."

"Yes, you believe what you say or have to defend family?"

He shrugged. At the moment he wasn't certain of

either and had no intention of admitting it to her. He believed in family and would someday tell her how his had stood by him even when he made foolish decisions. Ah. What was the point? She'd already pointed out her belief that he had a perfect family but not everyone did. He took that to include herself.

In what category did the children belong?

Jeannie had joined Sammy to chatter excitedly about her "horsey" ride. The two of them came to Brewster to stroke his side.

Sammy stood before Sadie. "Miss Sadie, can Logan stay for supper?"

Sadie's eyes suddenly revealed nothing. "I'm sure he's expected at home."

Her reply made Logan want to stay if only for the hope he might again see the welcome he thought he'd witnessed when he'd passed her in the door of the temporary schoolroom. He was beginning to think he'd only imagined he'd seen anything of note. But perhaps he could discover why she held such suspicions about the children's father. Not that Logan was blindly believing in the man's goodness, but he was prepared to withhold judgment until he found him and discovered the truth.

"Annie knows to expect me when she sees me."

Sammy grabbed his hand. "Then you can stay?"

Logan could not believe how much he wanted Sadie to invite him. How badly he wanted to see any sort of welcome. How desperately he wanted to tell her of his frustration at trying to learn anything of Mr. Weiss. He needed to let her know of his plans to go to Wolf Hollow as soon as he could get away. "Only if it's okay with Miss Sadie." He waited, his heartbeat slowing as she considered her answer.

Sadie wanted to refuse to invite Logan to join them for supper. Almost as much as she wanted him to stay. For no other reason than to hear his news. Except she had to *insist* it was the only reason. Had to deny a desire to see if she'd imagined the feeling between them when he was in the schoolroom at noon. And most certainly not because she enjoyed his company. No. Not that. No, she must not invite him to stay.

She would simply tell him she didn't have anything prepared for supper, which was mostly true. "We'd be glad to have you join us for the meal." How had those words come from her mouth when her brain insisted he should leave?

"Thank you. Sammy, do you want to help me take care of my horse?"

"Sure do. Can I lead him?"

Logan handed the reins to Sammy, but he didn't turn around and leave. No. He held her gaze so firmly she couldn't think past this moment. Couldn't hear her usual warnings. Didn't want to hear them. Instead, she let herself fall into his deep look, her mind racing toward—

"I'll be right back." Logan tilted his head in a goodbye gesture and followed Sammy.

Sadie found her senses, though they felt a bit shaky. What was wrong with her? It wasn't like she and Logan had anything in common besides the care of the children and, even on that, they were divided. If he had his way, he would find the father and reunite the family. And if she followed her instincts, she would see they were never returned to the man. She knew fear and loathing when she saw it. Logan, with his ideal family, had no notion of what she feared for the children.

Turning, she met Beth's scowling presence. "Why did you invite him? He's been here all day. He should go home."

Sadie wanted to hug away the girl's resentment but knew Beth would shrink away from such intimacies. She hated that she glimpsed so much fear and loathing in Beth's eyes. "You have to trust me when I say Logan will not hurt you and I will make certain of that."

Beth shifted, suddenly interested in something out the window. She mumbled something. Sadie couldn't catch everything, though she guessed the girl said, "I've heard that before."

If Sadie needed any more convincing that all was not as it should be in this family, Beth's behavior and words provided it.

"Would you like to help me prepare supper?"

Beth shrugged. "I can make supper for us just fine. You and him can have your own meal."

Sadie caught Beth's shoulders and turned her so they were face-to-face. "I don't know why you are so angry at Logan, but I suspect your anger is misplaced. I'm guessing you're angry at someone else and Logan is simply handy for you to vent on. Which hardly seems fair to me." She couldn't have explained to anyone why she defended him so vigorously, apart from knowing it was futile and damaging for Beth to allow her experiences to color every corner of her life. "I invited him and he will be treated politely while he is here. He's helping the best way he can."

Beth's eyes darkened. For a moment, Sadie thought the girl was softening, and then Beth shrugged away.

"My ma would not want me to be rude," she murmured.

"I'm sure she wouldn't. I'm also certain she would want you to ask for help if you needed it and I don't mean only accepting my offer of a home."

Beth stiffened. For a brief moment, Sadie thought she might reveal more of what had happened to them. Instead, she grabbed a paring knife. "Do you want me to peel potatoes?"

"I'd appreciate it." Logan's uncle had provided Sadie with pork chops, and, while Beth peeled vegetables, Sadie browned the meat, covered it with brown gravy and put it in the oven to cook.

Logan and Sammy came inside, Jeannie trotting along beside them.

Beth took a step toward her little sister.

Logan's eyes narrowed and his mouth drew back in a tight line, giving Sadie pause to wonder what had gone on throughout the day. She needed to talk to Logan alone and find out.

"Children, supper will be a few minutes. Why don't you go out and play or go for a walk? Mind you, don't go too far. I'll call when supper is ready."

Beth ushered her sister and brother out the door rather hurriedly, ignoring Jeannie's protest that she didn't want to go outside.

Sadie waited until she could see the children playing at the lumber pile before she turned to Logan. "First, tell me what you found out about their father."

Logan sank to the nearest chair and rested his elbows on the table. He pressed his fingertips to his brow and massaged it.

Sadie's gaze followed the movement of his fingers—long, strong fingers, yet gentle as she'd discovered when he'd caught her tears. She swallowed hard and informed her longing heart that she did not ache for more of those comforting touches.

Logan sat up with a deep sigh. "I asked around town. The good news is the blacksmith remembers the man and provided a bit of a description. So we know he's been around. The bad news is no one else can recall the man except for Uncle George. My uncle says he was here a couple of weeks ago, but the blacksmith is certain it was longer ago than that." His crooked smile told her he had found the news disappointing. "Their stories vary so greatly I wonder if they are talking about the same man."

"I suppose a lot of men go through town or come for supplies. It would be hard for the businesspeople to keep track of everyone."

He nodded. "I'd like to go to Wolf Hollow and look around, but I feel I need to stay and keep an eye on the girls." He rolled his head back and forth as if his neck muscles had knotted. "Not that they seem to appreciate my concern. Or, I should say, Beth doesn't."

"She's wary. And perhaps with good reason."

Those words made Logan lean forward, his expression defensive.

Before he could offer his argument, she spoke again. "What did they do all day? I kept thinking of them. Beth should be in class, but Jeannie is too young to attend school so Beth needs to be here." She paused to consider the options and could think of no other solu-

tion. "This seems to be the best arrangement for now."
She repeated her question. "What did they do?"

A faint smile curved his mouth. "Mostly Beth did
her best to avoid me and to keep Jeannie away from
me. The little one wanted to talk, but she seemed to understand her big sister wouldn't approve. So I talked."
His grin widened.

"What did you talk about?" She admitted it was
more than curiosity that prompted her question. She
wished she'd been a little bird perched on a nearby
branch, hearing his every word. She would not try to
explain why she cared except there was something
about Logan that transcended all her warnings and
threatened all the cautionary barriers she had erected
in her life. Which, in itself, should be cause for alarm.
But if any bells rang, she didn't hear them and was
prepared to ignore them.

"I told them what it was like growing up with two
older brothers and a little sister." He looked deeply into
her eyes and seemed to read her lonely heart.

She listened hungrily as he told of family ups and
downs. How they supported one another through the
tough times.

He grew thoughtful. "Jeannie asked if I had a mama
and papa. I told her things about my mother I haven't
thought of in years."

"Like what?" She hung on his words. They were a
balm to her soul.

"She said things like, 'Your family is forever. Take
care of each other.' As boys, we were often rough. But
if we hurt one of the others, she would take us aside and
say, 'Treat others like you would want to be treated.'
She'd ask if we would want to be hit or punched in

the stomach or have our toy snatched away—whatever unkindness we were guilty of."

"Where was your pa?" She'd met him and found him a likable man with a steadiness that his sons mirrored. But had he always been so?

"Pa was always there for us. He taught us to be men." Logan talked about the fun of learning to ride, to rope, to take care of the animals. "'Above all,' Pa would say, 'we take care of our womenfolk.'"

How she wished she'd had siblings. More than that, she'd longed for a loving, supportive family. She could point out that not all families were like the Marshalls, but there seemed no value in doing so. She'd said it already.

The smell of supper cooking brought her back to her responsibilities, and she hurried to the stove. The potatoes were done and she drained them, as well as the carrots she'd set to cooking earlier. "Would you call the children in?"

"My privilege." He opened the door and hollered, "Supper."

Her mind stalled. *Privilege.* The word echoed through her. That's how family should be viewed. The members should come first, even before business partners. Family should guard and protect those who were part of it. She sucked in overheated air. Too bad not everyone saw it that way.

Sammy rushed in first, Jeannie trying to keep up. Beth followed more slowly, her expression guarded. She carefully skirted around Logan.

"Children, would you please set the table?" Sadie watched from the corner of her eye, wondering if Beth would find a way to avoid being near Logan.

The girl kept carefully to the opposite side of the table as she put the plates around and helped Jeannie with the silverware. Quietly she asked Sammy to put on the cups and fill a pitcher with water.

The children were a family that took care of one another.

The knowledge served to increase Sadie's loneliness. She shifted her gaze to Logan. He watched her. There was no way, she told herself, he could see inside her and read her hurting feelings, but his eyes— so warm and so filled with comfort—made it difficult for her to breathe. She couldn't think. It took every ounce of mental strength just to jerk her gaze to a spot beyond his shoulder and suck in a deep breath. She dared not let him see what was inside her. If he did, his shock and disgust would know no end.

She couldn't allow that to happen even though she wanted nothing so much as to find acceptance and shelter.

In his arms? Her eyes returned to him and rested on his broad shoulders.

Why would she think such a thing? It wasn't that they had anything in common apart from the children.

It wasn't as if all his talk of a supportive family could ever include the likes of her.

It wasn't as if all the things he cherished could be within her reach.

Chapter Six

Logan had gladly accepted Sadie's invitation to join them for the meal and now sat at the table facing Sadie with the girls on one side and Sammy on the other.

Sammy talked nonstop about the horse ride. "I'm going to get my own horse. He's going to be big and black and he'll buck when I tell him to. But I'll never fall off because it will be a trick between the two of us." He slowed and grew serious. "How much does a horse cost? I suppose I'll have to get a job." He turned eagerly toward Logan. "I guess you could use a helper. Maybe you'd like a partner."

Logan chuckled, his gaze shifting from the boy to Sadie, and there it stalled. She and Beth looked at each other. Their looks went on and on, their expression so serious, so full of something he couldn't interpret, that he longed to ask them what they thought or at least be granted the ability to read their minds. Why were they so guarded, so suspicious? What had brought them to this place, and, more importantly, what would it take to bring them out of it?

"I could work for you on Saturday," Sammy said with so much hope that Logan nodded.

"I 'spect I could use a helper. It would make the work go faster." He suspected it would have the reverse effect, but he wouldn't mind if it kept Sammy happy. "Would you like to help me start on some swings and maybe a teeter-totter?"

The boy almost squirmed off his chair in excitement. "I'm your man."

Logan's grin came from the depths of his heart and, wanting to share his enjoyment of the child's eagerness, he again looked at Sadie, hoping she and Beth had stopped staring at each other. His wish was rewarded. Sadie grinned at him, obviously sharing his amusement. She said, "Sure hope his eagerness for work lasts for many years."

"It will. It will. I'll work even harder when I get bigger." Sammy scraped up the last of the food on his plate, determined to grow up as fast as possible.

"I be big, too." Jeannie stretched as tall as she could in her chair. "I help, too."

Beth favored Logan with a fiery look, wrapped her arm about Jeannie's shoulders and pulled her close. "You can help me."

Jeannie crossed her arms in a defiant gesture. "I wanna help Logan."

"Well, you're too little," Beth said.

"I not. Am I?" Jeannie appealed to Logan.

Logan looked from one sister to the other. The older one so defensive, so protective. He didn't like to admit Sadie might have some call for her suspicions. What but some unhappy experience would explain Beth's determined rejection of every offer of friendship? What other reason could there be for shielding her little sister so fiercely? He shifted his attention to Sammy, who watched his sisters with a look Logan could only describe as defiant. Was it a different reaction to the same circumstances?

There seemed only one way to discover the truth—locate Mr. Weiss and have him answer a few questions. Logan would make certain he answered the hard ones.

When was he to find the man when he'd told Sammy they'd work together on Saturday? He needed at least half a day to go to Wolf Hollow and ask around.

"Sammy, you can help me Saturday. You can, too, Jeannie, if Miss Sadie and your sister give permission." He didn't look at Beth, knowing refusal would be written all over her face. "I won't be here until afternoon though. I have an errand to take care of."

"Aw. Half the day will be gone by there."

"Can't be helped." Logan allowed himself to look at Sadie. Her eyes questioned him. He'd pull her aside later and explain his plans.

Jeannie squirmed away from Beth's protective arm and leaned closer. "Mr. Logan, are you somebody's papa?"

Logan brought his gaze to the child, wondering where this question would lead. "No, I'm not."

"Why not?"

Beth leaned close to Jeannie and told her to hush. Jeannie pointedly ignored her big sister and waited for Logan to answer.

"'Cause I'm not married."

Jeannie studied him long and hard. He could almost hear her thinking. She shifted, glanced from him to Sadie. "Is Miss Sadie married?"

Logan met Sadie's gaze, felt a fragility in her look and wondered at its meaning. What had happened in her family to make her this way? He added discovering the reason to his list of things to do.

Realizing Jeannie waited for his answer, he brought his attention back to her. "No. She's the teacher."

"Oh." More thinking. "Teachers can't be mamas?"

Beth caught Jeannie's hand and squeezed hard enough to force the little girl to scowl at her. "You ask too many questions."

"How else I gonna learn?"

Beth rolled her eyes.

Logan chuckled. "Indeed. And the answer to your question is that some districts insist their teacher isn't married, but we can decide whatever we like here."

Jeannie bounced up and down. "Oh goodie. Then why don't you and Miss—"

Sadie jumped up from the table so quickly that her chair tipped backward and she grabbed it to steady it. "Who wants some cookies? Logan's aunt Mary was kind enough to send us some." Not waiting for an answer, she hurried to the cupboard and filled a plate with Aunt Mary's famous oatmeal cookies. She returned to the table and stood a moment behind her chair.

Logan held his breath. Would she sit again or rush off to do something else? He took in her heightened color and rapid breathing. He knew Jeannie had been about to suggest he and Sadie marry. Was the prospect so distasteful to Sadie that it sent her into a flurry of activity?

She need not worry. She had far too many things she kept hidden. Twice before he'd made the mistake of getting involved with women who were not com-

pletely open and honest with him. He didn't mean to
repeat the mistake even with a gal who made his heart
push against the walls he'd erected.

He glanced about the table. These kids deserved
a family. And wasn't Sadie doing her best to provide
a temporary one despite her arguments that family
wasn't always a good thing? What did her words mean
when her actions proved the opposite?

Jeannie swallowed a bite of her cookie. Her bottom lip began to quiver and tears slipped down her
cheeks. She sucked in a shuddering breath. "Mama,
I want Mama." She choked out a sob, bent her head
over her chest, her half-eaten cookie clutched in one
hand, and cried.

Sammy shook his head. "Every night like clockwork
she runs out of sweetness."

"I'll take care of her." Beth lifted the sobbing child
and Jeannie pressed her face to her sister's shoulder.

Beth took a step toward the bedroom, then turned to
Sadie. "I'll do the dishes after I get her settled."

Sadie waved her away. "You look after your sister.
That's far more important."

Beth looked ready to argue, but Jeannie's crying
urged her to forgo it for now and she hurried into the
other room. Sammy slipped outside before anyone
could ask him to help with the dishes.

It provided Logan with the perfect excuse to depart,
as well. He pushed to his feet. "I must be on my way."

Sadie followed him to the door. "Good night."

Two words? Nothing more? No explanations?
"Sadie, don't be offended by things Jeannie says."

Pink returned to her cheeks and she shifted her gaze

to a spot behind him. "Of course I'm not. She's only three."

"Exactly. And missing her parents. I will find their father and see that the family is reunited. Those children deserve it."

The pink in her cheeks intensified. Her eyes flashed. "What those children deserve is a safe home."

"I'm not arguing against that."

She pressed her lips together and her eyes darkened. A shiver touched her shoulders. She stiffened. Her nostrils flared.

"Sadie, what happened to make you see family as so…?" He couldn't even think how to describe her reactions. "So undesirable?"

She blinked. Her eyes had grown expressionless.

He stared. It was if she had disappeared behind a thick wall. Without thinking he reached for her, wanting to bring her back, wanting to comfort, to offer a healthy portion of the love his family had provided all his life. He touched her shoulder, felt her stiffen.

"I—" She swallowed loudly.

Please tell me. Please let me help.

She lifted her chin, giving him a look so cold that ice crystals raced along his veins. She stepped back, forcing him to lower his arm to his side.

"What makes you think anything happened?"

"Only your blatant defensiveness."

"You're imagining things. Perhaps your privileged way of life makes you judge those of us who haven't had the same good fortune. Why do you refuse to believe that not all families are a wonderful thing?"

Her accusation made him appear naive and overly idealistic. "I don't refuse. I'm simply not ready to judge until I find Mr. Weiss and give him a chance to explain what's going on."

"You do that."

"I plan to. That's what my Saturday morning errand is. I'm going to go to Wolf Hollow and look around. Until I find him, I will be here every day to work on the schoolroom and keep an eye on the girls while you teach. I'll spend every other moment looking for Mr. Weiss." He decided to shift the topic in the hopes of erasing the glittering hardness from her eyes. "Soon you'll be able to teach right next door to your living quarters."

"I'm looking forward to the time I can both teach and supervise Beth and Jeannie."

Her words burned.

"Goodbye." He jammed his hat on his head, spun about and strode toward his horse. Her meaning couldn't have been clearer. At such time, he would no longer be needed.

Or welcomed?

Sadie leaned on the door, willing her breathing to return to normal, willing her heart to calmness…without great success. *What happened in my family? They ignored my pain. They chose someone else above me. They made me feel I was to blame. Made me feel dirty.* Her insides twisted and coiled. Her throat grew tight. Tears pressed against the back of her eyes. If only she could tell someone how much their choices had hurt her. How, even now, she longed for arms of comfort, words of acceptance and healing, even though she knew better than to expect them.

She straightened, faced the room. Thankfully, the girls were still in the bedroom and Sammy was outside.

Her gaze fell on the remains of the meal. A task to do. Just what she needed. She put one foot in front of the other. Reached the table and took one dirty dish after the other and carried it to the cupboard. She carefully put away the uneaten cookies. With measured slowness, she filled the basin with hot water and washed each dish with meticulous care. Step by step, action by action, her life returned to normal.

She was Sadie Young, schoolteacher. She would care for these children as long as she could. Pain shafted through her innards. Her knees wavered. Never would she have a family of her own, a love of her own. A man who cherished her. The selfish, vile act of a family friend had made that impossible for her. No man would want her even if she could bring herself to ever trust a man to treat her decently.

Beth came from the bedroom. "She's finally asleep." She took up a towel and began to dry dishes. "It's hard for her to understand what's happened to us."

Sadie's hands grew still. This was the most Beth had ever said about their situation. She slowly faced the girl.

Sadie thought the dish Beth dried got more attention than it required. The studied indifference was so familiar it tore at Sadie's heart. *Lord, please give me the right words.*

"Do you mean your mama's death?"

Beth nodded, still not looking at Sadie.

"Honey, I am so sorry about you losing your mama." She caught Beth's shoulders to turn her toward her.

Beth kept her gaze on Sadie's throat. "Do you know where we can find your father?"

Beth's eyes jerked upward, collided with Sadie's. She opened her mouth. Snapped it shut. But before she turned back to the dishes, Sadie saw something in her eyes that made her shiver. Fear. Stark fear.

"Beth, where is he?"

She shrugged.

Sadie knew she would not get another word out of her. Sammy had slipped inside a moment ago, quietly so as to not draw attention to himself. She glanced toward him. He sat with his back pressed to the side of the cot, his eyes wide and watchful. "Papa is—"

Beth spun around so fast the towel flapped about her waist. "Sammy, no."

Sammy clamped his lips together and nodded.

Sadie studied the pair. What were they hiding? What were they afraid of? "I hope you both know you can trust me."

"Yes, ma'am," Sammy mumbled.

"Beth?" Sadie prodded. "You do know that, don't you?"

Beth nodded but refused to look at Sadie or speak a word.

"Just don't forget." The dishes were done. "It's time to do some lessons."

Sammy protested, but Beth seemed eager for anything that made further conversation about her father difficult. Sadie soon discovered the girl read well. At least her education hadn't been neglected.

Throughout the evening, Sadie found a degree of forgetfulness in the ordinary things of life—listening to Sammy and Beth read, preparing lessons for the next day, getting ready for bed. Even in her usual practice of reading her Bible and silently praying—her prayers encompassing the children in her care and each of her students—she found solace.

But as soon as she turned out the lamp and lay in the dark, her thoughts ran rampant. She thought about Logan and his probing questions. Logan and his steadfast belief in the goodness of family. Logan and his gentle touch. Her hand went to her shoulder, where his fingers had warmed her. And—she added with a silent wail—had made her want to run into his arms.

She slowed her breathing. She knew she could never expect shelter in a man's arms. She was used and soiled. Instead, she must focus on protecting these children and accepting Logan's help only on their behalf.

Until they could discover what had happened to Mr. Weiss and until she could learn the truth about his relationship with his children, she must see Logan every day and every day remind herself that she could not accept comfort or expect understanding from him.

Armed with determination, girded with the acceptance of who she was, she made it through the next two days without speaking to Logan about anything except the children. And even those conversations she kept to a minimum. It was relatively easy so long as she kept busy with a myriad of tasks.

Lessons to prepare, homework to supervise, clothes to alter for the girls. She'd have to sew something for Sammy soon. His two shirts were threadbare. And he still managed to change without letting her see his back, which only served to increase her suspicions. Then there were meals to prepare, the rooms to tidy and the classroom to keep clean and organized. After school, she took Beth and Jeannie to the classroom in an attempt to avoid contact with Logan. Sammy stayed with the man despite Beth's order to accompany them.

"I'm learning my job," he claimed.

Sadie often felt Logan's gaze on her, knew he wondered if she purposely avoided him, but she dared not look at him, or try to explain. It would take only one touch from him and she'd forget to guard her secret. Not only would she suffer for such a lapse, she feared what would become of the children. As soon as the townspeople realized she was an unsuitable woman she would lose her job and the children would be taken away.

Friday, Logan showed up as usual, in time to be there before Sadie left for school. He didn't go directly to work. Instead, he stopped at the living quarters and leaned against the door frame as she gathered up her books in preparation for crossing the street and spending the day with her students.

She darted a glance his direction. "Did you need something?" She grabbed at a pencil that rolled away.

"An answer."

Her heart stalled. The children were all outside, providing her no protection from his probing look. Was he remembering his question as to what had happened in her family to make her so jaded? She stalled for time by rearranging her books several times. When she thought she could speak calmly, she said, "An answer to what?"

"I'm sorry if I offended you and that's the reason you are avoiding me."

"Oh, but you haven't offended me." *Frightened me, yes, offended, no.*

"Then give me a reason."

Breathe in. Breathe out. Breathe in. Breathe out. But despite her slowed breathing, her heartbeat hammered in her head. A reason? Where would she begin? He'd never understand her pain, because he had a loving supportive family. Still, she ached to tell him because he showed concern. Because his touch was gentle and inviting. And…she silently wailed…because he stood for something she had never had and never would have.

"I've been busy trying to take care of these children and teach my students."

"What can I do to help ease your burden?"

"It isn't a burden. I didn't mean it that way."

"Would it help to talk?"

Something inside Sadie's chest opened like petals on a blossom, welcoming sunshine, rain and new life. To be heard. To be understood. To be comforted. Yes. Yes. It would help to talk.

But no. No one must ever know. The knowledge would destroy her.

He continued as if she'd answered in the affirmative. "I'll come over after school and help you clean the classroom. We can talk as we work."

She grabbed at the petals' edges, trying to bring them back into the tight knot she must keep. "The children—"

"Will be okay. Beth is very responsible." His laugh was short and mirthless. "She'll likely welcome some time away from us. Me, especially."

Sadie glanced at the clock. She did not have time to discuss this, to make him change his mind, or she would be late. "Fine." She stepped outside. "Come on, Sammy."

Sammy trotted ahead of her across the street.

Sammy usually ignored her during school hours. She understood his need to put distance between them in the classroom. But when he stopped at the door and held it for her to enter, an unfamiliar joy filled her heart. She tousled his hair. "Thank you."

"Aw. It's nothing. I just remember how Ma told me I should always be a gentleman."

"She would be proud of you."

Grinning, he went through the room and out the back door and joined the others who had gathered to play before school began.

Mrs. Weiss would be proud of her children. She'd also be concerned for their well-being. "I'll protect them," Sadie whispered. Even if it meant opposing Logan. He would be expecting some answers when he showed up after school. And she could not provide them. How was she to divert him?

She pondered the question throughout the day without reaching a satisfying answer. She couldn't tell him the truth and her conscience would not allow her to lie, which left her floundering for other topics. The hours alternately raced by like a runaway wagon or slowed to a crawl like the wagon had hit a bog.

Emily put up her hand and Sadie acknowledged her. "Miss Young, it's ending time."

She glanced at the clock. "Indeed, it is." She couldn't hold the children back. "Put away your books and you may go. Have a good weekend."

The children left in a flurry. Sammy paused at the doorway. "You coming?"

That would provide the perfect escape, but she couldn't bring herself to take that route. "No, I want to clean the room." She remained behind the desk, her fingers tightly twined as Sammy left. She was sitting there when Logan strode in, his blond hair uncovered and his blue eyes bright. As always, he gave the impression that all was right in his world. Likely it was.

He crossed to stand in front of her.

She felt his study of her and kept her gaze on the desktop.

"Hard day?"

She shook her head. "Not particularly."

"It's been days since we've had a chance to talk about the children."

Avoiding him, except when surrounded by others, had made such conversations impossible. "They seem to be settling in well." Or was she only hoping it was so? She lifted her eyes to his. "Don't you agree?"

His smile was so gentle, so warm, it tipped her heart sideways. "Jeannie is turning into a little chatterbox despite Beth's best efforts to make her stay away from me. And Sammy is eager to learn. He's an energetic child." Logan's smile flattened. "Beth remains distant." He leaned against the closest table. "The two little ones are happy, outgoing children. But Beth—" He shook his head, finding her a puzzle.

Sadie got to her feet so she could meet Logan's eyes without tipping her head back so far. "Every time their father is mentioned, both she and Sammy grow very tight-lipped. I'm sure they are hiding something. But what?" Besides the harshness of an abusive father? "Could Mr. Weiss be running from the law?"

"I never considered that possibility, but whatever is delaying the man, I intend to discover the reason and return him to his children. I asked Jesse to inquire about Mr. Weiss," he said, mentioning the sheriff who seemed almost part of the Marshall family. "I wonder if he's learned anything."

There was nothing Sadie could say. Logan had repeatedly stated his intention. She could only pray that the truth would be revealed and the children protected.

She looked around the room. Friday afternoons meant giving the place a good cleaning.

Logan studied the room, too. "I didn't realize how dark it is in here." Two small windows let in a limited amount of light.

"I leave the back door open when the weather is nice enough." But too often a cold wind made her choose the gloom over the penetrating chill of early spring.

Logan pushed to his feet. "What needs to be done?"

She directed the moving of all the furniture to one side of the room so the floor could be properly cleaned. Logan grabbed the broom and started sweeping before she could protest. She got water and a rag and washed off the tables. As soon as Logan was done sweeping, he moved the furniture to the other side in order to do the other half of the room. The floor clean, she and Logan arranged the tables and chairs back in order, then she tidied and dusted the shelves while he washed the windows until they glistened.

"Soon you'll be in the new schoolhouse with lots of windows. That will make your days more pleasant."

"I'm looking forward to it." Except for one thing. Logan would no longer have a reason to be in town. She admitted she would miss his company and his support even though she rejected it so thoroughly.

"What will you do when you're finished at the school?" she said.

He paused in his task and stared out the polished

window. She waited, wondering what had taken his thoughts away from where he stood.

He stepped back from the window and ran his rag along the top of the nearby boxes. "I've neglected my family long enough. Pa wants me to check on the line cabins. Conner has a horse he wants help with. I told Annie I would put up another clothesline for her, and Grandfather is feeling ignored."

Sadie ducked her head, unable to watch the determination in his every move. He talked like he was the only one who could do any of those things, but one thing was clear—his family would always come first. *Even before a wife?* It was a silly question and why did it matter to her?

A little later they completed their tasks and came face-to-face.

"Are we done?" he asked.

She looked about the room. "It looks good. Thank you."

"You're welcome, but I'm afraid we've failed to complete the task."

"Really." She gave the room another look, searching for missed corners and saw none. "What didn't we do?"

"We didn't talk about how you are doing. This morning you were about to tell me why you've been avoiding me."

No, she wasn't. "How can you say that when you are there every day?" And had stayed for supper more than once. She wasn't about to admit to anyone, including herself, how lonely the last two suppers had been without him even though Beth said it was nice not to have "that man" staring at her. Sammy had countered with a lament that it didn't seem fair that he was the only man at the table with Logan gone. And Jeannie had started her evening whining earlier than usual. But she couldn't tell him any of that. Couldn't make him think they'd all missed him.

They stood too close and she should have realized it sooner. Now it was too late as he laid his hand on her shoulder. "People can breathe the same air, sit at the same table, even tend the same children and still avoid each other, even worse, avoid being honest with one another."

His words, spoken so firmly, brought her about to look into his stormy eyes.

"Are you speaking from experience?"

He nodded.

"You were married?" she whispered, unable to comprehend the possibility.

"Not me. Dawson. His first wife made his life miserable."

Sadie knew Dawson was a widower. His daughter, Mattie, was one of her students. Her friend, Isabelle, had married the man.

Logan's hand still rested on Sadie's shoulder and it seemed he sought something from her. What did he want? Honesty? She could not give him that. Instead, she turned her thoughts to what his words revealed about himself.

"You sound like you've had experience with a dishonest person other than your sister-in-law."

He didn't say yes or no, but his eyes told her the answer.

"But how can that be? Your family is so—" She struggled for the right word. "Morally upright. They have such high standards." Something that left her groveling at their feet.

"I've made my mistakes. Mostly in trusting people outside my family."

She waited, willing him to continue.

"Women." His voice grew hard. "Women who let me believe they were one thing when they were something entirely different."

"Different? How?" Her voice sounded from a hollow spot inside. He could well be speaking about her.

"There was Nola Mae, who led me to think she was a sweet young girl. I let myself believe her even though she refused to attend church and tried to get me to do things I wasn't comfortable doing. When she wanted to go to Wolf Hollow I followed her, thinking she needed my protection." His words were sour as green apples. "She only wanted to dangle me along while she enjoyed time in the company of other men."

Sadie's cheeks burned as she understood his meaning. "And when you discovered her secret, what did you do?"

"I got a job in a mine and tried to work day and night to forget it. I might have killed myself doing that except Pa and Conner came and persuaded me to come home. I was so ashamed I would have refused, but they said Ma wasn't well. I went home, my tail between my legs. Ma hugged me and told me to forgive myself. I found healing in the bosom of my family and promised Ma I would be more careful who I courted in the future."

Sadie could see how he fought against self-accusation, but she struggled with envy that his family had welcomed him home and forgone judging him.

"I thought I was smart enough to know when a

woman was sincere, but I soon found out I wasn't."
He told about meeting a girl when she and her mother
moved into the boardinghouse. "Paula. She was pretty
and sweet, came to church with me, met my family and
charmed them."

To Sadie, this girl sounded ideal and she wondered
why Logan spoke with such bitterness.

"Then one day there was a robbery at the store
where Grandfather and Pa kept the payroll after it came
in on the stage. There were four riders with bandannas
over their faces, but I recognized Paula." He shook his
head. "I convinced myself I was mistaken. But she had
disappeared at the same time. Jesse and my pa and a
posse tracked down the thieves and they ended up in
the territorial prison."

"You were wrong about Paula?" She meant he was
mistaken in thinking he recognized the girl.

"So very wrong. She had befriended me in order to
learn about the payroll. What's more, she was married
to one of the men." He'd taken her question to mean he
was wrong about who Paula really was and what she
wanted. His pain twisted his features.

She pressed her hand to his arm. "That's terrible.
You poor man."

He shifted and her hand fell to her side. Heat raced
up her neck. She'd been too bold and he had objected.

His gaze moved away and his jaw muscles clenched
and unclenched. "I thought I would be disowned by
my family, but they didn't even blame me. They said
they had been as mistaken about her as I had." His look
came to her, blue as lightning, making her take a step
back. "So I guess you can see why I think family is so

important and why people need to be given a chance even when they make mistakes."

His story left her shaken. How could a woman be so careless with what had been offered to her in the Marshall family? Even more condemning for her was the knowledge he would not let anything harm his family, especially association with a fallen woman.

She must protect her secret at all costs.

Chapter Seven

As soon as Logan realized how desperately he wanted to cling to Sadie, how much he emotionally leaned into her, he dropped his arm to his side and shifted so he looked at the door into his uncle's store. Why had he told her about his foolishness in misjudging not one, but two, women? He normally did his best to put those incidents behind him.

He'd only wanted to know why she had been avoiding him these past two days, three counting today. There had to be a way to get her to tell him what was the matter.

"Are you finding it too much work to care for the children as well as be the teacher?"

She gave him a look so challenging it was all he could do not to cringe. "Has someone suggested I have neglected my duties?"

"I didn't mean it that way. But if you need more help with the children—"

"The children practically take care of themselves. What are you suggesting?"

He lifted his hands, palms out in a placating ges-

FREE Merchandise and a Cash Reward† are 'in the Cards' for you!

Dear Reader,

We're giving away FREE MERCHANDISE and a CASH REWARD!

Seriously, we'd like to reward you for reading this novel by giving you **FREE MERCHANDISE** worth over **$20** retail plus a CASH REWARD! And no purchase is necessary!

You see the Jack of Hearts sticker above? Paste that sticker in the box on the Free Merchandise Voucher inside. Return the Voucher today… and we'll send you Free Merchandise plus a Cash Reward!

Thanks again for reading one of our novels—and enjoy your Free Merchandise and Cash Reward with our compliments!

Pam Powers

Pam Powers

P.S. Look inside to see what Free Merchandise is **"in the cards"** for you!

W

e'd like to send you two free books like the one you are enjoying now. Your two books have a combined price of over $10 retail, but they are yours to keep absolutely FREE! We'll even send you 2 wonderful surprise gifts and a Cash Reward†. You can't lose!

REMEMBER: Your Free Merchandise, consisting of **2 Free Books** and **2 Free Gifts**, is worth over $20 retail! Plus we'll send you a **Cash Reward** (it's a dollar) which is really the icing on the cake because it's in addition to your FREE Merchandise! No purchase is necessary, so please send for your Free Merchandise today.

Get TWO FREE GIFTS!
We'll also send you 2 wonderful FREE GIFTS (worth about $10 retail), in addition to your 2 Free books and Cash Reward!

Visit us at:
www.ReaderService.com

Books received may not be as shown.

YOUR FREE MERCHANDISE INCLUDES...

2 FREE Books **AND** 2 FREE Mystery Gifts
PLUS you'll get a Cash Reward†

FREE MERCHANDISE VOUCHER

2 FREE
BOOKS
and
2 FREE
GIFTS

Please send my Free Merchandise, consisting of
2 Free Books and **2 Free Mystery Gifts** PLUS my
Cash Reward. I understand that I am under no
obligation to buy anything, as explained
on the back of this card.

102/302 IDL GLGZ

Please Print

FIRST NAME

LAST NAME

ADDRESS

APT.#   CITY

STATE/PROV.   ZIP/POSTAL CODE

NO PURCHASE NECESSARY!

HLI-N16-FMC15

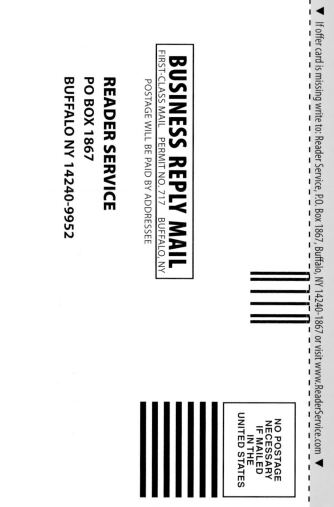

▲ If offer card is missing write to: Reader Service, P.O. Box 1867, Buffalo, NY 14240-1867 or visit www.ReaderService.com ▲

BUSINESS REPLY MAIL
FIRST-CLASS MAIL   PERMIT NO. 717   BUFFALO, NY

POSTAGE WILL BE PAID BY ADDRESSEE

READER SERVICE
PO BOX 1867
BUFFALO NY 14240-9952

NO POSTAGE
NECESSARY
IF MAILED
IN THE
UNITED STATES

ture. "Sadie, I'm only trying to guess the reason you're so distant."

"And, like I said, you're imagining things." She looked about as if checking every detail of the room. "We're done here."

Why did he get the feeling she didn't only mean cleaning the room? And why was he so reluctant to end the day? An idea sprang into his mind. "You've served me supper several times. Let me return the favor. Let me take you out for the meal."

Was she surprised? Pleased? Displeased? Her expression gave away nothing.

"I don't know," she said after a moment's contemplation. "What if Jeannie starts to cry like she does every evening?"

"We'll eat early and take her home before she can get overtired."

"Sammy doesn't have a clean shirt. I was hoping to make him a new one over the next few days."

"I have a better idea. Come on." He took her hand, pleased that she didn't pull away, and led her into the store area. "Uncle George, we need a couple of shirts for Sammy."

Sadie slipped from his grasp and stood a distance away from him, her look wary.

He glanced about. Although no one else was in the store, perhaps she was afraid someone would enter and find her holding hands with him. The thought stung. He tried to tell himself she only meant to be circumspect, but he curled his fingers into a fist and wished she would be so glad to hold his hand or even let him hold hers that she wouldn't care who saw them. Uncle

George led him to the shelves of ready-made clothing, allowing him no time to dwell on the matter.

"Here are some that would likely fit the boy," Uncle George said, laying a half-dozen shirts before them. "Let him try them on and choose which ones fit. Bring the others back."

Logan selected three. "Do you like these, Sadie?"

"They look fine." She seemed distracted. Logan tried to think why. Was she reluctant to lose her excuse to refuse joining him for supper? Well, he didn't intend to let her avoid it.

"I'll take these," he told his uncle. "Let's go see what Sammy thinks of them." He took Sadie's elbow and guided her across the street.

The children were in the yard, laughing about something.

Sammy saw them approach and hollered, "Hi, you're home."

Beth's laughter died. Her expression soured and she headed for the house. Jeannie would have run to them, but Beth saw her intent and caught her hand.

Logan's shoulders sank a good two inches. "Will she ever accept me as a friend?" he asked Sadie.

"Don't be upset. She's simply cautious around men."

"I know you're going to say 'and likely with good cause' but I don't want to believe her father has made her afraid. Fathers are supposed to protect and guard their children. I can hardly wait until tomorrow when I go to Wolf Hollow. The man has to be there and if he is, I aim to find him."

They reached the door and stepped inside, Sammy hot on their heels. Logan would have liked more time to talk to Sadie about his plans for the next day and how he hoped and prayed to find good news.

"Children," Sadie said. "Logan is taking us to Miss Daisy's Eatery for supper." It was the only eatery in town. "Won't that be fun?"

"It's just across the street." Beth made it sound like that made it less than appealing.

"We'll go early." Sadie had obviously decided not to let Beth's attitude upset her. Logan decided he would do the same. "Beth, can you help Jeannie into a clean dress?"

Wearing an angry scowl, Beth took Jeannie to the bedroom.

"Hey, pardner, I brought you some shirts. You can wear a spanking-new one to the restaurant." Logan held out the three shirts. "Which one do you want to try on?"

Sammy gave the shirts wide-eyed study. "For me?"

"If they fit. Here, try this one." He picked the blue one that seemed to draw Sammy's eyes the most.

"Okay." He slipped his worn shirt over his head and reached for the new one.

Sadie stood behind Sammy. Her gaze dipped to his back and she pressed her fingers to her mouth. She crooked her finger to indicate Logan should look.

He helped Sammy get the shirt over his head, allowing him to move around so he could see Sammy's back. The glisten of tears in Sadie's eyes warned him he would not like what he saw and she was right. Red welts crossed Sammy's back from one side to the other. One still had a scab on it. Without thinking he gently touched it.

Sammy jerked about, yanking the shirt to his waist.

He faced Logan with a mixture of fear and defensiveness in his eyes.

"Son, who did that to you?"

Sammy's only answer was a scowl.

"Did your pa do this?" Logan persisted.

Something flickered through Sammy's eyes too fast for Logan to know if it was denial or acknowledgment.

"Do you want me to find your pa?"

Nothing but a dark scowl.

Beth and Jeannie came out of the bedroom and Sammy quickly tucked in his shirt. "Can I keep this one?" he asked.

"It's yours." Logan rubbed the back of his neck where an unfamiliar tightness had developed.

The three children marched from the room and into the yard. Neither Logan nor Sadie moved. With movements so jerky they hurt, he faced her.

Her wet eyes shouted anger and pain. "I'd hoped I was wrong," she whispered.

"I will find the man and get an explanation." He knew children got whipped, but this was more than that and he meant to find out what had driven a father to treat his children so terribly. "Do you think he's done the same to the girls? Beth especially?"

Sadie rocked her head back and forth. "I've seen both girls' backs and there are no marks like we saw on Sammy, but something has happened to Beth." She ground down on her teeth. "I don't like to think what it might have been."

He didn't, either. He reached for her hand, pleased when she grasped his. Together they would see that these children got a good and safe home. "We'll get some answers tomorrow."

* * *

Sadie had suspected it all along. She'd believed it from the beginning, but seeing proof did not give her any satisfaction. She would have given anything to be wrong. This child had been hurt enough times to leave a maze of scars. Her skin felt like a dozen spiders crawled up and down her arms. She choked back a bitter taste in the back of her throat. She had reached for Logan's hand but slowly withdrew from his grasp and went to look out the window toward the town square. How could people hustle back and forth as if everything was normal? Didn't they understand a little boy had been hurt?

"This is the other side of family." Each word stung her tongue. She felt Logan at her side.

"I can't believe what my eyes saw is true," he said.

At least he didn't pretend it was simple correction of a child by an adult. Though the evidence made denial futile. He stared out the window, his mouth set in a hard line. "I will find the man and demand an explanation."

"Explanation! What excuse could he have? It's not like he's a—" She caught the final word between her teeth before it escaped. No, he wasn't a partner. He was a parent. She slowed her breathing. "Parents should protect their children, not hurt them." She stopped, again slowed her breathing, forcing herself to speak calmly. "And if the parents fail to do so, other adults should step in and do it." Like Aunt Sarah. What would she have done without that refuge?

She would offer the same refuge to these children.

She shifted to the other window to watch them. Jeannie twirled about, enjoying her new dress found in the box of clothes Annie had sent.

Beth stared down the alley. Sadie looked the same direction even though she suspected there was nothing to see. On one side of the alley, ashes remained from the recent fire, and across the alley were the clean backyards of the buildings that had been spared. Nothing both she and Beth hadn't seen many times before.

No, she suspected the girl saw something in her memories.

Sammy hunkered down at the far corner of the yard, his shoulders hunched to his ears.

Beth turned slowly and studied her brother. She spoke to him. Sammy shrank further into himself.

Sadie wished she could hear the words, especially when both of the children looked toward the house.

Even across the distance she could see the defiance in their postures and the set of their mouths.

"Do you suppose Beth acts the way she does because she's protective of her brother and sister?"

Sadie brought her thoughts to his question. "That might explain her behavior." She wished she could believe it was so.

"You think otherwise, don't you?"

She gave a halfhearted shrug. She could see no point in telling him her suspicions. Even putting them into words proved too painful. "If we're going to get them fed before Jeannie runs out of sweet, as Sammy says, we should go."

He started for the door but she didn't move. How was she to keep her emotions under control? Indeed, how was she to take her next breath and not break down?

She stiffened. This was not about her, and for the sake of the children she must be calm, show no shock, which could serve to make them feel it was their fault. She would provide strength and safety. Her determination in place, she followed Logan outside. "Children, are you ready?"

Jeannie ran toward them. The other two didn't move, studying the adults, gauging how they would react to their discovery.

Sadie regretted that she had not warned Logan to hide any sign of distaste. She should have told him the children would misinterpret any such expression as being condemnation toward them. It was too late now. All she could hope to do was signal him with a look.

But he swept Jeannie off her feet and swung her overhead, earning himself a throaty chuckle.

His eyes met hers and she knew she would not have to warn him.

The thought eased her tension on one front and increased it on another. What would it have been like to know such understanding on her behalf? Would that acceptance disappear if he knew the truth about her?

She shifted her attention toward the children. She wasn't going to test the idea. "Come along."

Beth and Sammy joined them. Beth's expression was wary, Sammy's defiant.

Sadie pretended not to notice. "I've eaten at Miss Daisy's several times when I was living in the hotel. She always serves a great meal. Maybe I should take lessons from her."

"You're a good cook," Beth said.

"Thank you. You are, too." The girl made noon dinner for herself and Jeannie every day, and sometimes there were leftovers for Sadie to enjoy.

"Mama taught me." Beth's voice caught.

"She'd be proud of you." They reached the café and their conversation ended as they stepped inside. Immediately Sadie was engulfed by the warm, welcoming smells of meat, potatoes and pie cooking.

"Miss Sadie." Dorie bore down on them. She was short and thin and very energetic. Her sister, Daisy, cooked, and Dorie served the customers with enthusiasm. She looked ready to hug Sadie but, instead, grabbed her hands and squeezed them. "So nice to see you again."

When the children edged to Sadie's back, Dorie would have none of that. "And these are the young ones sharing your quarters." She planted her hands on her hips and studied the trio. "You look like Miss Sadie is taking good care of you."

Jeannie, still in Logan's arms, returned her study. "And Logan, too."

That raised Dorie's eyebrows. She shifted her attention to Logan. "It's nice to see you taking an interest in the children."

Logan grinned. "We need to feed them before this little miss hits the end of her day." His grin came to Sadie, and at the look in his eyes she almost forgot how to think...as if they shared a sweet secret.

"You find a place and I'll bring out the meal."

Sadie had learned there was one meal served...take it or leave it. But after tasting a few of the meals, she knew no one had a problem with taking it. She led the way to a table big enough to accommodate them. They had barely got themselves settled before Dorie began bringing out laden plates.

Logan waited until a meal had been placed before them all. "I'll give thanks." Obediently the children bowed their heads. Sadie drew in a sigh. How was she to ensure these children were given the safety and security they deserved? As she'd said to Logan, how long before someone raised an objection to her caring for them? How long before the single objection increased into a public uproar? Especially if the truth about her came out.

"Dear Father in heaven…"

At Logan's words, she quickly bowed her head and closed her eyes, silently adding her own prayer to his. *God, help me. Please give me the strength and wisdom to care for these precious children. Help us discover the truth about their father. Help…* She didn't finish the thought as Logan said, "Amen." Nor was she sure she could have. She needed help in so many directions. She could hardly wait for the meal to end so she could hurry home. But not until the children were in bed would she be able to truly examine the situation. Until then, she must keep her emotions under control.

The children ate quickly and quietly. Sammy and Beth sat with their backs to the wall, facing the room. Every time the door opened, both sets of eyes jerked in that direction and Sadie saw fear flicker through their eyes. The children watched the newcomer, and when they were certain it wasn't someone they dreaded, they sucked in air.

Sadie gave Logan a look she hoped told him to take note of the children.

He tipped his head slightly to indicate he did.

Sadie's appetite fled and she couldn't finish her meal. She knew what it was like to dread the appearance of a man she feared. How the thought coiled and recoiled inside her stomach like something alive and venomous. How it caused a person to jerk awake in the dead of night, so caught in the throes of terror that it was impossible to breathe. How one learned to listen at corners, slip away silently for fear of being discovered alone and unguarded.

I will not allow these children to go back to such a man, she vowed, although she knew there was little she could do to prevent it. A father had rights to his children that could not be taken from him.

God, protect them. The prayer cried through her innermost being.

Logan and Sammy had cleaned up their meals. Food remained on Beth's plate, as it did on Sadie's.

Jeannie held her fork and had stopped eating. The child's eyes glazed and her lips started to tremble.

Sadie pushed to her feet. "If everyone is done, we better be going."

Already Sammy and Beth were on their feet. As Beth reached for Jeannie, the child whimpered and lifted her arms to Logan, who scooped her up and hurried to the door.

"I'll settle up later," he called to Dorie.

They hurried across the street and into Sadie's living quarters. Logan tried to transfer Jeannie to Beth, but the little one wailed and clung to Logan.

"Should I...?" He tipped his head in the direction of the bedroom.

Sadie was about to give permission for him to take Jeannie there when Beth planted herself in the doorway. "I'll take her." Ignoring Jeannie's cries, she pried the little girl from Logan's arms, went into the bedroom and firmly closed the door behind them.

Jeannie's protests rang through the small quarters along with Beth's quieter, calming, firm voice.

Sammy stared at the bedroom door for a moment, then dashed outside.

Sadie blinked at the boy's sudden departure.

Logan rubbed his forehead. "This has not turned out the way I'd hoped. It was supposed to be a pleasant break for all of you."

"I'm sorry." She couldn't begin to say what she was sorry for as regret after regret twisted through her, the rope of them growing tighter and tighter until she wondered something didn't snap. So many things she wished could be different. The fear and pain she saw in the children. Beth's guardedness. Sammy's back. The failure of parents to provide protection. Her own past. Even her growing dependence on and trust in Logan.

She knew better than to allow it. Yet she was powerless to end it. She needed him to help find the children's father. To help with Sammy. To finish the schoolhouse.

To be a rock to lean on.

No. God is my rock and salvation. I need no other.

But for the first time since her parents had let her down, she allowed herself to think how pleasant it would be to have someone in her life she could trust.

She pushed aside every wayward thought. "Thank you for supper. It was lovely."

"You're welcome." He touched his hair. "I've left my hat at the diner. I'll have to go get it." He reached the door and paused. "I'll be back at noon." He studied her with blue-eyed concern. "I'll speak to Sammy." His look went deeper, offering sympathy and concern. "I feel I am leaving you with a mess."

She brought forth a smile that went no farther than her mouth. "We'll be fine."

"I hope so." Still he lingered at the doorway. "We'll get to the bottom of this. I promise." The skin around his eyes crinkled as if he had an amusing thought. "But if you don't stop looking so worried, I might be tempted to wrap my arms about you and hold you tight." He lifted one shoulder in a mocking gesture. "Though I don't suppose it would solve anything." He sighed deeply. "Tomorrow I will go to Wolf Hollow and see what I can learn. Good night." He pulled open the door and left.

In the other room, Jeannie's cries died away and Sadie knew she must have fallen asleep. Poor little tyke. Sadie waited, but Beth did not come out of the bedroom.

Through the window, she watched as Logan spoke to Sammy. Sammy nodded.

They both glanced toward the house. Logan continued to talk and Sammy stood up taller.

Sadie smiled. Whatever Logan said had turned Sammy from an unhappy boy into one ready to face whatever life handed him.

Like Logan offering her a hug had done for her.

No, he hadn't given it, and they both knew doing so would have solved nothing except perhaps to temporarily relieve the anxious tension within her. It would simply return with increased strength afterward.

Logan rode away. Sammy came to the house. Hearing him, Beth returned to the living area and the two of them sat down to do lessons without any urging from Sadie.

She found it difficult to concentrate on her own work.

Not until she lay in her bed, the two girls asleep in the big bed and Sammy asleep on the cot in the other room, did she feel free to evaluate the day and her own reactions.

Determined to sort things out in order to keep her heart steady and her thoughts focused, she lay awake staring up at the darkened ceiling. Everyone—child or adult—deserved a rock.

She thought of Logan's arms about her, solid as a rock.

With a sigh, she snuggled into the covers. Tomorrow she would have a firm talk with herself about how she must not depend on him.

It would hurt too fiercely if he should ever learn her secret.

Chapter Eight

The next morning Logan left the ranch early, intent on getting to Wolf Hollow in good time. He'd had a restless night, waking himself several times with his own moans. The sight of Sammy's back permeated his sleeping thoughts. Sadie had been right all along, and it shattered Logan's belief in the goodness of family. But without family, what would happen to these children? Their mother was gone and if their father didn't take care of them, they would be orphans. He wasn't familiar with the laws concerning orphaned children, but if Sadie wasn't allowed to keep them they'd be sent to an institution or parceled out one at a time to generous people.

He would not allow it.

He'd find the father and make him do right by his children, though at this point, Logan wasn't sure reuniting them with their father would be a good thing.

He rode down the rutted street of Wolf Hollow. The whole town was dirty, the buildings nothing but hastily erected shacks except for the saloon at the far end of town with its garish false front. This early in the morning, the place was practically deserted.

He decided to ask at the saloon first and dismounted in front of the building. Inside, the red wallpaper and large mirrors screamed at him. The chairs sat upside down on the tables and a man was bent over a broom sweeping up last night's debris.

"Hello?" Logan called.

The man jerked about. "Pretty early in the morning for business."

"I'm looking for someone. Mr. Weiss." He gave the description he had. "You know of him?"

The man shook his head. "But I'll ask the boss. Boss," he hollered, and then turned back to Logan. "He'll be here directly."

Logan leaned against the door frame as he waited for the boss man. After a few minutes, a large, rotund man entered from a back room.

Logan repeated his inquiry. The big man looked Logan up and down. Logan waited. He wasn't leaving without information.

The man adjusted his braces. "I might know of this Mr. Weiss. But, last I heard, he was dead."

"Dead?" That wasn't possible. The children would have said so. "You sure?"

"Nope. Just what I heard."

Logan unwound from the door. "Guess I'll ask around and see what else I can learn."

"Help yourself." The man returned to the back room and closed the door.

Logan moved on. He asked at various places. Heard various reports.

"Heard he lost his wife. Wonder what happened to the kids."

"Heard he got into a fight with some claim jumpers."

"Ain't seen him in quite some time."

"Never heard of him."

He was able to get rather garbled directions to the Weiss mining claim and made his way out there only to be greeted by half-a-dozen men with rifles who ordered him off the location.

"Don't want no claim jumpers nosing around here."

"I'm trying to locate a Mr. Weiss," he called.

"Nobody by that name here."

Logan's frustration grew. People here were none too friendly to strangers. If they knew Mr. Weiss's whereabouts they weren't about to tell him.

He glanced at the sun. Time to head back. He had a promise to keep and he needed to talk to Sadie about what he'd failed to learn.

Sammy waited for Logan in the school yard when he rode in. "Thought you might have changed your mind."

"Nope. You had dinner yet?"

Sammy nodded. "A bit ago."

Logan had eaten a lunch Annie had packed for him, so there was no reason to delay the afternoon activities he'd promised Sammy. None, that is, except his desire to see Sadie and tell her his news.

Sadie stepped out, Jeannie riding on her hip. Jeannie caught at the hairpins holding Sadie's hair up and her loosened hair fell down her back, ripples of brown and gold.

Sadie shook her head and laughed, her eyes shining with affection for the child in her arms.

Logan couldn't tear his gaze away from the sight.

He'd always thought Sadie an ordinary-looking woman. He was wrong—she was beautiful.

Sadie shifted Jeannie and saw Logan. Pink flooded her cheeks. "I didn't know you were there."

"Just got here." His tongue felt thick. His words sounded hoarse.

Sadie put Jeannie down and ducked her head to scoop her hair into a roll at the back of her neck and fasten it in place with the remaining hairpins.

"We's gonna build something," Sammy said.

Beth stepped outside, her arms crossed over her chest, her expression harsh. What did she know that she wasn't telling?

Logan sighed. He really needed to find out what was going on with them. But how was he to do so? She might never trust him enough to tell him. And he'd been able to learn nothing of value in Wolf Hollow.

"I need to talk to Sadie alone for a few minutes. Beth, would you watch your brother and sister? Sadie, let's sit on that bench." He indicated the nearby town square. The morning had been cool, but the sun had warmed the air to a pleasant temperature.

Sadie said nothing as she accompanied him to the bench. They sat side by side. He leaned over his knees, his hands dangling. "I failed."

"In what way?"

"I couldn't find their father, and the information I got was so mixed-up it's hard to know what is true and what isn't. One man was certain Mr. Weiss had died." He sat back and they both shifted so they looked at each other. "Is it possible?"

Sadie darted a glance toward the children, who sat on the woodpile watching them. "Surely they'd tell us if he was dead. Unless—" She caught her bottom lip between her teeth. "Unless they don't know." Her words were a low whisper. She turned to him, her eyes wide with distress, and she caught his hand and held on tight. "What are we going to do?"

She'd reached for him. The thought filled his heart with a delicious warmth. In her distress, she had reached for *him*.

He cupped his other hand over hers, a silent promise to take care of things, to protect her. His gaze shifted to the children. Protect them, as well. He turned his thoughts to her question. "I don't think they know where their father is. We'll just have to keep looking for him and caring for them until we find him."

"I worry…" Her eyes brimmed with tears.

He glanced about. A couple of men came out of the nearby hotel. Two women stood outside his uncle's store. A wagon drove past them. "Sadie, don't cry. Especially not here. I will have to take you into my arms and this is not an appropriate place."

She laughed a little and swiped at her eyes. "I'm not going to cry."

"Good. Now tell me what's worrying you."

She sniffed. "How long before the school board decides I can't teach and also have children in my care? How long before someone decides a single woman isn't the best person to have them?"

He chuckled softly and squeezed her hand, gratified when she squeezed back. "First, Pa and Grandfather are two of the three board members and I can guarantee they aren't going to make a fuss." He'd speak to them tonight and ensure that. "As to the other matter, I don't see why anyone would complain about you giving these children shelter unless they were willing to do it. So I think you're safe for now."

"Until you find the father."

He nodded.

"And then they go back to a man who can hurt his boy. And fill Beth with fear."

He squeezed her hand again. "We won't be able to stop it. No one can take a man's children from him. But I give you my promise. I will make sure he knows I won't accept having those children hurt."

"All he has to do is move on."

"I will follow him wherever he goes and appoint someone in my place to ensure the children's safety."

"There is some comfort in that." She watched the children for a few minutes. "If only we could do more. It's awful not to be able to trust your own parents." Her voice caught and tears clung to her lashes.

"Sadie," he hissed. "I won't be responsible for my actions if you cry." Did she realize how much she had revealed to him with those words? *Not to be able to trust your own parents.* That was her story, but he wished he knew the details.

Sadie might have been tempted to sit there the rest of the afternoon, clutching Logan's hand, except for Sammy waiting impatiently for Logan to go back so the two of them could work together. And then there was the small matter of the promise to herself, made repeatedly throughout the morning, that she would not allow herself to grow any fonder of him.

She and Beth had done the laundry together, a task normally done on Mondays by most women. But Saturday was the schoolteacher's only free day.

"Beth, what is it you aren't telling us?" she'd asked the girl as they hung wet garments on the clothesline running from the corner of the schoolhouse toward the back alley.

Beth had continued pegging Jeannie's dresses and her nightgown to the line.

Just when Sadie had decided Beth wasn't going to answer, the girl spoke. "Why do you think there's something?" she'd asked, picking up another garment, making it impossible for Sadie to see her eyes and judge her emotions.

"You know I saw Sammy's back, don't you?" She hadn't wanted to distress the girl, but Beth needed to understand that she and Logan were prepared to help her. "You can trust us to help you."

Beth's chin had jutted out. "You don't know everything."

"I don't pretend to, but if you would tell me I could perhaps help you."

Beth's hands had grown still on the pillowcase she'd been fixing to the line. Her gaze went down the alley as it often did. Her shoulder had twisted and then she'd brought her attention back to the clothesline. "Don't recall saying I need any help. We was managing just fine, you know."

Sadie knew nothing of the sort and so did Beth. "I don't mean to upset you." She had gone to Beth's side and draped her arm across the tense shoulders. "I'll leave it for now." She had wanted to assure the girl they would all be safe with her. But could she give that promise and keep it? She took some comfort from the fact Beth didn't shy away from Sadie's touch. "Beth, I'm concerned about you and your brother and sister."

Beth nodded. "I know. Thank you."

Sadie had heard the tears in Beth's voice, but before she could pull the girl into her arms, Beth had turned away, returning to the laundry.

There seemed nothing more she could do at the moment.

And now for Logan to return with no real news of the children's father, only such contradictory statements that it was impossible to guess which might be true. However, she could not sit here all day; nor could he. She turned to him. "I wish we knew the truth about Mr. Weiss and his whereabouts."

"Me, too." He got to his feet and held out a hand to assist Sadie. "I will continue to make inquiries and look for him. In the meantime, let's do what we can to make the children happy." His sweet, promising smile drove away the shadows.

From the beginning she'd been doing her best to make life good for the children. Perhaps he meant his words to remind her, to help her focus on what they could do rather than what they couldn't, which was find Mr. Weiss.

At least Logan no longer insisted that being with family was the best thing for them. He only said it was nigh impossible to forbid the father his rights.

"I have an anxious young lad waiting to help me build something."

She managed to stop staring at Logan's encouraging smile and look at Sammy, who stood beside the lumber pile, watching Logan. He shifted from one foot to the other. He jammed his hands into his pockets and a few seconds later pulled them out. His shoulders went up and down, indicating a deep sigh. Sadie chuckled. "He's getting a little restless."

Logan chuckled. "I hope I can put all that energy to good use."

Together they returned to the yard. Logan went to Sammy's side, handed him a shovel and indicated he should start digging a hole.

Sammy set upon the job eagerly.

Beth had withdrawn to the corner of the house at Logan's approach, one hand holding Jeannie. Jeannie would have none of it and broke free to run to Logan.

"I help, too?"

Logan grinned at the child. "In a bit. Why don't you help Sadie take the clothes in?" He smiled across the yard at Sadie.

He might have given her pearls and diamonds for the way her heart rejoiced. What would it be like to really share a family…children…with him?

Her breath caught somewhere between her ribs and her throat, and she strove to remember that such dreams were not possible for her.

Jeannie tugged at her hand. "I help you?"

Grateful for the distraction, she unpegged the dry items and folded them, then handed them to Jeannie, who placed them in the wicker laundry basket with great care.

They took the basket in when it was full and put away the items that didn't need ironing.

"I can iron now," Beth said.

It bothered Sadie that Beth seemed to always be concerned with work. Had she been punished, threatened, somehow made to be afraid if she didn't keep busy and get things done? But hadn't her mother died recently?

Sadie shrugged mentally. So many things about this family did not make sense. So many details were missing. "Maybe we'll do something fun this afternoon."

"Fun? What about the ironing?"

"It can be done later." At Beth's dubious look, Sadie grew determined to do something simply for enjoyment. "What would you like to do?"

Beth looked uncertain. "Make cookies?"

Sadie shook her head. "Something that isn't work."

Beth's eyes widened. A small smile tugged at her lips and she glanced about the room. But she ducked her head before she revealed anything more to Sadie.

"Anything," Sadie urged.

Beth's gaze found a small picture Sadie had created out of her dried flowers. Again, she turned away almost, but not quite, before Sadie understood what she was looking at.

"Would you like to make a picture like that?" Sadie asked.

Beth sucked in a tiny gasp and let it out slowly. She shook her head. "I couldn't do that."

"Sure you could. Come. I'll teach you how."

"I go help Logan." Jeannie dashed out the door before either Sadie or Beth could say yes or no.

Sadie let her go. She'd be safe with him. She propped the door open, letting in refreshing air and allowing her to watch Logan and the children.

"Let's set out the material on the table for making a picture. That will give us lots of room." She handed Beth the box of supplies and took the book that contained her pressed flowers. She'd learned to clamp the covers of the book tightly to achieve the best results.

She undid the clamps and gingerly opened the pages

to reveal a collection of flowers, some whole, some only petals. As she showed Beth, she explained what she did. "You can do a number of things. If you choose canvas, you can draw or write on it before you add the flowers. You can make stationery cards." She showed Beth a few things she had made. "I'm going to make a picture for my aunt Sarah for Christmas. What would you like to make?"

Beth simply stared at the examples Sadie had shown her.

Sadie wondered if she even breathed. "Would you like to make a picture to keep?" That way she'd have something to remember Sadie by. The thought of having these children taken away sent a pain slicing through her middle. She glanced out the door. Logan was helping Sammy dig a hole. Jeannie held a hammer with two hands, her tongue poking out the side of her mouth as she concentrated on trying to hit a nail.

Sadie chuckled.

Beth looked up and followed the direction of Sadie's glance. She half rose, then settled back down, a smile playing at the corners of her mouth.

Jeannie lifted the hammer and whacked it, though there didn't appear to be much power in her blow.

Beth laughed. "The hammer is too heavy, but she'll never give up. She's always been a determined one."

Sadie's insides filled with candy-sweet enjoyment of Beth.

Beth sobered. "Ma used to say it was up to us to protect Jeannie. She said she'd run headlong into danger and never give it a thought." Beth lowered her head but not before Sadie saw her eyes glisten.

"And you've done exactly as your mother would want," she said with gentle firmness.

"I hope so." Beth sighed and touched the pink petals of a rose Sadie had dried before she left Saint Louis. "Mama's favorite flower was the rose."

"Then you must use those petals and make a picture in remembrance of her."

"Can I? You don't mind?" Beth looked at Sadie with such yearning that Sadie squeezed her shoulder.

"I'd be pleased if you did."

Slowly, almost fearfully, Beth lifted one pink petal and placed it upon the canvas Sadie had given her.

"Put things where you think you'd like them, then glue them." She had found a special glue that didn't darken the petals.

Beth placed petals here and there. She chose different flowers. And as she worked, she began to talk almost as if she didn't realize she did so. "Mama said the first thing she was going to do when we got us a nice place to live was plant a rosebush. She said her own mama had a lovely rosebush on either side of the doorway." Beth's hands grew idle. "I feel bad that Mama never got to plant her rosebush."

"I hope you get a chance to plant one for her."

Beth looked up, her eyes searching the distance. With a tiny sigh she bent over the picture again. "I might. When I grow up."

Sadie could not miss the hopeless note in Beth's words, as if she wondered if that time would ever come. A shiver snaked across Sadie's shoulders. Whatever secret these children were hiding, it carried more than a hint of danger and despair. Sadie would like to see the children in a place where they didn't have to fear what lay ahead.

"I think she'd like that." Sadie turned her attention to her own picture, intending to create one showcasing the wildflowers and leaves of Montana.

Beth tipped her head back and forth and studied the arrangement of her flowers. "Did you say I could write something on the canvas?"

"Yes. I've done Bible verses and little sayings. Or even a word. You can practice on a piece of paper if you like." She indicated the little store of paper she kept in the box of supplies.

Beth found a piece she liked and sat with the end of a pencil pressed to her lips. After a bit, she carefully printed the words, *Mama, I miss you.* "Is this okay?"

Tears clogged Sadie's throat. She swallowed them back. To think of the sadness these children carried with them. "Oh Beth, I'm so sorry." She sat next to Beth and gave her a sideways hug.

Beth leaned against Sadie, her breathing rough. After a second, she straightened. "It's okay. Mama knew she was dying and told me what it would be like. I miss her, but I have Sammy and Jeannie to think about and take care of." Her voice hardened. "I look after them as best I can."

"Your mother would be so proud of you and so am I."

"You?" Beth's gaze sought Sadie's. "Why do you care?"

Sadie couldn't very well say because she knew what it was like to be abandoned by one's parents. Not that Beth's parents had abandoned her. At least not her mother. For a moment she wasn't sure what to say. "If

I ever had children of my own I would want them to be just like you and Sammy and Jeannie." It was the truth. And the impossibility of it about ate up her insides with sorrow. She touched Beth's cheek, and when Beth didn't shy away, Sadie's throat again clogged.

They studied each other for a moment. Sadie knew she saw longing and fledgling trust in Beth's eyes. Perhaps soon there would come a time when the girl trusted her enough to tell her the secret she and Sammy shared.

They returned to making pictures. Sadie gave a few pointers on centering the words on the canvas and getting them all the same size. Beth was meticulously careful.

"I want something Mama would be proud of."

Sadie blinked back the tears that were so close to the surface that afternoon. "You're doing an excellent job. I couldn't do better myself."

Beth smiled at her. "Thanks."

Thanks to you for having such a beautiful heart. Perhaps someday she would feel free to say the words aloud but not yet. Their relationship was still too fragile.

An excited cry from outside drew their attention to Logan and the other children.

With help from Logan's uncle George, two poles had been dropped into the holes Sammy had helped dig. The two poles were joined by thick piece of wood, from which hung two lengths of rope. The two men, with two children assisting them, tamped dirt around the posts, then nailed braces on either side of the poles to stabilize them.

"A swing," Sammy cheered. "Can I try it?"

Logan glanced toward the door. "I think this calls for a celebration. Come on out, you two."

Beth didn't need a second invitation and was out the door ahead of Sadie, who followed almost as eagerly. Seeing playground equipment, if only one swing, gave Sadie reason to think she would soon be teaching the children in a proper classroom with a proper play area.

And she'd be able to keep an eye on Beth and Jeannie while teaching.

Her footsteps slowed. Her throat tightened. It would also mean Logan would no longer have any reason to be in town. Hadn't he said he was anxious to be done so he could join his father and brothers out chasing after cows? Or something like that.

It was what she'd expected from the beginning, and if she hoped to protect her fickle heart it couldn't happen too soon.

Jeannie jumped up and down. "I wanna swing."

Logan caught the child and lifted her to one hip. His gaze captured Sadie's and she forgot every other thought at the way he smiled at her as he said, "Behold! The first piece for the playground."

She grinned, almost as excited as the children. "It's lovely."

"I couldn't have done it without help."

Sammy's chest expanded several sizes at the acknowledgment. "I did good. Right?"

"You and Jeannie both did good. And I expect Beth was doing just as good helping Miss Sadie."

"She's an excellent help," Sadie said, draping her arm across Beth's shoulders.

Beth flashed a shy smile and ducked her head.

Pleasure as sweet as honey filled Sadie. The children were growing more and more at ease around her and Logan. She found Logan's eyes again and shared a promise-filled glance at Logan.

Promise of what?

She too ducked her head. There existed only one promise she could make to herself and that was to guard the truth about what she was. Perhaps she was more like the children than she cared to admit. The thought troubled her. Were they hiding a past as shameful and hurtful as hers?

Sammy had been fidgeting from one foot to the other and could contain his excitement no longer. "Are you going to get to use the swing?"

Logan put Jeannie on her feet, keeping hold of one hand. He reached his other hand toward Sadie. "Let's hold hands and make a circle around the swing," he said.

Knowing she should refuse to take it, she nevertheless lifted her hand and slipped it into his grasp.

She reached for Beth, who took Sammy's, and he took Jeannie's. They stood around the swing.

"Why we doing this?" Sammy asked.

Logan gave a deep-throated chuckle. "So I can hold Miss Sadie's hand."

Her cheeks burned. She would have jerked her hand free, but he squeezed it, making it impossible.

"Aw, that's yucky," Sammy said with a great deal of disgust.

"I'm joshing." Logan grinned at Sadie. "But that pink sure looks good on you."

She looked anywhere but at him. Somehow she managed to find her voice. "I know that isn't the reason. So why are we standing like this?"

He half sobered, though the mischief in his eyes remained as strong as ever. "Didn't I say we should have a celebration?"

"Sure hope you don't think we're going to dance around like a Maypole dance." Sammy sounded so disgusted that Logan chortled.

"Hey, that's a mighty fine idea." Logan paused. "Unless someone has a better one."

"I think we should take turns trying it out," Sammy said somewhat emphatically.

"We used to have a swing," Beth said. "Mama said it was the best sort of fun. She said a person could dream of all sorts of wonderful things as they were flying through the air. Maybe we could think about Mama for a moment."

It was the longest speech Beth had made and everyone silently agreed.

Sadie couldn't guess what the others thought in that moment of silence as she thanked God that she had found these children before it was too late. *Please help me keep them safe. Help us discover the truth about their father.*

Logan smiled at each one. "Let's thank God for allowing us this little pleasure." He bowed his head and offered a simple prayer both of thanks and blessing. "Amen."

"Now can we swing?" Sammy asked. At his question the children let go of one another's hands and clustered around the upright poles.

"Yes. But why don't we let Beth go first?" Logan said.

Beth shook her head and moved away from the swing. She turned from the others.

Sadie went to her side and cupped her hand over Beth's shoulder. She knew the girl was finding the moment too emotional. "It's okay. We'll let the others go first."

Beth nodded.

Sammy climbed to the swing seat. "Logan, push me."

Sadie turned to watch the pair.

"Higher. Higher. I'm flying." Sammy laughed and laughed.

"My turn. My turn." Jeannie waited at one side.

Sammy slowed and got off. Jeannie got on and Logan pushed her.

The little girl laughed. "This is fun."

After a bit, she got off.

"Who's next?" Sammy looked at his big sister, but Beth shook her head. "Teacher then."

"Me?" Sadie had not thought she'd have a turn. "Oh, I don't think so."

"Come on. It's fun." Sammy grabbed her hand and pulled her toward the swing.

"It's fun." Logan's voice teased and tempted at the same time. "You'll like it."

"Seems to me I've heard that before." But she dismissed the dark memory of that man's words. They had no place on a day like this, and she allowed herself to be pulled forward and sat on the seat, tucking her skirts under her to keep them under control.

Before she could think to ask him not to, Logan gave her a push. She soared upward, the air brushing her face, erasing all her arguments and blowing away all her worries. She dipped backward. Her hair tore free of the pins and billowed around her face. Logan pushed on her back again, his hands warm and firm. As she arched upward again laughter pushed from her. Joy raced into her heart.

Up and back, with Logan keeping her swinging high. Her laughter rang out with each upward sweep, cleansing and renewing her like nothing she'd ever before experienced.

Then it was time to return to earth. "Enough," she said, and slowed. She got off. "That was fun. Thanks." She couldn't look at Logan, instead brushing her skirts with her fingers and re-pinning her hair.

"Your turn." Sammy grabbed Logan's hand and pulled him to the swing seat.

"I don't know—"

"It will be fun. You'll enjoy it." Sadie repeated his words to him and had the satisfaction of seeing him roll his eyes. She laughed from pure joy.

He sat down. "Who is going to push me?"

"I will." Sammy pushed and grunted. He pulled and pushed but managed to get Logan to move only a few inches. "You sure do weigh a lot."

Sadie covered her mouth, barely able to contain her mirth. It brimmed from her eyes and puffed out her cheeks.

Logan gave her a stern look. "I can't help it if I'm big. Blame my father and my grandfather."

"Teacher, Beth, help me."

Sadie grabbed Beth and pulled her to Sammy's side. This was too much fun for any of them to miss out. Jeannie stayed at the side at Sadie's request. Sadie grabbed the ropes on either side of Logan. "Each of you grab down by the seat and, at my count, let's pull him back." They did so. "Now on three. One, two, three."

They backed up, pulling Logan as far as they could and they pushed him as they released him. He added his own push and came back with a whoosh.

Sadie and the others stepped out of his way as he pumped higher.

A chuckle rumbled from his mouth. "This is fun. I haven't swung since I was little."

"I guess that was a long time ago," Sammy said with so much disgust Sadie burst out laughing. Even Beth covered her mouth, vainly trying to contain her mirth.

"You saying I'm too big?" Logan planted his feet on the ground and came to a halt. In a movement so swift none of them had time to react, he grabbed Sammy and started tickling him. "Am I too big?"

"Yes." Sammy giggled and squirmed.

Logan tickled his armpits, his sides and under his chin as Sammy squealed.

"Am I still too big?"

"Yes." Sammy barely got the word out between his laughing and squealing.

More tickling and giggling and squirming. "Am I still too big?"

"Yes." The word was so breathless Sadie wondered if Sammy could get in enough air.

Logan stuck Sammy's head under one arm and let the boy squirm, trying to get free.

"Okay, you're not too big," Sammy said.

Logan released him and the two of them grinned at each other.

"That was fun," Sammy said.

"Anytime." Logan faced the rest of them. "Anyone else care to tell me I'm too big?"

"Me. Me." Jeannie wrapped her arms about his leg.

He swung her into the air and tickled her so gently that Sadie's eyes stung. He turned and his eyes met Sadie's, and he stopped playing with Jeannie and shifted her to one hip. The look between Sadie and Logan went on and on until nothing else existed but the two of them. Nothing else mattered but the hope of the future. Perhaps one—

Beth mumbled something about "just like him." She rushed past them to the house.

Sadie stared after her, too shocked to think.

"What was that all about?" Logan asked, his eyes filled with disbelief.

Sadie shrugged and waggled her hands.

Sammy retreated to the stack of lumber, his expression watchful.

Logan looked from Sammy to the little girl in his arms, now clinging to him, a tear resting on her eyelashes.

"I'll go see what's wrong." Sadie hurried to the house.

Beth lay facedown on the bed. Sadie wondered if she cried but, after watching a moment, could detect no rising and falling of her back or hear any sobs. She sat on the side of the bed. Beth shifted away. Sadie tried not to let the action hurt.

"Beth, what's the matter?"

"Nothing."

"Something must have bothered you to send you running to the house." She ached to comfort the girl, hug her and assure her everything would be okay. She knew Beth would not accept it.

Beth sat up on the other side of the bed. "Well, if you must know. It's too soon."

"Too soon for what?"

Beth got up and marched from the room without answering.

Sadie stared at the floor. Too soon? Did she mean to enjoy fun after their mother's death? From what Sadie knew it had been only a few weeks. Or was it a few months? The information was so mixed up. Did she feel they should mourn longer?

Or did she refer to something else entirely?

If only Beth would tell her, but Sadie knew she wouldn't.

She left Beth staring out the window and went outside to join Logan. They moved away from where the two younger children played together at the swing.

"What's wrong?"

She told him what Beth had said.

"What does that mean?"

"I hoped you would have some idea." She told him what she had thought it meant.

"But why all of a sudden? It isn't like we haven't played with the children already."

"I know and I thought we'd made some progress this afternoon." She told him how Beth had opened up as they'd made flower pictures. "Maybe talking about her mother brought the pain all back."

"These children have been through so much. I wish I could track down the father and get things sorted out for them. They deserve to know where they belong."

"And feel safe," Sadie added. She waited, wondering if he would argue that family provided a safe place. Surely not something he could truly believe was always the case after seeing Sammy's back.

"Agreed." His gaze caught hers and held it so firmly

she couldn't look away. At the way he regarded her, the strength and goodness she saw in him and knew existed, her heart lightened. He lifted a hand to her cheek and brushed his fingers along the side of her face. "We will work together to make sure these children are safe."

She leaned into his hand. Beth's words reverberated inside her head. *Too soon.* Slowly she turned her head, forcing him to pull his hand back even though it was the hardest thing she had done in some time. She stifled an urge to run to the house as Beth had done and throw herself across the bed.

Not only was it too soon now to think about opening up her heart to him.

It would always be too soon.

Chapter Nine

Logan rode toward home. Sadie hadn't invited him to join them for supper. He told himself that was okay. After all, she had laundry to finish, perhaps ironing to do. She had the children to care for. Saturday-night baths.

He would have helped her if she had asked.

How had the day gone from bad to good to bad again? When he'd returned from Wolf Hollow and told Sadie his disappointing news, he felt the two of them were finally united in what they wanted for the children—safety and security. The feeling had grown by huge leaps when they had gathered around the swing. It had wavered a bit when Beth raced off, but when Sadie returned and looked like she might melt into his arms he thought the day couldn't get any better if it had rained pennies from heaven.

Then she'd stiffened and it seemed she might run to the house just as Beth had done.

Beth's words banged around inside his head. *Too soon.* Was he guilty of expecting too much too soon?

Which raised a question he could not answer. What did he expect?

He was almost home and sat on the knoll overlooking the ranch, studying the place. Home. Family. The words ran round inside his head like panicked calves. He shook off the confusion and galloped the last few yards to the barn.

Conner glanced up at his approach. "Someone trying to catch you?"

Logan swung down from his horse. "Nope. Just anxious to be home."

"Little hard to believe that when you find every excuse to be away. You spending all your time with that little schoolteacher?"

Logan unsaddled Brewster as he considered his answer. "I'm not gone all the time. Besides, I'm only trying to get the schoolhouse finished as quickly as possible." He waited a second, then added hastily, "And find Mr. Weiss so the children can be reunited with their father."

Conner leaned against the nearest post, watching.

Logan knew his brother had something to say and would say it in his own good time. He began to brush his horse down.

Conner sighed. "Doesn't it seem like the man would be looking for his kids, not the other way around?"

Logan straightened and stretched his neck muscles. "Unless the man is injured, being held hostage, or any number of things."

"Like dead?"

"Yeah, that's one possibility." He told Conner what he'd found out at Wolf Hollow.

"If the man is dead, what happens to the children?

Won't the authorities find relatives? Or put them in an orphanage?"

"You think that would be better than leaving them with Sadie?" He hadn't meant to sound so defensive, but Conner had pointed his finger on the very thought that had been plaguing Logan. If he found out for certain Mr. Weiss was dead, what then? Sadie would never forgive him if he had any part in taking the children away. And he couldn't blame her.

"Nope. But don't suppose my opinion counts a whole lot."

"Well, Jesse is the sheriff and he's practically family. Wouldn't we be able to make him see the children are better off with Sadie than moved to—" He lifted one hand in a gesture of frustration. "Anywhere."

Conner grinned. "Maybe you're just wanting an excuse to continue visiting Sadie. Why not just court her without any excuses?" He unwound from the post and strode from the barn.

Logan stared after him. Court her? He'd like to except for a couple of hitches. First, every time he thought she might welcome his interest, she pulled back. He couldn't help but wonder why and he would not allow himself to believe it was because of him. But maybe it was. How could he know if she didn't tell him? Secondly, she had this thing about how families fail. How parents abandon their children. It was a belief that could not exist between them. Until she told him what had happened to make her feel that way—what secrets she hid—he knew he could not follow the desire of his heart. He'd learned that lesson too well to repeat it.

He finished taking care of his horse and went to the

house, where he was soon surrounded by the chatter of the family.

This was what family was to him. Warm, accepting and loving. They had healed from the death of his mother. He had never confessed to anyone that he blamed himself for her illness. She'd known of his situation in Wolf Hollow and had worried about him.

The family had also survived the behavior and rejection of Violet, Dawson's first wife. He had a responsibility to do nothing to add anything more to the family's pain.

But what if Sadie could see how good family could be?

He studied the food on his plate though his thoughts were far from eating. He could learn to care for her very deeply, but not so long as she hid the facts about her past and let them color her opinion about family.

Meanwhile, he would continue to search for Mr. Weiss and help Sadie with the children. Perhaps, in time, he could get her to confess what her family had done to make her so guarded.

The next morning he prepared for church as usual. They always went unless the weather or impassable roads prevented it. He joined the others for breakfast.

Annie buzzed about, chattering like a magpie. Conner and Logan looked at each other. Logan raised his eyebrows and shook his head. He had no idea why she was so keyed up.

Pa and Grandfather discussed the need to move the horses to a different pasture.

The family sat around the table. Logan glanced toward the chair where Ma used to sit and where Annie now sat. An ache sucked at his insides.

Again, words tangled in his brain. *Family, home, responsibility.* Why did they race about rather than settle down? Was it because he wanted Sadie to share the same values and he knew she didn't?

The meal was over and Annie hurriedly cleaned up. Logan and Conner helped while Pa went out to get the wagon to take Grandfather to church.

"I've got plans with Carly," Annie said. "I won't be coming home after church."

"We'll starve," Conner said, clutching at his stomach.

Annie flicked a towel at him. "Or you could make yourself a sandwich. There's plenty of bread, some roast beef and a hunk of cheese."

Logan had thought he'd invite Sadie and the children out to the ranch for the afternoon, but Annie's announcement made him reconsider that plan. Maybe he could suggest something else that they could do together.

Pa and Conner said they were riding horseback into town. That left Logan to take Grandfather. At first he thought it would mean he couldn't spend time with Sadie, and then he realized it needn't. If he could involve Grandfather in an activity it would be a good way to let Sadie see the value of family.

He helped Grandfather to the wagon and they drove to church. A cold wind blew around them as they traveled.

"Sure hope we aren't in for a storm," Grandfather said. "But my old bones tell me otherwise."

"Do you want to go back home?" He had no desire to be caught in a storm with the old man.

The wind subsided. "There, it's all over. I want to go to church. There's something about that young preacher I like."

"He's a straight shooter, isn't he?"

For a few minutes they talked about the new preacher, then arrived in town and joined the other wagons and riders headed for church.

Logan slowed as they drew close to the schoolhouse. He didn't see Sadie or any of the children. He journeyed on to the church, glancing at those entering. Still no sign of Sadie and her entourage. Were they already inside?

He helped Grandfather from the wagon and stayed at his side as the older man hobbled toward the door. They stepped inside. It took a moment for his eyes to adjust to the dimmer interior. Before they did, a little body pressed to his legs.

He reached down and touched Jeannie's head. "Good morning." He looked around and located Sadie and the other children sitting nearby. Sadie's smile welcomed him. Beth's scowl did not, and Sammy looked ready to bolt. He shifted his gaze back to Sadie, finding solace in her steady look.

"I knowed you'd come." Jeannie's sweetness smoothed his insides.

He took her hand. "Jeannie, this is my grandfather."

Wide-eyed, she took in his canes and white hair. "How old are you?"

Sadie gasped but Grandfather chuckled. "I'm ancient." He turned toward Sadie. "Do you mind if we sit by you?"

"Of course not." She and the two children slid down to make room.

Jeannie still held Logan's hand and pulled him into place. She sat by Sadie and wriggled and smiled as Logan sat beside her, Grandfather next to the aisle.

"Good morning," he said. And could think of nothing more. It simply felt right and good to be here with Sadie and the children on one side, Grandfather on the other and Dawson, Isabelle and Mattie sitting a few rows ahead. His pa and Logan sat by Dawson and Annie sat with Carly. Yes, this felt just about perfect.

The hymns they sang settled into his heart with warmth and familiarity.

Preacher Hugh Arness opened his Bible. "'But Jesus said, Suffer little children, and forbid them not, to come unto me: for of such is the kingdom of heaven.'" He closed his Bible and leaned forward. "Is there anything more precious than a child?"

Logan turned his head enough to see Sadie. She had turned to him. Their gazes met and melded. No words were necessary. They both agreed these children deserved love and care.

The preacher went on to talk about God's love for them as children, then shifted to say that God had given parents to help with the task. Logan watched Sadie's hands twist together and wondered why such comforting words would unsettle her. He promised himself he would ask the next time they had a chance to be alone.

Then the service ended. Logan introduced the two older children to Grandfather.

Beth even smiled. Logan couldn't help but wonder why she seemed to like the old man while she continually rebuffed Logan's attempts at friendship.

Sammy shook Grandfather's hands. "Can I go now?" He didn't wait for permission but darted out the door.

The rest followed more sedately. In the yard, Logan hesitated at Sadie's side.

Grandfather gave him a squinty-eyed look. "You gonna say something or just stand there? Ask the gal if she'd like to go for a walk after dinner."

Logan chuckled. "Would you?" he asked the blushing Sadie.

Sadie grinned at Grandfather before she turned to Logan. "Why don't you bring your grandfather over for tea and cookies and then, yes, I'd like to go for a walk."

"I accept." Grandfather practically crowed with delight. "Come on, boy. Let's go."

Logan chuckled. "I'll see you a little later," he said to Sadie and waved to the two girls. Sammy played with a couple of boys some distance away. He'd see the boy later.

He followed Grandfather and helped him into the wagon. Grandfather waited until they turned down the street to say, "I thought I might have to jump in and do all the asking back there."

Logan snorted. "Seems to me you did."

Grandfather rumbled his lips. "A gal likes to know she's important enough for a man to make a little effort, you know."

"If you say so."

Grandfather patted Logan's shoulder. "You can take my word for it."

They drew in at the back of the store and went into the living quarters to join Aunt Mary and Uncle George for dinner. It was one of Grandfather's rituals…sharing this time with his younger son.

"Grandfather, why are you in such a hurry?" Aunt Mary asked as Grandfather attacked his dinner.

"Got me a date."

Logan snorted.

Grandfather fired Logan a challenging look. "Tea and cookies."

Aunt Mary stared. Uncle George's hand, with his fork loaded, stopped halfway to his mouth.

"You're seeing a girl?" Aunt Mary, bless her heart, spoke without the disbelief that filled her eyes. "Courting her?"

"Yes and no."

Logan grinned. He loved the way Grandfather kept the family on their toes.

Uncle George put his fork down. "Is it yes or no? It can't be both."

"Yes, I'm seeing a girl and, no, I'm not courting her. I'm leaving that to Logan if he isn't too thick to see the possibilities."

Logan about choked. Too thick? But he knew better than to let Grandfather's goading get under his skin.

"Oh, you mean Miss Young, the schoolteacher." Uncle George neatly dismissed Grandfather's claims. He turned to Logan. "Have you had any success in finding Mr. Weiss?"

"Afraid not." He gave a report of his trip to Wolf Hollow.

"That's not very helpful," Uncle George said. "Have you asked Jesse to look for him? After all, he's the sheriff."

"He's been asking around, too, but hasn't learned anything more than I have."

Grandfather shoved back his chair. "I'm done." He

looked at Logan's plate. "You gonna take all day to finish that?"

Logan toyed with the food for a second or two just to let the old man know he wouldn't be rushed. Though he was likely more anxious than Grandfather to cross the street and visit Sadie and the children, he wasn't about to admit it. Grandfather stood, tapping one cane and then the next in an impatient drumbeat.

Logan drew his fork across his plate and scooped up the last of the food. "Guess I'm done. Are you ready, Grandfather?" he asked with a great deal of pretended innocence.

Uncle George chuckled as Grandfather grabbed his coat and struggled into it, not allowing Logan to assist him. "I'm always ready," he grumped.

Logan knew better than to ask ready for what? Grandfather had a whole list of things he'd been able to do better than most men when he was able-bodied.

They thanked Aunt Mary for the meal. Logan grabbed another stool from the store and they crossed the street to the school yard. Logan shortened his stride so as not to rush his grandfather.

Grandfather examined the window trim and the siding as they went by the wall. "I'll have a look inside the room before I leave. See that you're doing a decent job."

Logan chuckled, not a bit put out by the old man's words. "Bear in mind you taught me everything I know."

"Harrumph. And still you don't know enough to court the pretty schoolmarm."

"And still." He echoed Grandfather's words. Let him make of it what he would. They reached the entrance to the living quarters and Logan knocked.

Sammy pulled the door open. "Sadie said we had to wait for you to come before we could have dessert."

"It's only cookies," Sadie said somewhat apologetically. "But do come in and join us." She smiled at Grandfather and the old man practically preened. Logan had a sudden urge to jump in front of Grandfather and inform the old man that he had seen her first.

She shifted her gaze to Logan, her smile warm and welcoming.

He swallowed hard. "I brought another stool."

Grandfather groaned. "She ain't blind, is she?"

"No." He set down the stool and removed his hat. Too bad he couldn't erase the silly words as easily. He turned back to the room and saw amusement in Beth's eyes. So she liked seeing Grandfather tease him, did she? In that case, he would encourage the older man. "Oh no," he drawled like a backwoods hermit. "Her looks real good."

Sadie caught his meaning and colored up like a fresh spring rose.

Grandfather chortled.

Beth covered her mouth, but she didn't succeed in completely muffling her laugh.

Logan let his gaze find Sadie, wanting to share with her his pleasure at the change in Beth. If it took a crotchety old man to produce this change, he might bring his grandfather along every day.

They settled around the table. Somehow Logan ended up at one end, facing Sadie at the other. This was exactly the way things should be.

Sadie poured tea and passed the cookies.

"Who made the cookies?" he asked.

"Beth did." Sadie smiled at the girl.

"They are sure good. Thank you." He watched Beth for some sign that she would accept his compliment.

She glanced at Grandfather.

"You're a fine cook for one so young," Grandfather said.

"Thank you." Beth slowly brought her gaze to Logan. "Thank you, too."

Her thanks wouldn't seem like much to most, but to Logan it was big. Especially after the scene last night.

Sammy edged forward on his seat. "You started the ranch, didn't you?" he asked Grandfather.

"Sure did, son. Why, when I came out here, there wasn't anything but grass and coyotes. I slept in a tent and listened to them howl not ten yards from where I lay. Now, there's a lonesome sound."

Sammy peppered the man with questions about what it was like. "That was some adventure." He sat back. "My life is so boring."

"Let's keep it that way," Sadie said, giving Logan a look of such hope that he almost got up and went to her side. He'd promise to make sure Sammy didn't get into any serious mischief.

She shifted her attention around the table. "Anyone want more tea?"

No one did.

Grandfather gave Logan one of those looks...telling Logan something without using words. Half the time Logan didn't know what he wanted and the rest of the time, he ignored the look. Let Grandfather say what he wanted rather than expect people to read his silence. He ignored him this time too.

"Thought you were going to take Sadie for walk." Grandfather made it sound like Logan should have grabbed Sadie by the arm and dragged her from the room. He continued, "Now don't be shy. I'll stay with the young ones. I expect we can amuse each other." He turned to Sadie and, before Logan could get a word out, said, "He'd like you to accompany him for a walk."

Sadie laughed. "Why, thank you, Logan. I'd be pleased to go with you."

Again Beth covered her mouth and again failed to hide her laugh.

Sadie took a shawl from the hook by the door and Logan took his hat, and they stepped outside.

Beth's laughter and Grandfather's deeper chuckles followed them.

"At least she likes him." Logan knew there was a hint of regret in his words.

"I'm glad to see it. Aren't you?"

"Of course I am." He could hardly admit a degree of regret that Beth didn't seem to like him near as well.

"Don't you worry." Sadie tucked her hand around his elbow. "She likes you, but she's afraid to show it."

He pressed her hand to his side, finding comfort in her touch. He let himself believe it meant Sadie liked him. He meant to make an opportunity to talk to her about what made her so resistant to family. He wanted to know the secret behind her fear and erase it.

Chapter Ten

The wind had a cold bite to it and Sadie pressed just a little closer to Logan's side, welcoming the shelter of his large body. If she also enjoyed the comfort of being next to him, well, perhaps she could allow herself the privilege for a short time. She knew it would be temporary at best. She could allow nothing more. Her history had the potential to destroy not only her but his family, as well. And that would destroy him.

But for the present, because of the cold wind, she would ignore all the warnings inside her head. "I expect your grandfather was quite a character in his younger years."

Logan snorted. "He's quite a character now."

She chuckled softly and resisted the urge to press her cheek to his shoulder. "That's true. But you're very fond of him, aren't you?"

"I am. He had as much input into my upbringing as my parents. He takes any failure on my part as a failure on his. Which reminds me, he said he wants to have a look inside the schoolroom before he goes so he can make sure I've done a good job."

"Does it bother you that he is like that?"

"Not a bit. Because I know he is proud of me. Even when he acts like I can't manage on my own, he'd be the first one to stand back and say I could and tell me afterward that I'd done a good job."

"I sensed that. I think Beth does, too."

"She really relaxed with him, didn't she?" he said, and they grinned at each other as they thought of how his grandfather had elicited laughter from the girl.

Side by side they walked past the church and continued on by private homes. They passed a pussy willow tree. She pulled him to a halt and stared at the tree. Wouldn't she like to have some of those to add to her dried-flower collection?

As if reading her mind, he pulled a pocketknife from his pocket, cut off several sprigs and handed them to her.

She brushed her cheek against the furry catkins. "Thank you." She lifted her gaze to his and, at the brightness of his smile, her heart kicked against its traces. She could almost let herself believe he looked upon her with fondness. With gentleness. With claiming.

But if he knew...

"Shall we continue?" He crooked his elbow toward her.

She tucked her hand into the shelter of his arm and they went farther down the street.

"Did you enjoy Preacher Hugh's sermon?" Logan asked.

"He's very direct." Enough to make her uncomfortable at times.

"I couldn't help noticing that something he said seemed to upset you."

She was so sure she'd hidden it. "What did I do to make you think that?"

"You twisted your hands."

She could say her gloves were uncomfortable. Or that her hands were cold.

Logan stopped walking and turned to face her. He put his hand over hers where it rested, warm and safe, on his forearm. He exerted just enough pressure that she couldn't pull free without making it look like she was upset. She didn't want to give him that impression.

"Will you tell me what bothered you?"

Even without looking directly at him, she felt the power of his gaze. How was she to answer him? She couldn't admit that she'd wondered why her parents couldn't love even half as much as God did. Yes, she cherished God's love for her, but sometimes it would be nice to know a human love she could trust. But she pushed aside her own pain and thought of the children. "Like the preacher said, is there anything more precious than a child? It upsets me to think Sammy and likely his sisters have not known that sort of love from those in authority over them."

He squeezed her hand. "I understand. But at least we are able to offer them love and protection while they are here."

And then what? She wouldn't say the words. They'd discussed this so many times. A father had rights. Who was to challenge them? Would it do any good if she or anyone else did? But perhaps if someone with recognized authority spoke up...someone like Logan's grandfather...things might change.

If she got a chance, she'd speak to the older man.

Something stung her face.

Logan looked around. "It's snowing. We'd better get back before this turns into a storm."

They returned to the house far faster than they'd left. By the time they reached the door, the snow fell heavily, driven sideways by a strong wind.

They burst inside. Logan leaned against the door to push it shut.

Sadie hurried to the stove to warm up.

"Grandfather," Logan said, his voice full of urgency, "we have to go. It's settling down to a spring storm."

The older man didn't move. "I'm not going anywhere in that cold wind."

"But we have to go."

"Nope. We can stay here."

Logan opened his mouth to argue, but Grandfather Marshall didn't give him a chance. "There's plenty of room here. I'm sure Sadie won't mind if we stay until the storm ends."

Sadie waggled her hands. "Certainly." What else could she say? And surely the storm would pass as quickly as it came.

Logan shrugged. "If it's okay with you then I guess there's no reason to leave. I'll take the horse and wagon to the livery barn." He was gone before any of them could protest.

Sadie tried to watch him out the window, but the snow obscured everything. She pressed her hand to her throat hoping he would make it back safely. That's when she realized she still clutched the pussy willows and found a jar to put them in.

The others had returned to their activities. Jeannie

perched on Grandfather's knees. Beth and Sammy sat on the floor at his feet as if they had been listening to stories or playing a game.

Sadie could not relax. Not with Logan out in the snow. She didn't realize she stared at the door, waiting for his return, until Grandfather spoke.

"Don't you worry, missy. He'll be okay."

She jerked away from the door and hurried to the cupboard. No doubt Logan and his grandfather would be there for supper. She'd have to prepare something.

As soon as she pulled out food, Beth joined her, and they began to make a chicken potpie from the leftover meat from dinner.

The door rattled and Sammy ran to welcome Logan, who stumbled in covered with snow. He rubbed his hands. "It's turned awfully cold. I hope Pa and the others get home safely or find shelter somewhere until this is over."

"They would have been home long ago," Grandfather said, but one look at his face and Sadie knew he wondered about the rest of the family, as well.

"Come to the stove and get warm." She handed Logan a towel and he rubbed the snow from his face and hands.

She tried not to look at him. She tried not to think how she felt safe and scared at the same time. It was good that Beth was more relaxed with Grandfather there. It was not good that Sadie felt tenser. She couldn't turn around without encountering Logan. He'd been there before, she chided herself.

But not confined to the house by a snowstorm.

Would he take advantage of the situation?

No, because the children and Grandfather were there.

But if they weren't?

She dared not answer. To say he wouldn't meant she trusted him, and that frightened her. But to say he would...well, that stung her heart and conscience because she knew he wouldn't.

What was she to do? She was truly stuck between her warming heart and a raging blizzard.

At the moment she had only one option—make the best of it. Keep everyone occupied. First, feed them. As she and Beth returned to preparing the meal, Grandfather regaled them with stories of past blizzards.

Soon the food was ready and they crowded about the table.

She asked Grandfather to say the blessing.

"My pleasure." He bowed his head. "Father God, we are grateful for food, family and friends, and for safety from the storm. Not just snowstorms but the storms of life. May we always be safe. Amen."

Sadie didn't look at either men. Safe? Would she ever truly feel safe again?

As regular as clockwork, Jeannie fussed as the meal ended and Beth took her to the bedroom. The little girl settled quickly, and Beth rejoined them and helped with dishes.

Grandfather kept the conversation filled with teasing and stories so that the evening passed pleasantly, but, as the time ticked by, Sadie's insides grew tighter by the minute. Were they going to spend the night here? Where?

"Grandfather," Logan said, interrupting another story that had the children mesmerized. "We should make our way over to the store and stay with Uncle George."

Grandfather raised his bushy white eyebrows. "In this storm? Why, I'd be blown clear off my feet and end up in Mexico."

Beth grinned and Sammy laughed.

"The storm is not going to let up and we can't stay here."

"Why not?"

"It's too small."

Grandfather harrumphed. "There's a whole empty classroom just beyond that door." He pointed to the door that opened into the schoolroom. "A dozen men could sleep there."

Logan lifted his hands to the air. "Did someone invite you?"

Sadie couldn't help it. She laughed. "You are both invited to stay and you don't need to sleep in the cold schoolroom. You can share Sammy's quarters. Right, Sammy?"

The boy nodded eagerly. "Mr. Marshall," he said to the older man, "you can have my bed and I'll sleep on the floor with Logan."

"Don't mind if you call me Grandfather."

As easily as that, it was settled. The only thing that wasn't settled was Sadie's insides. It was one thing to share care of the children with Logan and even to share mealtimes. It was quite another to have him there at night. She stole a glance at Beth. The girl's face was tight, her eyes hard. As if she had the same thought.

Could she have the same reasons?

The possibility had hovered in the back of Sadie's

mind for days, and she'd pushed it away. How could she contemplate such a thing?

But she couldn't deny the possibility, either.

A shudder crossed her shoulders.

Logan sidled up to her. "Are you okay?"

How was he always so attuned to her every mood? She nodded.

"Do you want to go see the classroom?"

She'd gone in many times, anxiously planning when classes would be held there, but feeling crowded in her small living quarters, she agreed.

"This is a good time for you to check and make sure the windows and door are tight against the elements," Grandfather said.

Sammy jumped up and was about to follow when Grandfather said, "Let me tell you about a storm that had us stranded at school when I was a youngster."

Sammy looked from Logan to Grandfather, trying to decide which direction to go, then settled back down at Grandfather's feet.

Sadie waited, wondering if anyone else would join them. No one seemed interested so she and Logan went alone into the cold room, darkened by the swirling snow outside each window. She hurried from one window to the next, running her finger along the bookshelves lining the wall beneath the windows.

Logan followed on her heels, not saying anything yet occupying her thoughts.

"I can hardly wait to fill these shelves and to see desks lining the room." She turned to picture the arrangement and, instead, came face-to-face with Logan.

"Does it bother you that we are staying here?" he asked.

She tried to shake her head no, but it went round in circles, instead.

"If it's just me, I can go across to the store."

"No!" The word came out more forcefully than she planned. "It's storming too much. You wouldn't be safe."

He edged closer. She could feel him with every breath.

"Is that the only reason?"

Hearing the uncertainty in his voice, she lifted her eyes to his and was caught in something she couldn't escape. Be it need or want or loneliness or anxiety, she couldn't say. She only knew she didn't wish to be responsible for it.

"I don't mind if you stay here." She might as well admit the truth to herself. She would feel safe with him there. And his grandfather, she added hastily. The storm could not harm them with two Marshall men to protect them.

She simply must guard her heart.

He cupped his hand to her face. "Sometimes you're about as skittish as Beth. Like you're afraid of me." His soft voice made it impossible for her to think. "It makes me want to hug you and promise you I will never harm you or let anyone else harm you."

She leaned into his hand, wanting to trust his promise. But a knot behind her heart tightened, reminding her of her lost innocence and the rejection by her parents.

Sadness sucked at her. Her breath caught in a half sob.

"Sadie, I—" He didn't finish. Instead, he tipped her

face upward and caught her lips in a kiss so sweet and tender that she instinctively leaned into him.

He lifted his head, pulled her into his arms and rested his chin on her hair. "I didn't know how else to say how much I want you to feel safe with me."

She did feel safe. For the moment. And she let the moment be enough, even knowing it couldn't last.

Her secret was not the sort of thing that would make her welcome in a family, and family was all-important to him.

But she'd accept his comfort and offer of safety for the present.

Sammy laughed loudly about something, and Sadie and Logan broke apart. The moment had come to an end. Reality must replace dreams.

They returned to the other room, pulling the door closed behind them.

Logan sat on a chair and concentrated on Grandfather's stories though he'd heard them many times before.

He shouldn't have kissed Sadie. Not that he regretted it. He'd been about to ask her what secrets she hid, but Sammy's laughter had stopped him.

And he couldn't say if he'd regretted it or welcomed it.

If it was a secret he could dismiss then they could look to a future. But if it was a destructive secret...

What would he do?

He considered several possibilities: she was a wanted woman; her family were outlaws; she'd stolen from someone and had a price on her head. None of the scenarios he came up with made sense. But if one of them was true, she'd have to flee once her secret was out. What would he do?

Would he leave with her?

He looked at his aging, crippled grandfather, considered Dawson's recent marriage, thought about Annie and her need to pursue her own life. Could he leave them to cope on their own?

He shook his head. He couldn't believe Sadie would be guilty of any of those things.

The evening passed pleasantly enough. Sadie made popcorn and brought out a board game. Grandfather turned the game into a lively competition, making them all laugh.

Then it was time for bed. Sadie produced blankets for Logan and Sammy, then she and Beth went to the bedroom and closed the door.

Grandfather took the bed and Sammy and Logan spread blankets between the table and the stove.

"This is just like the cowboys do, isn't it?" Sammy said.

"Cowboys learn to sleep in lots of different places," Logan agreed. "To hear Grandfather talk, you'd think they purposely chose a bed of rocks or cactus, but we usually try and find the most comfortable place. Sometimes we'll cut evergreen boughs to make a soft bed."

Grandfather made a mocking sound. "Surprised you don't carry a mattress with you so you'll be really comfortable."

Logan pretended to give it serious consideration. "Never thought of that."

Grandfather chuckled. "I hope I don't live to see the day."

They settled down. Sammy fell asleep almost at

once, and soon Grandfather was snoring loud enough
to drown out the sound of the storm.

Logan lay awake staring at the ceiling. There were
so many uncertainties in his life at the moment. The
children's missing father. His growing feelings toward
Sadie, and her continued resistance. Until he settled
them to his satisfaction, his life would continue to feel
unsettled. There was little he could do about it but pray,
and he did so. *God, help me find Mr. Weiss. Help us
learn the truth about what the children are afraid of.*
He wished he hadn't seen the marks on Sammy's back.
Wished he didn't wonder at the cause of Beth's skit-
tishness. *Help Sadie learn to trust me.*

He smiled into the darkness. He had kissed her. It
had been a purely instinctive move to comfort and assure her. But it had instantly become more in his mind.
It had become a promise, a possibility…a dream.

His smile flattened. The dream was destined to be
dashed unless she felt the same way. Unless she trusted
him enough to tell him what she was hiding.

The storm still raged the next morning. Logan made
a path to the woodshed and brought in more wood.
When Sadie handed him a cup of coffee accompanied
by a smile, he thought again of possibilities.

Jeannie ran to him and he picked her up and pressed
his cold cheek to her neck making her giggle.

Sammy rocked back and forth on his heels. "Guess
there won't be any school today 'cause of the storm."

Logan put his coffee cup on the table so he could
ruffle Sammy's hair. "You don't sound disappointed."

Sammy grinned. "I'm not."

Logan checked on Beth. She was setting the table
but darted a look toward him. He saw the guardedness

in her eyes and something more—longing and uncertainty. He knew the latter had nothing to do with the weather. "We are all safe and I intend to keep it that way." He hoped she would understand he meant more than shelter from the storm.

"Did you sleep well, Grandfather?"

"Like a log."

He chuckled. "Yeah, I heard you sawing them all night long. I expect everyone did."

Sammy nodded. "I did."

Logan brought his gaze to Sadie. "Did you hear him?"

Her eyes twinkled. "I heard a loud noise. Like the rumble of a wagon over a rough road. Was that him?"

He fell into her warm look. He let himself believe she held nothing back as she met his gaze.

"I'm not that loud," Grandfather protested.

Sadie turned to Grandfather and chuckled. "I might have been imagining it."

"Why do you think we make you sleep downstairs?" Logan asked.

"You didn't hear me, did you?" Grandfather looked to Beth for sympathy.

Her face innocently blank, she looked around the room. Her gaze came to Logan and stalled there. "I honestly thought it was Logan."

"Me?"

Grandfather was the first to realize Beth was teasing Logan, and he slapped his leg and laughed. "Oh, you are a sneaky one. You almost had us fooled."

Logan chuckled. "Beth, I see you've been taking lessons from Grandfather."

Beth's eyes danced and she ducked her head.

Logan wanted to hug the girl. He met Sadie's eyes and saw she shared the same joy over Beth's teasing. He wanted to hug Sadie, too. Instead, he hugged Jeannie. "Your sister is a tease, isn't she?"

Jeannie nodded.

Breakfast was ready and they gathered around the table. Like a family.

The thought jerked his head up and he looked from one place to another. Apart from the three children, and him and his grandfather, they weren't a family. But a family didn't have to be related by blood or marriage. Family was also formed by bonds of love.

After breakfast dishes were done, Sadie insisted the two older children must do lessons.

Sammy complained. "What's Logan going to do?"

"I'll help you." Soon they were around the table. Sadie and Beth worked together on an essay. Logan helped Sammy practice his sums, and Grandfather and Jeannie read a children's book.

Logan lifted his head to find Sadie's gaze on him. A smile filled her eyes and tugged at the corners of her mouth. Joy warmed his heart. If not for the dangers of a spring storm and concern about the safety of his family members, Logan might like the storm to last for several days, keeping them shut in, safe from the outside world.

But they had barely finished dinner when Sammy looked out the window. "It's stopped snowing." He rushed to open the door. The sun shone blindingly on the fresh snow that was several inches deep. Logan knew the warmth of the sun would soon melt the snow and mire the trail in mud.

"We have to get home." He pushed away from the

table. "I'll get the wagon." He hurried from the house. He must get Grandfather home before the trail became impassable for the wagon.

He returned as soon as he could and hurried to the door. Grandfather waited with his hat and coat on and his canes in his hands.

Jeannie looked past Logan to the wagon. "You're leaving?"

"Yes. We have to get home."

"I don't want you to go." Wailing, she threw open the door leading to the classroom. Her shoes pitter-pattered across the floor.

Logan stared after Jeannie. He left every day. Always had. Why did she now object? Or was it Grandfather's leaving she objected to?

"Better go see if you can calm her down," Grandfather said.

Sadie and Logan both headed for the door and crossed the bare floor to Jeannie, who sat in a huddle crying.

They squatted at her side. "Honey, you know I have to go home," Logan said.

"No." Jeannie clutched an arm about his neck. "I want you to stay." She grabbed Sadie with her other arm and pulled her close. So close that Logan could feel her breath, watch the sadness in her eyes. He tipped his head so their foreheads touched.

"I don't want anyone to go," Jeannie wailed.

"Honey, I'll be back tomorrow. But I have to get Grandfather home."

Jeannie's cries deepened, tearing Logan's heart to shreds. He reached for Sadie, clinging to her hand, feeling her sorrow as well as his own, like a raging storm blinding him to every bit of reason. He would stay if he could.

Responsibilities and proper conduct made it impossible.

Jeannie sniffed back a sob. "Nobody loves us."

As one, Sadie and Logan drew her closer. Logan shifted so his arms circled both of them. He couldn't speak for the tightness in his throat. All he could do was hold them and promise himself he would somehow make things better for the children and for Sadie.

That meant discovering the truth about all of them.

The truth might hurt. He knew that. But without the truth, there was no future for any of them and especially not a future that included him.

"Honey, I love you. And I promise I will return tomorrow morning. Is that okay?"

She nodded none too happily.

"I love you, too," Sadie said, her voice husky. "And I'll be here."

"You have to go to school."

"Beth will be with you when I'm there and so will Logan."

"I know." She grew thoughtful and turned to Logan. "Will you play with me when you get here?"

"Of course I will." Had he been so busy working that the poor child felt she didn't matter? "Are you okay now?"

"I'm okay." She bounced to her feet and trotted back to the kitchen, where she announced to one and all that Logan was going to come and play with her tomorrow.

Logan and Sadie sat shoulder to shoulder. He felt her sadness clear through and wrapped an arm about her and pulled her close.

She shuddered. "I feel I've let them down."

He caught her chin with his free hand and turned her to face him. "You've given them security, safety and a good home. You've treated them well. What's more, you love them."

Tears sheened in her eyes and she nodded. "I don't want them to go, especially to a father who hurts them."

He caught a tear from each cheek and his heart cracked wide open, weeping silent, dry tears into his innermost being. He could not abide her pain and pulled her close to kiss her. She leaned into his embrace, returning the kiss. Whether offering comfort or seeking it or both, he could not say; nor did it matter.

Their lips clung, their arms tightened. His heart would forever be changed.

"Did you two get lost?" Grandfather called.

They slowly parted, smiling into each other's eyes. Logan rose, pulled her to her feet, and they crossed the schoolroom. He dropped her hand at the doorway and waited for her to enter the kitchen. Then he slowly closed the door behind them, feeling as if he closed the door to that part of their relationship, as well.

He helped Grandfather to the wagon. The family crowded into the doorway to wave goodbye. Beth sucked in her bottom lip and blinked. She would never say so, but she didn't want Grandfather to leave. It was reassuring to see the girl reveal some emotion besides resistance. It renewed his determination to find the children's father and end their uncertainty.

Logan returned the next day as promised to be greeted by Jeannie, waiting eagerly to be played with. Sammy was still there, too, though Sadie had already gone to the classroom. Did she want to avoid him? Had his kisses made her uncomfortable?

He grinned. Not because she didn't enjoy them. He knew that. She had given as much as he.

"What do you want to play?" he asked Jeannie.

"Can't catch me." She took off running through the patches of snow, splashing the slush about her legs. She'd soon be wet to her knees.

He ran after her, swept her off her feet and tickled her.

"Can't catch me," Sammy said, and Logan chased him, Jeannie bouncing up and down on his hip. He snagged Sammy with his free arm and lifted him off his feet.

"I got you both. What am I going to do with you?"

They wrapped their arms about his neck.

"You could give us piggyback rides," Sammy said.

"Okay." He shifted Sammy so the boy clung to his back and, still holding Jeannie, he galloped about the yard, giving Sammy a rough ride.

Sammy hung on like a bronc rider, laughing all the way.

"My turn," Jeannie said when Logan stopped to catch his breath. He squatted so Sammy could dismount and shifted Jeannie to his back, giving her a less vigorous ride, Sammy yelling and chasing after them.

Logan came to a halt in front of Beth, who watched them play. He lowered Jeannie to the ground and studied the older girl. Did he see a hint of mischief, perhaps even a yearning to play?

One way to find out. "Let's play tag. You're it." He touched Beth on the shoulder and darted away. The younger children ran away squealing.

Beth hesitated then went in pursuit of Jeannie, easily overtaking her. "You're it."

Logan danced about Jeannie, almost letting her tag him and then darting away. After a few tries, he let her catch him, then spun about and ran after Beth.

She raced away, ran around the schoolhouse. He pursued her and just before she reached the safety of the door where he knew she meant to run inside and slam the door in his face, he tagged her. "You're it."

She turned and faced him, a dozen different things racing over her expression. Exhilaration at the thrill of the chase quickly faded to uncertainty. He watched her struggle with a desire to retreat and one to continue this game. Then determination darkened her eyes. He wished he knew if the latter meant she would allow herself to enjoy playing with him or if it meant she would retreat to her cautiousness.

A bell rang.

He jerked toward the sound.

Beth's eyes grew large. "Sammy is going to be late."

"I'm going." Sammy ran for the store.

"I better get to work, too." Logan resumed the finishing details on the schoolroom. He would soon be done and have no more excuse to come to town every day.

None but three children who looked forward to his visits and a lovely schoolteacher whom he'd promised to help with the children.

He experienced a deep regret that he would not see them as frequently as he wanted.

Chapter Eleven

That week the children seemed to settle into a comfortable routine. Logan sensed a huge difference in them, as if they allowed themselves to believe this would be permanent and perhaps even that he could be trusted. Every day he continued putting the finishing touches on the schoolhouse. If Grandfather knew he spent almost as much time playing with the kids, there might have been a ruckus.

Or maybe not. Every morning before Logan left and every evening when he returned, Grandfather required a report…but not on the work. He wanted to know about the children and about Sadie.

"Bring them out Sunday," Grandfather said. "I'd like to spend the afternoon with them."

Logan was glad Grandfather hadn't asked to have them visit Saturday. He meant to spend the morning asking around Wolf Hollow again.

Sammy begged to be able to help him, so Logan made the same arrangement as the previous week. He would be away for the morning and come to the school at noon, when he and Sammy would work on a project.

"Join us for dinner," Sadie said, her smile so welcoming Logan couldn't have refused if a hundred reasons had appeared.

"On one condition." He kept his amusement to himself as three children and one schoolmarm looked both guarded and interested.

"Depends on the condition," Sadie said after some seconds of consideration.

"Let's make it a picnic." He laughed at the relief on her face and knew without looking at Beth that she wore a matching expression. "The weather is sunny and warm. The flowers are blooming. Last week's snowstorm was simply winter having one last fling." The warm sunshine had melted every bit of snow and dried the ground. "I know a perfect spot just south of town."

Sadie nodded, a smile on her lips and a flash in her eyes that made Logan mighty pleased at his suggestion.

"I'll make a lunch while you're gone."

"Great." He sketched a goodbye wave and rode away, but his thoughts lingered back at the schoolhouse. Saturdays were busy for Sadie. Already she had laundry flapping on the line. He knew she would bake, clean the small living quarters and undertake likely a hundred other chores. But she deserved a little fun, too, and he meant to see that they all had an enjoyable afternoon. Even while helping Sammy on a project.

He reached Wolf Hollow and again asked about Mr. Weiss. Again he received confusing messages. Two men thought they'd heard Mr. Weiss had died. Some had heard he'd taken his family and moved on to a more suitable place. At this answer, Logan tried to gain some information about the family to see if they spoke of the same Weisses, but, to his discouragement, he learned nothing of value. He again tried to find Mr. Weiss's gold claim, but there was no mine in his name. He must have sold the claim.

Frustration clawed at his insides as he returned to Bella Creek.

Sammy stood at the back of the lot bouncing on the balls of his feet. "He's here. He's here," he screamed loud enough to inform the entire town.

Logan grinned. There was nothing like a welcoming child to drive away the feeling of failure from his morning. Sammy raced toward him and Logan reached down and pulled the boy up behind him to ride the last twenty feet to the house.

Sadie came out and smiled up at him, the bright sun causing her to tent her hand over her eyes.

He resisted an urge to jump from his horse, sweep her off her feet and kiss her until neither of them could remember why they shouldn't. At the moment, he couldn't think of a single reason.

Jeannie crowded to Sadie's side. "We goin' on picnic?"

Logan jumped to the ground to swing Jeannie up in the air. "You think it sounds like a good idea?"

She nodded, her eyes shining with anticipation.

Beth sat at the table, a full basket covered with a checkered cloth in front of her. She kept her attention on the window across the room but didn't succeed in hiding a twitch of a smile.

Today, Logan decided, was going to be a good day. "Is everyone ready?"

Sadie nodded and Sammy yelled he was.

"Let me take care of my horse and then we'll be on our way."

"We're not riding?" Sammy conveyed shock and disappointment.

"I only have one horse," Logan pointed out. "Besides, it's close enough we can walk." Only half a mile and if he could do it, so could those more used to walking than he.

"I'll carry the basket," he said.

Sadie reached for a lacy shawl. "Sammy and Beth, will you each carry a blanket?"

With Sadie at his side, the girls following and Sammy racing ahead, they marched down the alley.

Kate stepped out of the doctor's house. "It looks to me like you are going somewhere."

"On a picnic," Sammy told her.

She smiled. "Have fun."

Logan waved. "Thanks. We intend to." He winked at Sadie, bringing a splash of color to her cheeks and making Kate laugh.

"It's for the children," Sadie protested.

"Of course it is." Kate grinned widely. "I didn't hear anyone suggest differently." She waved and returned inside as Logan and his little army marched onward.

"You needn't have given her the wrong idea." Sadie kept her voice soft, but there was no mistaking the warning in her words.

He pretended injury. "I only said we meant to have fun." He chuckled. "And I do. Don't you think the children deserve it?" *And so do we.* The atmosphere in the home was strained so much of the time. "The children are finally starting to relax."

"It's good to see."

Contentment made him swing the basket in one hand and take her hand on his other side and swing it, too. "It's a great day for a picnic." The sun was warm overhead and the sky, a cloudless blue. They reached the pathway leading through the trees. The pines were dark and shadowy, the aspen and willow heavy with buds.

Sadie slowed and sucked in a deep breath. "It smells so fresh."

"It smells green." Beth's voice was round with awe, and no one corrected her that green was a color not a smell.

They followed the narrow path in single file, the sound of the creek growing louder. They broke through the trees to a grassy slope. The creek rushed over smooth rocks on its way to join Wolf River some miles away.

Sammy immediately started throwing rocks in the water.

Jeannie squatted down and examined the rocks, exclaiming how pretty they were.

Beth and Sadie stood near the creek watching and listening to the sounds of nature while Logan watched them, pleased to see them enjoying the moment. However, he couldn't remain an observer any longer and went to Sadie's side, close enough that her shawl brushed his arm. She smiled up at him and he congratulated himself on having had this good idea.

Sammy raced up to them. "We gonna eat? I'm hungry."

"Me, too." Jeannie gave them a sweet, begging look that made both Sadie and Logan chuckle.

"Now that you mention it, I'm kind of hungry too."

Sadie went back to where the blankets and basket had been left.

Logan hurried after her and spread the blankets while she smoothed the checked tablecloth on the ground and soon had the food set out. Logan's mouth watered at the bounty—thick sandwiches, a dish of dill pickle spears, and little biscuits with butter and jam.

"Beth?" Sadie called softly.

The girl turned from watching the water gurgle by and joined them, her gaze thoughtful. "Mama loved picnics. Remember that, Sammy?"

Sammy's normal exuberance quieted. "I liked it best when we went away from town and it was just us."

Beth turned to Jeannie. "Do you remember our picnics?"

"Mama put a blanket on the floor and we ate like this." Jeannie looked around at the five of them sitting in a circle.

Beth nodded. "That was our winter picnics."

Sadie glanced to each child. "Do you think she might like you to keep having picnics and remembering her?" Her gaze rested on Beth.

Beth nodded slowly. "I think she'd like it." Beth's eyes met Logan's briefly, and in that glance he saw something he had not seen before. He wanted to believe it was gratitude but would settle for it being only acceptance. Anything was better than the outright rejection he'd endured so far.

He asked the blessing over the food and Sadie passed the sandwiches around.

Logan did not want to let this sense of peace go to waste. "Beth has made me think of something. Let's go around the circle and everyone tell of a favorite memory about their mother." To his right, he heard Sadie's sudden gasp. He ignored it. Perhaps she would reveal something about her family under these circumstances.

"I'll start," he said. "My ma used to read to us after supper during the winter months. She did it right up until she passed." He didn't say that he had missed many of those evenings as he followed his foolish heart, but it was a good reminder to be careful and not repeat his mistakes. He glanced at Sadie. He understood she had not been completely open with him but couldn't believe it was because of something that would hurt him or his family.

Sammy sat next to Logan. "Mama let me help make cookies and I liked that."

Beth chuckled. "You ate so much cookie dough that Mama used to say she wondered if she should bake you."

Brother and sister smiled at the memory.

Jeannie was next. She nodded. "I 'member Mama rocking me in the chair."

Logan's throat tightened. Sadie cleared her throat.

Jeannie brightened. "Now Beth rocks me."

The air lightened at her happiness and all eyes shifted to Beth. Logan wondered if she would refuse to share. After all, she had talked about her memory of picnics with her mama.

But Beth smiled at her brother and sister. "I remember what Mama said when each of you was borned. She told me each of us was a gift from God and we should never forget it. Do you remember?"

Sammy nodded, but Jeannie looked uncertain. "Me, too?"

Beth hugged her little sister. "Yes, you too."

Slowly, guardedly, Logan turned to Sadie. The children looked at her, as well.

She didn't say anything. Her expression, if he had to describe it, was shielded. Thoughtful perhaps.

"Tell us about your mama," Sammy said. "What's she look like? Where do your parents live?"

So she'd told the children her parents were alive.

"They live in Saint Louis. My mother is pretty, I suppose."

"Does she look like you?" Sammy persisted.

Logan noted that Beth didn't try to hush him and looked just as interested.

"Anyone want some biscuits and jam?" Sadie passed around the sweets, but the children weren't diverted.

"Does she?" Sammy asked again.

"I don't think I look like her. I guess I'm not like either of my parents."

Logan wondered if she realized she hadn't said she didn't *look* like them...only that she wasn't *like* them.

"Don't you like them?" Sammy looked puzzled.

This time Beth shushed him, but Logan wondered the same thing.

"I like them fine," Sadie said quite emphatically. "I just don't see them a lot."

Jeannie went to Sadie and put her arm about her neck. "Did your mama read to you and take you on picnics?"

Sadie shook her head and pulled the little girl to her lap.

Logan wanted to pull them both into his arms at the way Sadie's throat worked. She kept her head down, her cheek pressed to Jeannie's head.

Beth reached over and squeezed Sadie's hand. "You can come on picnics with us," she said.

"And you can read to us," Sammy added.

Sadie looked up, her eyes glistening with tears. "I can't think of anything I'd like better."

They finished up the food and put away the picnic items and then the children went to play, leaving Logan and Sadie alone. She sat staring toward the creek, but he wondered what she really saw.

He edged closer and leaned back on one elbow, watching her, wanting to somehow comfort her. He sat up, wrapped an arm about her shoulders and pulled her close, pleased when she offered no resistance. He pressed a kiss to the top of her head, felt her shudder and tightened his arm to still her trembling.

If only he knew what to say, but words were far too inadequate.

Sadie pressed to Logan's side, clinging to his strength and comfort. If only she could believe both would be offered if he knew the truth about her. It was on the tip of her tongue to confess it all. But she was afraid. Afraid of his reaction, afraid of being abandoned and alone again. No, he wasn't like her parents. He was strong, protective…and very principled. But she'd thought her parents possessed the same qualities.

She shifted her thoughts to the children. How sweet that they had opened up. They were beginning to feel safe with her. And Logan. They needed Logan as much as they needed her. For the children's sake she dared not risk anyone finding out the truth and bringing an end to this partnership.

Jeannie and Beth wandered hand in hand up the

creek bank, examining everything. Sadie smiled, thinking how Jeannie would want to know about every bug, every leaf and every rock, and how gently and patiently Beth would explain.

Sammy played at the water's edge, building a little barrier with rocks, diverting water into a puddle.

Sadie told herself it was time to move, to end this need for Logan's comfort, but she lacked the strength to do so. She had a four-year hollow of need that ached to be filled.

Logan shifted without releasing her. "I'm sorry if our talk about mothers made you sad."

What could she say? And he hadn't really asked a question. She simply breathed quietly.

"It did, didn't it?"

And now he had. How was she to answer? With the same words she'd been giving him all along. "Like I've said repeatedly, not all families are ideal. We don't all have the privilege of being born into one like the Marshalls."

"There are others ways of finding family besides being born into it."

His idea intrigued her and she waited, wondering, hoping he would explain.

"Take those three out there. You've given them the sort of family they deserve."

She shook her head. "I'm only temporary. What will happen when you find Mr. Weiss?"

His frustration was obvious as he told of another fruitless visit to Wolf Hollow. "But I won't give up until I find the man. The children deserve to know what's become of him."

She sighed wearily. "They will never feel safe until

they know." It was wrong to wish ill for a person, but perhaps the father had died of disease or accident. That would free the children from their fears. But would the authorities take the children from her? She shivered and Logan's arm tightened again.

They sat in silence a moment before he again spoke. "There are still other ways to get a family."

"I suppose." All of them were out of her reach, so she hoped he'd drop the subject.

He leaned back, pulling her along so they both rested on an elbow facing each other.

He brushed a strand of hair off her cheek and tucked it behind her ear. "Do you ever think about marriage?"

His question sliced through her, and his gentle touch left her floundering for footing. She wasn't sure what he meant, but it was another subject she didn't wish to pursue. "How can I not when Isabelle and Dawson wedded last month." Everywhere she looked she saw husbands with their wives, children with parents, young people courting. "Of course I think about it."

He trailed his finger along her cheek. "I mean for yourself."

She swallowed hard. He had no idea how much she longed for the acceptance and security of a husband who would love her through good and bad.

He didn't wait for an answer, instead pulling her close and claiming her lips in a kiss so full of promise and possibility that she couldn't think. If he asked her right there and then to marry him she would say yes and pray that the truth would never come out to destroy them.

"Sammy." Beth's panicked voice jolted them to their

feet to look toward the children. Sammy had fallen into the creek.

Logan was on the run immediately. He waded into the shallow water and plucked up the boy.

"I want the log," Sammy protested, trying to catch a floating tree.

"Forget the log. You're freezing." Logan carried the wet boy to the shore and stripped his shirt and pants off him without giving Sammy a chance to protest.

Sadie wrapped him in the blankets and held him tight, the cold of his little body penetrating through the blankets and turning her insides icy. "We need to get him home."

"I'll carry him." Logan scooped the boy into his arms. Beth clutched Jeannie's hands, her face wreathed in worry. Sadie grabbed the picnic basket and they hurried back through the narrow path and up the trail toward town.

Logan threw open the door of Sadie's living quarters and paused only to toss Sammy's wet things over the clothesline. Sadie rushed in on his heels. "I'll make a hot drink." She filled a pot with milk and set it to warm while Logan rubbed the boy all over until Sammy giggled. It was good to see that he no longer flinched when touched.

"You can stop now. I'm okay."

Beth found dry clothes and he slipped into the bedroom to get dressed.

A sober bunch sat around the table drinking warm milk.

Beth set down her cup with a thud. She shuddered.

Sadie sent Logan a concerned look. Would this set back the progress they had made with the girl?

Beth lifted her head and directed her gaze at Logan. "Thank you for rescuing him."

"You're welcome, but he was never in any real danger. The water is only a few inches deep."

"I know, but he would have drowned before he'd given up trying to bring that log to shore." She rolled her head at her brother's stubbornness. "Ma used to say she was grateful he wasn't born twins."

"Aw, she did not." Sammy stuck out his bottom lip.

Beth chuckled. "'Fraid she did, but only when you were getting into more trouble than usual."

"I never get into trouble."

Beth grinned widely. "I doubt if you'd find anyone here agreeing with that."

Sammy turned to Logan, his eyes wide with appeal. "Do I get into trouble?"

Sadie winked at Beth. *Let's see how Logan handles this one.*

"You might get into mischief once in a while." He held up his hand to stop Sammy's protests. "Grandfather always says that a mischievous boy is simply looking for something useful to do. Guess that's what you need. What do you say? Should we go make some teeter-totters?"

Sammy was instantly on his feet. "That will keep me out of trouble."

Chuckling, Logan followed the boy outside.

Sadie stared after them. Logan understood little boys in a way she never could. Sammy needed his influence. She had to be grateful that Logan had left off talking to her about marriage to rescue the boy.

Only she couldn't deny a hint of regret.

Chapter Twelve

Logan prepared for church with particular care. Sadie had agreed to bring the children out to the ranch after church. He wouldn't admit that she had hesitated. Wouldn't let himself believe it was because he had asked too many questions yesterday—and gotten few answers. Today he hoped to get some of those questions answered and a whole lot more that he hadn't asked and fully intended to.

He paused as he brushed his hair and stared into his own eyes. Yesterday he'd asked if she would ever consider marriage, and in the back of his mind he had wondered if she would ever consider marrying him. It would provide a permanent home for the children.

But what if the father returned and claimed them? Did he want to be in a marriage that no longer had the children as a reason? Or was there another reason that he wasn't willing to admit?

He sighed and finished with his hair. Thankfully Sammy's fall into the creek had stalled Logan's wayward thoughts.

There were too many unknowns concerning Sadie for him to even think of such things.

He smiled. But so many pleasing knowns. She loved children. She enjoyed fun times. She had a strong faith. Plus a sweet smile that turned his insides upside down.

"Logan, I'm ready to go," Grandfather called. "What's taking you so long?"

Logan chuckled. Grandfather was as anxious to see Sadie and the children as he. He clattered down the stairs and out the door, helped Grandfather into the wagon, and they were on their way.

The children waited outside the church as he drove up. He helped Grandfather down and the two of them joined the children. Jeannie reached up and put her hand over Grandfather's, bringing a chortle of joy from the old man. Sammy would have dragged Logan forward, but moderated his enthusiasm out of concern for Grandfather's slowness.

Beth hung back and, behind her, Sadie watched and waited.

Logan's gaze met hers and for all his awareness of the others, he and Sadie might have been alone on a desert island.

She stood in the shadow of the doorway, making it difficult for him to read her gaze, but her lips curved ever so slightly, as if she found the situation to her liking. As if she found his presence to her liking. Was she thinking of yesterday and the kiss they had shared? Was she anticipating time and opportunity for more of the same this afternoon? Somehow, he would make sure there was such.

Grandfather jabbed his elbow against Logan's. "Boy, are we going to stand out in the sun all morning?"

Logan jerked his gaze away and took a step forward, then his eyes returned to Sadie. She still watched him, her expression thoughtful. If only she'd tell him what those thoughts were.

They found a pew to accommodate all of them, and he ended up with Grandfather on one side and Jeannie on his other. Next to Jeannie sat Sadie. He couldn't keep from smiling his pleasure.

Grandfather leaned close. "You're looking a mite lovesick."

A frown quickly replaced Logan's smile. He leaned over to whisper to the old man. "It's getting so a man can't even enjoy a Sunday-morning service without being misjudged."

Grandfather chuckled. "If that's what you want to call it."

Logan faced straightforward as Preacher Arness stood to open the service. He shared the hymnal with Grandfather. He forced his complete attention to the delivery of the sermon. He tried to pretend Sadie wasn't so close he could hear her singing and enjoy it. Could breathe in the scent of her—something akin to a mixture of wild roses and fresh laundry with a hint of chocolate cake. He might have succeeded if not for Jeannie, who, halfway through the service, patted his leg and drew his attention to her.

She knew better than to whisper in church, but as soon as she had his attention, she pulled herself to his lap and leaned her head on his shoulder.

He shifted so his elbow didn't drive into Grandfather's side.

The movement brought his other elbow in contact with Sadie's. She didn't move away. In fact, he allowed himself to think she might have leaned just the slightest bit toward him.

After that he missed most of what the preacher said as his mind whirled with her nearness.

Annie had said she'd make dinner, so after church he led his little group out to the wagon. He'd put up another bench, so Sadie and Beth sat behind him, Jeannie between them. Grandfather sat at Logan's side and Sammy sat in the back.

"'Twas a good sermon, I thought," Grandfather said as they turned down the Mineral Avenue on their way out of town. "What did you think, Sadie?"

"Pastor Arness is a forceful speaker."

Grandfather grunted and Logan grinned. She had answered the question without saying anything to indicate she heard the sermon. Perhaps she had been as distracted as he had been.

"What about you, Logan?" The old man watched Logan, a knowing smile on his face. "What did you think of the sermon?"

"It was good. I wonder if the preacher has had any success in locating his family." Hugh Arness had taken the preaching position in town in order to allow him to search for his missing wife and little boy.

"Dreadful thing." Grandfather shook his head. "Brings to mind the time you were away."

"I wasn't lost and I wasn't a child."

"Where was you?" Sammy asked.

"I was in Wolf Hollow." He could feel the children considering his words.

"I don't remember ever seeing you," Sammy added.

"I expect it would be before you were there." He could be grateful they hadn't seen him at his worst. He shifted so he could glimpse Sadie, wanting to know if she recalled what he'd told her about that time in his life.

She smiled and nodded.

He turned forward again, satisfied with her acknowledgment.

Grandfather chortled. "You're looking a mite—"

He had no intention of letting the old man finish, knowing he would use the same word as he had in church. *Lovesick.* "Oh, look." He pointed upward. "A hawk."

Grandfather didn't even bother looking. "Ain't fooling me, boy."

Logan kept his thoughts to himself. He wasn't trying to fool anyone. Except maybe himself.

The children had never been to the ranch, so Logan pulled to a halt as they topped the last rise before the ranch. The buildings lay spread out before them.

"You live here?" Sammy's voice brimmed with awe. "Which house is yours?"

"I live in the big house. The smaller one to the right is where my brother Dawson and his wife, Isabelle, live with little Mattie. You know her? She's in school."

"Yeah. She's a girl."

He shifted so he could watch Sadie and the children as he pointed out the various buildings. "And past the barn is the same creek that flows by the town."

Sadie turned from studying the view to meet his eyes. "It looks like home." Her voice was round with what could be any number of things, but her eyes told him that she longed for a place that felt like home to her. For a heartbeat and then a second, he thought of offering her a permanent place here.

And then she tore her gaze away, leaving him suspended between dreams shared with a woman just like her and reality of his guardedness toward her.

"My stomach is so hollow it's kissing my backbone," Grandfather said, by way of reminder they were going home to eat.

Sammy laughed at Grandfather's comment. "Mine, too," he managed through his amusement.

Logan gave another glance at Sadie, hoping for a return look from her, one that would tell him what he wanted to hear. He jerked his attention forward. What did he want except to know why she refused to talk about her parents? Even if they had been unkind, or worse, didn't she know she could trust him to be sympathetic?

This afternoon, he had a plan to learn everything about her. He wanted to know of every hurt, every delight she'd ever felt. He wanted to know the happy and sad moments of her childhood and the challenges she'd conquered as she grew up.

They reached the house and he helped everyone down. Except Sammy, who jumped out and bounced on his feet as he looked about at everything. Old Jimbo, a hired hand whom Grandfather said came with the place, jogged over with his peculiar bowlegged gait.

"I'll take care of the outfit," he said.

Sammy watched Jimbo with wide-eyed curiosity. "How old are you?" he blurted out.

"Sammy!" Beth gave his arm a jerk.

"Don't mind his asking," Jimbo said in his reedy voice. He bent over and picked up a clod of dirt. "You see this?"

Sammy nodded.

"How old is it?"

"There ain't no way of tellin'," Sammy said, doing his best to imitate Jimbo's stance and his laconic way of speaking.

"Same with me." Jimbo tossed the dirt to the ground and led away the horses and the wagon.

Sammy rocked back and forth on his heels, his admiration for the old cowboy clear.

Logan glanced at Sadie. She watched him, her eyes dancing with humor. Logan's thoughts scrambled.

Dawson, Isabelle and Mattie crossed the yard toward them.

"Annie invited us to come for dinner," Dawson said.

Sammy's eyes slowly went from Dawson's polished black cowboy boots, up his black-clad legs to the shiny silver buckle holding his belt in place. He admired the pearl buttons on Dawson's shirt and he gave the man a careful study. Then he shifted to imitate Dawson's stance, his arms crossed, one leg bent as he leaned back on the heel of his other foot.

Logan almost choked with amusement. Sammy had a fascination with cowboys. Logan would be sure to give him a good dose of ranch life while he was there.

Sadie and Isabelle caught hands and smiled at each other, then the children were introduced. More introductions were made as Conner joined them.

A little later, they all sat around the big dining room table. Annie had prepared a bountiful spread. Her friend, Carly Morrison, helped her serve the food. Carly wore a pretty blue-flowered dress out of respect for the Sabbath and her father, who also joined them. Most times when she came to visit Annie, she wore trousers.

Lively conversation accompanied the meal. Sadie sat at Logan's left, making it impossible to watch her and gauge her reaction to all the teasing and news sharing.

But he had his plans for the afternoon.

After generous slices of rhubarb pie, the men retired to the sitting room. At least Pa and Grandfather, Dawson and Conner did. Logan had other things in mind.

First he wanted to show Sadie and the children around the ranch. Then he wanted Sammy to have a taste of ranch life.

And then—well, his plan would have to wait until later.

Sadie had been to the ranch on several occasions. With Kate and Isabelle and Dr. Baker on the first day of their arrival, later as a guest of Annie's and, not so long ago, as an attendant at Dawson and Isabelle's wedding.

But never before had she had Logan as her personal guide.

"These are the horses we train and sell." He leaned against the top rail of a fence. The children climbed up to look over. Sadie would have peered through the space between the two top rails, but Logan would have none of that and lifted her up. "Put your feet on that rail."

He stood close to her, his arm around her waist to hold her steady.

She was in no danger of falling, but she might faint from the way her heart raced and her lungs tightened. She listened and nodded as he pointed out the different traits of each animal.

Sammy climbed up and sat on the top rail.

She grinned when she saw he had a straw in his mouth that he chewed vigorously.

"Think I could ride one of these horses?" He drawled his words, causing Sadie to grin even wider. She glanced at Logan, saw answering amusement in his eyes, and yet he spoke to Sammy with such earnest respect.

"These aren't ready for riding, but—" he pointed to another pen "—these others are. Maybe I'll ask Jimbo to let you ride one of them." He grabbed Sammy to keep him from falling off the fence as he bounced in excitement.

They moved on. Sadie's respect for Logan grew at his knowledge and his ability to explain things so the children could understand. And so she, completely unfamiliar with the workings of a ranch, could see how efficiently the Marshall Five Ranch operated.

They circled back to the barn and Logan called to Jimbo. "Can you give this young fella a ride on one of the gentle horses?"

Jimbo waved at Sammy to follow him.

"We'll leave him in your capable hands," Logan said.

When Sadie started to protest, Logan took her arm. "Let the boy enjoy being treated like a man. Besides, I have something more planned." They returned to the house.

"Beth, can you and Jeannie play with Mattie while I take Sadie for a walk?"

Beth looked as startled as Sadie felt at the request, then nodded and led Jeannie over to where Mattie played under the shade of a budding tree.

They retraced their steps past the barn. Sammy sat on the back of a white speckled horse and waved to them. Seeing their intention to go on, Jimbo touched the brim of his hat. "Have a good outing."

Logan pulled her hand around his arm. "I hope you didn't find the family conversation too much. Especially when so much of it is teasing."

She chuckled. "Not at all. In fact, it's rather refreshing."

"Refreshing? That's one way to describe it, I suppose." He gave a crooked grin.

"Truly, it's rather nice to—" She stopped before she blurted out the rest.

"Nice to—?" he prompted.

"Never mind. It was only a silly thought."

"Okay." Thankfully, he did not press her to finish. It was nice to see people so comfortable, so supportive, so kind to each other. Even their teasing was never cruel, never meant to hurt.

"Here we are."

She looked about and gasped. Purple crocuses, yellow buffalo beans and tiny bluebells. "Surely, it's early for so many wildflowers."

"This hill is protected from the north winds and gets lots of sunshine. There are often flowers here long before anywhere else."

She picked up her skirts and ran across the grass to the place where the flowers were most bountiful and sat down. Breathing deeply of the fresh air, she looked about. "It's so peaceful." She pulled her bag to her lap, drew out smallish a hardcover book. She reached for a sprig of bluebells and laid them carefully on a page of the blank book. Satisfied, she closed the book, then plucked a spray of buffalo beans and again spread them on a page and closed the book, squeezing the pages together.

"What are you doing?" he asked.

She knew he must find her little hobby silly, but it gave her lots of pleasure so she continued. "Pressing flowers." She chose several crocuses in full bloom and a couple that now had feathery plumes, and pressed each between the pages. "As soon as I get home, I will put these in a heavier book."

"You're collecting an awful lot. What are you going to do with them?"

"Save them."

"Huh." He sat back and stared at her. "Why?"

She chuckled, knowing she'd surprised him. "I use them to make pictures."

Now he really stared as he wondered if she was teasing him.

She grinned at him, enjoying his uncertainty. "I assure you, my pictures are beautiful."

"Guess I'd have to see it to believe it."

"Then I suppose I'll have to show you." Her fingers stilled. Had she just invited him to come for some reason other than the children? But at some point their relationship had shifted to more than taking care of the Weiss children and finding their father. She tried to tell herself it could not be, but, at the moment, surrounded by a riot of wildflowers, the breeze lifting the wayward hairs off her neck, she looked into blue eyes that matched the bright Montana sky and could think of no reason she shouldn't enjoy his company.

His smile softened and something dark and compelling held her gaze. She couldn't have looked away if she'd wanted to. Not that she wanted to. She felt as if he had opened his heart to her and asked her to belong.

"I was hoping we would get a chance to talk alone.

Seems we never do what with the children and—" He shrugged. "Well, we just never do."

Sadie didn't move except to breathe. Did he have something specific he wished to discuss? A distant bell rang. A warning sound that she ignored. Pretended she didn't hear. What, after all, could he talk about that would cause a problem? She'd never given him so much as a hint that she wasn't the sort of woman who make a good schoolteacher and a good surrogate mother.

He continued slowly, gently, his gaze holding hers. "I couldn't help but notice you didn't want to talk about your mother yesterday. In fact, you never want to talk about your family." He covered her hand with his.

Did he feel the trembling that came from deep inside? Or was it felt by her alone?

"I finally realized that you must have had an unhappy family situation, and I'm sorry."

She tried and failed to swallow the lump choking her.

He rubbed his thumb along the back of her hand. "I can understand why that might make you cautious about family, but you've seen my family. Seen how we forgive each other for mistakes, how we help each other even as we tease, how we hold up each other through the tough times."

Oh, if only it was that simple. But it wasn't. He must surely feel her vibrating.

He slid closer and pulled her to his side. "Sadie, what I'm trying to say is that you are safe with me and my family, just as the children are. I want you to know nothing will ever make me or my family turn away from you."

She wanted so much to believe it that she dismissed every contrary thought and lifted her teary gaze to his.

"Oh, Sadie." He tipped his head and caught her lips with his. A sweet promise of acceptance. All she had to do was forget the past and never mention it.

She wrapped her arms about him, pressed her hands to his back and drank in the offering of his kiss. When he pulled away, she made a small sound of protest and, with a deep-throated chuckle, he lowered his head and kissed her again.

A little later, hand in hand, they returned. They loaded the happy children into the wagon and made the trip back to town.

"I'd stay," Logan said at the door. "But I think it's best if I say good-night now." He kicked the door closed, the children inside, she and Logan outside. He tipped her chin up and gave her a gentle kiss. "I'll see you tomorrow." He backed up until he ran into the side of the wagon, then jerked around, climbed to the seat and drove away, turning around several times to wave until the wagon turned the corner and was out of sight.

Sadie went inside and did the things she always did. Fed the children, tidied the rooms and prepared lessons. But she moved automatically, her mind racing with the joy of acceptance.

Not until she lay in bed in darkness did those distant voices push forward and demand she listen.

He did not know the truth about her. Could she hope to forever hide it?

Chapter Thirteen

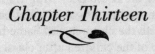

Sadie watched the children at play behind the store, but her mind was elsewhere. Over and over, she had replayed the recent events. Sunday and Monday a week ago, when Logan and his grandfather had been stranded at the schoolhouse, Logan had kissed her, not once but twice.

And despite every reason in the world she should feel otherwise, she had enjoyed both times. In fact, she might have invited them. Not in words, but likely her feelings had filled her eyes and she was learning that Logan was good at reading her feelings.

Then, this past Saturday and Sunday, she'd let herself inch closer to believing she could be accepted without anyone knowing her past. The Marshall family all seemed to like her. She could keep it that way by never telling about her father's partner.

But wouldn't the Marshalls want to know more about her family? Would they accept that she had her reasons for not wanting the two families to meet? Not that her parents would ever tell anyone what had happened to Sadie. But what if Logan pressured her to know more about her past?

Well, she could tell him about the early days when she was young and innocent. And she could tell him of living with Aunt Sarah. He would never even notice the missing months.

Convinced she could deal with life that way, she settled into a routine. Logan worked on the school, spent time with the children and Sadie taught school and took care of the children after classes.

Beth relaxed more and spent a lot of time on the swing or pushing Jeannie on it.

Sammy had always had an attitude of defiance toward their circumstances, but Sadie now saw that slip away to reveal a cheerful, cooperative child.

As for Jeannie... Sadie went out of her way to shower affection on the child and tell her how much she loved her. Logan did the same. Often Sadie would watch them together and her eyes would sting at their easy affection. Logan would make a wonderful father.

That thought had sent pain spiraling through her. She'd clutched her arms about her middle and turned from the tender scene of the big man playing with the small child.

Wouldn't it be ideal if she and Logan married and provided a home for the children? She swallowed back tears. That's when all her dreams, all her rational arguments came crashing down. She longed to tell Logan everything. Ached to have him hold her and comfort her. But her mother's words echoed inside her head. *It will ruin your reputation. It will ruin your father. It will ruin us. It will ruin you. Ruin. Ruin.* The words occupied her every thought.

She must protect Logan, the children and the Marshall family from the ugliness of her secret.

She glanced at the clock at the back of the temporary schoolroom. It was time to resume classes and she rang the bell, calling the children in from their play.

As she taught and supervised throughout the afternoon, she tried to come up with a plan for her life.

Perhaps she should move, find another position thousands of miles from Montana. But until she knew the children were safe in a loving home, she would not leave.

Could she take them with her? That way they would be safe from their father.

Her shoulders sagged. As Logan had said, the father's rights superseded all else.

Pain twisted a cruel fork through her insides. She loved the children and could not bear the thought of losing them. She bent over her desk, hoping anyone who looked at her would assume she pored over a book.

Eventually the pain lost its grip on her and she straightened. She'd not be making any changes until the children were taken care of. *Please God, I know it's selfish but I would sure like to keep them.* Would it be wrong to pray they would never find Mr. Weiss? Yes, it would. Until he was found, the future would be filled with uncertainty, which was not good for the children.

She had just ended classes and dismissed the students when Logan appeared in the doorway. Had he missed her so much he couldn't wait for her to cross the street?

A smile raced to her mouth. It fled as she met his eyes, saw the darkness in them.

"What's wrong?" She glanced past him. "Are the girls—?"

"I've come to take Sammy home." He reached for the boy, but his gaze held Sadie's.

She could not miss the heavy tone of his voice and hurried to his side to repeat her question, her voice rising. "What's wrong?"

"Sammy, please go wait with my uncle. Don't go outside. I'll be with you in a minute."

Sammy squinted at Logan. "No fair. You're gonna talk about me behind my back."

Logan gave a tight smile. "You've been good, so anything I have to say will be praise for your behavior. Now run along."

"Can I have a candy stick?"

"Yes. Tell my uncle I said you could."

Grinning happily, Sammy left the room. Logan closed the door firmly behind him and looked around as if expecting someone or something to be lurking in the corners.

Sadie's nerves twitched and she looked around, too, afraid yet not knowing why. Had one of the girls been hurt? No. He wouldn't delay if that was the case. But what—

Logan took her hand and led her toward one of the windows, where he peered out.

"You're making me nervous."

He glanced over at her, then resumed his study of the world outside the pane of glass. "I'm not sure what's wrong, but something is. Beth was playing with Jeannie on the swing. I heard her gasp. She grabbed Jeannie and ran to the house as if a bear were after her. I turned to see what had alarmed her. A man stood on the steps in front of the hotel. Nothing else."

"Was it Mr. Weiss? Has he finally come to see what had happened to his children? If so, he'd better have a very good explanation regarding his long absence, the condition he'd left the children in and, most of all, the marks on Sammy's back." She didn't bother adding a remark about the way Beth acted. If the girl had experienced anything like Sadie had, it was best if no one knew about it.

"I watched him until he went inside, but he didn't have a limp."

"So it wasn't their father?" Her shoulders sagged with relief.

"I went after Beth. She was in the bedroom, sitting on the floor in a corner, holding Jeannie tightly. I don't know if she said anything to her sister, but Jeannie hung around Beth's neck as if she, too, thought someone was after them. I squatted before them, afraid to get too close. Their fear was like a living, breathing thing in the room. I asked what was wrong. Poor Beth. She could hardly speak. All she said was, 'Get Sammy. Bring him home. Don't let anyone see him.' I asked why and she just rolled her head back and forth. I touched her shoulder and said I would. She practically jumped out of her skin when I touched her." Logan turned from the window, his eyes clouded with pain. "I thought she was over being so guarded around me."

Sadie ached for him. He had done nothing to earn Beth's fear, but she couldn't tell him her suspicions. "Maybe she sees all men as being like her father."

He looked past her. "We need to get to the bottom of this." He drew her after him across the floor to the

store area, where they collected Sammy and his pep-
permint stick. Logan asked his uncle to add two more
to his bill and selected two for the girls.

They each took one of Sammy's hands, crowding
close to his side to shield him from curious, prying
eyes, and hustled across the street and into the living
quarters.

"What's going on?" Sammy demanded all the way
and again as they stepped into the kitchen and released
him. He faced them, his expression hard. "Where's
Beth and Jeannie?" Suspicion colored his words and
his hands rolled into fists.

"In there." Logan pointed to the bedroom.

Sammy hurried across the floor. Logan followed
and signaled Sadie to come along.

"We need to find out what's going on."

They stood side by side in the doorway as Sammy
went to his sisters. He took one look at them and his
whole body tensed.

"It's him, isn't it?" He didn't wait for an answer and,
instead, sat beside Beth, crowding to her side.

Sadie drew her lips in and blinked as tears stung
her eyes. These children were genuinely afraid of their
father, though Logan seemed to think the man he had
seen didn't fit the description of the father.

Logan studied the children. "I'm going to get to
the bottom of this." He spun about and headed across
the kitchen.

Beth's eyes widened, though Sadie would have
thought it impossible for them to get any bigger. She
shifted Jeannie to Sammy, who held the little girl tight.
Beth bolted to her feet, pushed past Sadie and raced after
Logan, grabbing his sleeve before he reached the door.

"What are you going to do?"

Logan's shoulders rose and fell. "Whatever is wrong has something to do with the stranger I saw in front of the hotel and I aim to find out what it is. Enough of this fear and hiding."

Beth blinked back tears. "Please don't say anything about us. Please. Promise me." She wrung her hands as she pleaded with him.

Sadie wanted to hug the girl, hug all of them and assure them they were safe, but she feared to move. The moment was fragile with fear and tension, and one wrong move would send them all into panic. She wasn't sure what they would do in such a state.

Logan rested his hand on Beth's shoulder and she let him. In fact, Sadie thought the girl practically leaned into the touch.

Sadie wondered if either of them was aware of it.

"Beth, I won't tell the man you are here. I promise."

She sagged with relief.

"But I will get to the bottom of this. You can tell me yourself—" He waited, giving her lots of time to answer, but she only rocked her head back and forth. "Or I can find out some other way."

Beth stepped away from his hand and covered her mouth against a strangled cry. She studied Logan for a moment. "Remember, you promised not to say anything about us." She fled back to the bedroom and huddled down beside her brother and sister.

Logan's eyes dipped at the corners. His lips pulled in.

Sadie went to his side and touched his arm. She wished she could say something, but not a single word came to her mind. This whole situation brimmed with raging fear and drowning uncertainty.

He groaned and pulled her into his arms, leaning his face against her hair. "What is she so afraid of?"

Sadie pressed her cheek to the rough fabric of his shirt. Her suspicions—no, her certainty—about Beth's fears tore one ragged strip after another from her heart. Every searing pain carried her own pain and fear. What would happen if Logan knew what Sadie knew?

"She—" She choked, knowing she could not reveal Beth's secret any more than she could reveal her own. It would ruin them both. "I expect she has her reasons."

Logan didn't move, yet she felt him pull back into himself. "It would surely help if she'd tell me what they were." He eased away from her though his hands remained on her arms. "Just as it would help if you told me what happened to make you so wary." He studied her for a moment, as if reading her thoughts. "Did your parents hurt you?" His eyes narrowed. "Did your father beat you?"

She tried to look away, tried to cloak her thoughts, and wondered if she had succeeded.

He tipped his head in a quick nod. "It is something to do with your parents, isn't it? Are you ever going to tell me about it?"

She opened her mouth, but nothing came out. Nor did a thought form in her head, except for the dread and horror she had carried with her for four years.

Logan's expression went from sorrowful to determined, and he left the house.

Sadie went to the window to watch him stride from the yard. Her chest hurt and she rubbed at it, knowing the pain would ease but would never entirely go away.

Logan disappeared around the corner.

Her insides cried after him. *Come back. Let me explain.* She longed to have him hold her and erase the ached that festered in her heart. She pressed at her breastbone. Telling him the truth would destroy everything. She must remember that.

Jeannie whimpered in the bedroom and Beth made soothing noises.

Sadie sucked in air until her lungs could hold no more, then slowly released it.

All that mattered was keeping these children safe. She tiptoed into the schoolroom and peeked out the door to watch Logan go into the hotel.

Oh, to be a little bird and fly after him and hear what he had to say.

Logan's back teeth hurt from the pressure he put on them. To see the children so afraid was torture. To know Beth was so desperate she would appeal to him for a promise and even let him touch her without recoiling made his insides ache. He wanted her to learn to trust him but not this way.

But all that paled in comparison to the sheer panic he had seen in Sadie's face when he'd asked her to tell him what her parents had done. Suspicions grew in his mind. Things he didn't want to believe. But he wasn't naive enough not to know ugly, horrible things happened.

Still, to know in a newspaper sort of way was entirely different than thinking people he cared deeply for might have experienced them.

His heels thudded hard on the solid ground as he

crossed the street. As if he hoped he could stomp out the fear he saw in the children and Sadie.

He paused in front of the hotel to bring his raging emotions under control. He needed his wits about him if he was to discover the truth and protect Sadie and the children at the same time.

He slipped into the hotel unobserved.

The stranger banged on the counter. "Hey, where is everyone? I need service."

Logan ducked behind a big plant to listen and observe.

The proprietor stepped into sight. "Hold your horses. I'm coming." Bespectacled, thin as a whip, Mr. Hawkins often left the hotel to go next door and visit Dorie and Daisy at the café. He could keep an eye on the front of his establishment from where he customarily sat, but if his cup was still half-full of hot coffee, or his meal half-eaten, he finished before returning.

"Took you long enough." The man was overly aggrieved, in Logan's opinion.

Mr. Hawkins took his place behind the counter. "Are you looking for a room?"

"A room and some information."

"The first I can offer. Can't necessarily say the same for the second."

The stranger signed his name, laid down some coins and pocketed the key to his room. "I'm looking for my kids."

Mr. Hawkins drew back. "I do not have them." He glanced at the register. "Mr. Harlan Perrin."

Not Mr. Weiss. That would explain the confusion Logan felt at the conflicting descriptions and information he'd found. Even as Logan branded the name on his brain, he almost laughed at the shock in the Mr. Hawkins's face.

"Never said you did. There are three of them—a girl of twelve, a boy of seven and a little girl of three."

Logan's insides froze over. He was after the Weiss children even if he did have Beth's age wrong. She was thirteen. But who was he? Not their father. Was he the man Uncle George had seen but a different man than the blacksmith spoke of?

"They your kids?" Mr. Hawkins asked.

"I'm their stepfather."

"How did you come to lose them?"

Logan heard the suspicion in the hotel owner's voice and knew the stranger would have a hard time getting any direct information from him.

"I left them safe and settled out of town a ways, and when I come back they're gone. Don't know if someone took them or what."

"Sounds like something you should talk to the sheriff about. He's across the street and down past the town square. Can't miss him." Mr. Hawkins closed the register and shoved it under the counter to inform the man the conversation was over.

Logan slipped away while Mr. Perrin stared a challenge at the impervious Mr. Hawkins.

He scooted down the road to the Jesse's office and quickly let him know what was going on, including the children's reactions. "I don't like it. See if you can stall him." He hurried out the back way and returned to the schoolhouse.

Sadie jerked about as he entered the room, her hand going to her throat. "You startled me." She glanced toward the bedroom door and edged toward him. "They refuse to come out. What did you learn?"

He pulled her closer, both to ensure the children didn't hear and to find comfort in the contact. They moved to the far window and looked out. He wrapped an arm about her shoulders and spoke softly. "He says he's their stepfather."

She jerked about to face him. "No!" Tears filled her eyes. "That means both parents are dead. How awful." She pressed her face to his chest and shuddered.

He hugged her to his heart, wanting to end the fear she and the children shared. "It certainly is. And it makes me feel better to know their own father wasn't the one to hurt Sammy."

"Did you tell him where they were?" Her voice was muffled against his shirtfront.

"I didn't speak to him and Mr. Hawkins suggested he take his questions to the sheriff. I hurried away and spoke to Jesse. He'll do his best to delay the man, but he said he can't put him off more than a few minutes."

She tipped her head back. "Are you suggesting we should hide them? Where?"

"We could take them to the ranch. They'd be safe there."

"Yes. Let's do it. Hurry. I'll get them ready."

"I'll need to get a wagon." He was on his way before he finished the sentence. It seemed to take an eternity to reach the livery barn and hitch a couple of horses to the wagon he rented. Every moment dragged. He went down the alley to the school, hoping Jesse had delayed the stepfather.

Sadie was watching for him and hustled the children out as soon as he appeared.

Beth glanced over her shoulder and looked right and left as she raced across the yard, holding Jeannie by the hand. Sammy didn't waste a minute, either. "The three of you hunker down in the back." He turned to Sadie. "Jesse will be here soon, no doubt."

She nodded, her eyes troubled. "I'll be okay."

"I'll be back to make certain you are."

"Thank you. Children, enjoy your visit."

Beth reached for Sadie's hand. "Thank you."

Logan turned the horses about and, rather than set them into a trot, he pulled them to a halt. Jesse stood in the middle of the alley, blocking the way. And Mr. Perrin stood beside him.

Jesse at least looked regretful.

Mr. Perrin looked anything but. "I hear you took my children from my house while I was away." The voice grated against Logan's nerves.

In the back, Beth smothered a cry.

The knuckles of Logan's hands popped as he squeezed his fists tight. The faint sound hammered in his head, a bitter accompaniment to the muffled sounds of distress coming from the back of the wagon. If not for his friend, Jesse, at Mr. Perrin's side, Logan would be tempted to bolt the horses past the stepfather without regard for any injuries that might occur. He'd consider them justice injuries in repayment for the marks on Sammy's back.

"Don't suppose they happen to be in the back of that wagon." Mr. Perrin's voice had a peculiarly annoying quality to it, half overbearing, half whining.

Jesse lifted his hands in a gesture of apology. "He's their stepfather."

A clatter behind Logan drew the attention of all

three men in that direction. The children scrambled out the back and raced toward Sadie. She stepped aside to let them in, said something, then pulled the door closed behind them and, head up, chin jutted out, crossed the yard to stand by the wagon.

Logan kept his eyes on Mr. Perrin, but he felt Sadie's presence in the depths of his rolling emotions and welcomed it. He would have touched her shoulder, but his hands were firmly clamped to the reins and wouldn't uncoil.

"What seems to be the problem, Sheriff?" Sadie asked in a good schoolmarm's voice.

Logan was not fooled by her calm tone. He'd seen her like this before when she had gone to investigate Sammy's situation. He could have warned Jesse and the man beside him that there was no stopping her when she'd made up her mind. His hands relaxed and he almost grinned as he waited to see how she would deal with this.

Jesse's expression grew hard.

Logan could almost feel sorry for him. He had a job to do that was about to put him in conflict with both the schoolteacher and the Marshall family. It couldn't be easy. But Logan would not allow his friendship with Jesse to cloud his judgment regarding the children and their stepfather.

"This is Mr. Perrin," Jesse said. "He's come to get his children."

"That a fact. And I presume you asked him what arrangements he's made for them?"

Jesse opened his mouth but, before he could answer, Sadie strode to Mr. Perrin, her hands on her hips.

"Because we found them in dreadful circumstances. A house that was barely standing. No food."

Mr. Perrin waved away her protests. "I'll take care of them. Not that it's any of your business."

Uh-oh. Logan knew how Sadie would respond to such words.

"Sir, that is where you are wrong. I believe every adult has the responsibility to see that children are safe and cared for. I would never stand aside and ignore a child's need."

Mr. Perrin took a step back at her vehemence. Then he seemed to collect himself. "I'm their stepfather. Ain't no one gonna take those kids from me."

Sadie closed the distance between them. "Someone is going to make certain that the children are safe and properly cared for." She swung around to confront Jesse. "Isn't that right, Sheriff?"

Logan almost felt sorry for Jesse. Almost, but not quite.

Jesse blinked. "Of course I'll make sure of it."

Sadie eased back. "Fine. Then until you've checked things out and found them satisfactory, the children can stay with me." She marched away.

She passed Logan, sparing him a challenging, pleading look, and continued on, almost reaching her home before Mr. Perrin recovered from her onslaught.

"Now wait just one minute," he called. "What gives you the right to keep my kids? I'll be taking them with me." He started after Sadie.

Logan was on the ground before he took a second step. "You stay away from her. You hear me?"

Jesse stepped between the two men. "You're staying at the hotel. That's no place for the children. Leave them with Miss Young while you show me the home you have prepared for them." He guided Mr. Perrin around.

"I don't need to show you anything."

"I'll be the judge of that." At least they could trust Jesse to check things out.

"If you must know, I have a house in Wolf Hollow and arrangements with a woman to take care of them."

"Fine. Then you won't mind showing it to me."

Mr. Perrin scowled. "I sure ain't goin' back there today. I need a hot meal and a good night's sleep."

Logan held his position until Jesse had accompanied the man back to the street and out of sight, then he jogged to the house. He stepped inside and leaned against the door. The children peered out from the bedroom. Sadie stood by the table, her arms wrapped about her, her eyes wide.

Logan started to laugh, which earned him a scowl from Sadie.

"I don't see anything funny," she protested.

He stopped laughing though he couldn't stop grinning. "It was great to watch you stand up to that man." He reached for her hands and pulled her close to smile down at her. "You were magnificent."

Her cheeks grew pink.

As she looked up at him, the color in her cheeks deepened, perhaps because she saw the admiration and something sweeter, stronger and infinitely more enduring that filled his heart and likely his eyes. He shifted his attention to the children. "Did you see her?"

Beth nodded.

Sammy asked, "Where did he go?"

No need to ask who he meant. They all knew.

Logan told them what had been said.

Sammy and Beth looked at each other. Little Jeannie watched them both, trying to assess what the news meant.

"He'll be back," Beth said, a tremble in her voice.

"And he'll make us go with him," Sammy added.

Logan retained one of Sadie's hands as he crossed to where the children huddled. "I trust Jesse. He won't let the man take you if he doesn't have a safe place." His words fell into an empty pit of silence.

Sadie eased away and went to stare out the window as if seeing Jesse and Mr. Perrin still there. Logan glanced past her. The alley was empty except for the horses and wagon.

With a weary sigh, she turned and faced him. "Who will make sure he treats them right?"

"I will," Logan said. He looked from Sadie to the children and saw nothing but doubt.

Chapter Fourteen

Sadie moved to the cupboard, pulled out a bowl and stared into its emptiness, unable to think what she meant to do with it. How could he promise something when he didn't even know what he promised? And he didn't know because no one had told him the whole truth. And she couldn't tell him without hurting Beth even more than the poor girl had already been hurt.

She ran her finger along the rim of the bowl, wishing her world felt as smooth, but it was rough and fractured like broken pottery.

They had a reprieve of a day while Jesse went to Wolf Hollow to inspect Mr. Perrin's house. If it was anything like the last house he'd provided for the children, would Jesse refuse to let him take the children? Or would Mr. Perrin have rights that didn't allow anyone to interfere?

Lord, help me help these children be safe. Was there anything she could do? One thing came to mind.

She knew what she must do, and her hands flew as she prepared the dough for biscuits.

Seeing her intent, Beth joined her in preparing the evening meal.

"I have to take care of the wagon," Logan said.

Sadie nodded. The children didn't say anything. Jeannie didn't protest at him leaving. Sammy didn't beg to go with him. Sadie would have looked at Logan to see if he noticed and, if so, what did he think of it? But her mind was awhirl with her own plans.

Logan left. The tension in the room mounted, if that were possible. Sammy parked himself at the window. Nothing was said, but Sadie understood they watched for the stepfather, fearing he would return and not knowing what they could do to avoid him. They must surely have considered running away and hiding, and dismissed the idea as futile and provided an excuse for their stepfather's harsh punishment. She wiped her hands on the towel and went over and dropped the bar in place to lock the door. Logan had given them this added security after the first night when Sammy had been so afraid. She did the same to the door adjoining the classroom.

Beth waited until Sadie was back at her side. "Are you afraid?"

Sadie considered her words. If she said no, she would not be telling the truth, but would it increase the children's worry? Perhaps if she said yes, it might encourage Beth to speak of what happened. But she was reluctant to increase the fear in the girl's eyes.

"Let's just say I don't trust that man. I know he's whipped Sammy enough to hurt him and I think he's capable of a whole lot more evil." She watched Beth out of the corner of her eyes.

Beth shuddered. "I think so, too," she whispered.

Sadie stilled any reaction. This was the most Beth had said. Would she say more with some gentle prodding? "Has he ever hurt you or Jeannie?"

Beth looked ready to shatter into a thousand pieces. "No." The whisper barely reached Sadie's ears. Sadie wished she could be certain it was the truth. But how was she to know? More importantly, how was she to find out?

The door rattled and everyone froze.

Sammy's eyes widened. "I only looked away for a minute." But the object he held made Sadie think otherwise. It was a simple toy Logan had made for him with parts that could be taken apart and fitted together again. He had been distracted.

"Sadie, it's me. Open the door."

A collective release of pent-up air came at the familiar voice and she hurried to lift the bar and let Logan in.

"Was someone here?" He closed the door but didn't put the bar back in place.

"Just being cautious." She edged past him and placed the bar over the door.

He watched her, his eyes asking questions.

She met his gaze. Let him think what he wanted. She couldn't tell him anything more than he already knew.

"I think you can relax as long as I'm here," he said after long consideration.

"You won't always be here." Beth's sharp words startled them both. It sounded almost like she wanted him to stay.

Sadie's gaze returned to Logan's. She saw no rejoicing at this change in the girl, only regret that it should be born out of fear.

Logan stayed for supper even though no one thought

to invite him. The meal was a somber affair. Jeannie cried earlier than usual and wailed even after Beth took her to the bedroom.

The sound grated on Sadie's already frayed nerves. The peace and security she'd hoped to give these children lay in ruins around her feet.

Ruin. The word that echoed throughout her head and guarded her secret every bit as much as the heavy piece of wood locked the entrance.

Beth appeared at the bedroom doorway, looking weary. "She says she won't stop crying until you go to her."

Sadie started for the door.

"Both of you."

Logan fell in at her side. They went to the bed and sat on either side of the crying child.

She scrambled into Logan's lap and buried her face in his shirtfront, at the same time reaching out to find Sadie.

Sadie held her hand and rubbed her back.

Her gaze locked with Logan's and they shared the pain and worry of what Mr. Perrin's presence meant to the children. He brought up a hand and covered hers, and together they provided comfort to Jeannie, who quieted and was asleep within minutes.

Neither Logan nor Sadie made a move. If only, she thought, things could stay as peaceful as they were at this very moment.

Beth came to the doorway. "Is she sleeping?" she whispered.

"Yes." Logan eased the child to the bed and they all tiptoed from the room.

Sadie wanted to proceed with her plan. She'd

thought to leave the children alone with the doors barred, but wouldn't it be better to leave them with Logan? She would ask him to stay. She tried to think how to word her request in such a way he wouldn't wonder what she meant to do.

Finally, she said simply, "I have an errand to run. Logan, can you stay until I get back?"

"Certainly. I meant to stay until bedtime."

Just to be on the safe side, she finished for him.

Sadie put on a bonnet and wrapped a shawl about her shoulders. Three pairs of curious eyes watched her, asking where she meant to go.

"You aren't going to do anything foolish, are you?" Logan asked as she went to the door.

She smiled at him and then at Sammy and Beth. "Have you ever known me to do anything remotely foolish?" She didn't wait for their answer. "After all, I'm the schoolteacher and I always conduct myself wisely."

The children seemed to consider her answer adequate, but Logan's gaze remained wary. "Please be careful."

He needn't have added that. She intended to be very careful. She never put herself at risk. "Thank you." She meant for staying with the children but wasn't sure he took it that way. "I won't be long." She hurried outside and made her way down the street toward a certain house, where she knocked.

Mrs. Eugene answered the door and recognized her as the teacher. "Miss Young, how nice of you to visit. Come right in. The children speak highly of you."

"Mrs. Eugene, I'm here to speak to your husband. I know it's after normal business hours, but I thought seeing as he now works at home…" She trailed off. It was an imposition to expect the lawyer to answer her questions at this time of day, but he had worked from home since the fire that destroyed his office, as well as the other buildings in the block shared by the school and doctor's office. "I couldn't wait until tomorrow." Mr. Perrin might return before she could come after school.

"Oh that's quite all right. Follow me." Mrs. Eugene led Sadie to a small parlor that had been converted to an office. "Wait here while I get my husband."

Sadie perched in a chair and tried to calm her nerves.

Mr. Eugene appeared in a few minutes. "What can I do for you?" he asked after the introductory preliminaries were out of the way. "My wife said it sounded rather urgent."

"You know I have had the three Weiss children staying with me while the sheriff tries to locate their father?" Likely everyone in town knew.

"Yes, I know."

"Mr. Weiss is dead, but their stepfather has arrived wanting to take them." She told him of Sammy's back, the state of the house where they'd found the children and…she hesitated. How much should she tell him?

"There's more, isn't there?" he prodded gently.

"Only my suspicions. But Beth is very afraid."

Mr. Eugene nodded. "Has she said anything?"

"No."

"Do you think she would talk to me?"

"I can ask her." She could hardly imagine Beth would confide in a strange man, but perhaps she would recognize that Mr. Eugene had the power to help her.

"See if she will. We need more than suspicions."

"What about Sammy's back?"

"Again, no one has ever accused Mr. Perrin of being the one responsible. Yes, the evidence is clear enough, but to take children away from a parent, even a step-parent, will require the judge to order it, and he will want good hard proof. If the children, especially Beth, would speak out, it would help."

She had one last question. "If the judge says the children don't go back to the stepfather, would I be able to keep them?"

He drummed his fingertips on the desktop, deep in thought. The sound battered the inside of her head as she waited for his opinion.

He slapped the desk, practically jolting Sadie from her chair. "The judge is a reasonable man. Unless some-one else wants to take in three children, he'll likely say they might as well stay with you." Mr. Eugene's gaze bored into hers. "How will you care for them and teach at the same time?"

Before he could answer, he continued. "And if you don't teach, how will you be able to provide for them?" He nodded briskly. "Those are the sort of questions the judge will ask. In the meantime, see if you can get Beth to tell you more."

"I'll do my best."

He patted Sadie's hands. "See what you can do."

"Thank you." Mr. Eugene escorted her to the door and Sadie hurried back to the school, feeling rather exhausted by the visit.

She had thought to keep her errand secret, but Logan deserved to know the truth...at least about her visit to the lawyer. Even more than that, she yearned to share her thoughts and feelings with him.

And her secrets?

Her heart spasmed. Yes, she would love to think she could tell him and he wouldn't be dismayed, wouldn't turn from her as a soiled woman. That he wouldn't walk away never to return because of the shame her presence would bring to him. And his family. He'd made it abundantly clear that he would do nothing to hurt his family.

She drew in a shaky breath. Her own situation had no bearing on what she would say and do. All that mattered was the children and their safety.

She reached her living quarters, knocked and waited for Logan to open the door to her.

"Everything okay?" he asked.

She glanced around to assure herself that the children were safe and no stranger had entered the room. Seeing that all was normal, she spoke to Logan. "We need to talk."

He joined her. "We'll be right outside," he said to the children.

They closed the door behind them and moved to the swing, where they could talk without the children overhearing them and where they could also watch the door and the children could see them through the window.

Logan leaned against a swing pole and waited, understanding she needed a few minutes to collect her thoughts.

She faced him, wanting to be able to see his eyes, read his expression as she talked to him. "I suppose you're wondering where I went."

He showed no sign of judgment and she continued.

"I went to see the lawyer."

His eyebrows went up. "Mr. Eugene?"

"I wanted to find out if I could do anything to keep the children."

Logan touched her shoulders and she leaned into his hands. He seemed to know her visit had not yielded the easy answers she wished for.

"What did he say?"

"That we needed more than our suspicions to convince the judge not to order the children to go to their stepfather and that I would need a better plan if I hope to keep the children." She gave him a few more details.

His hands tightened on her shoulders. "It doesn't sound good, does it?"

"We need something to convince the judge."

"I'm not sure what we can do. Perhaps Jesse will learn something that will help the judge decide they can't go to the stepfather."

"I hope so." She knew she sounded as uncertain as she felt.

He lowered his hands to hers and squeezed. "Do you want to pray about it?"

"I'd like that." She bowed her head and waited for him to pray.

"Father, in heaven, we ask that You will bring justice to these children." His gentle voice smoothed the tension that had built since the news of Mr. Perrin's arrival.

She added her "amen" to his.

Logan held Sadie's hands and studied the top of her head as she stayed bowed. She gripped his hands like she never wanted to let him go.

Not that he wanted to leave. The children were afraid of their stepfather. Somehow he had to protect them. Just as he had to make sure Sadie was okay. She wanted to keep the children, and they were safe and happy with her. They had become a family. Sadie and the children. There must be something he could do to make sure they stayed with her.

And him? As he considered it, his answer came quickly.

He'd like to be part of a family that included Sadie and the children.

Sadie lifted her head. Her eyes brimmed with despair.

"Don't look at me like that. It makes me want to kiss away all your troubles right here in plain view of anyone who cares to look." He looked over his shoulder to the town square. It was empty. Everyone was home.

She sighed. "If only that were possible."

He leaned closer, planted a kiss on her forehead and drew back to smile at her surprise. "Does it help even a little?"

She nodded, her eyes smiling even before her mouth did. "A little, perhaps." Her gaze clung, and if they hadn't been in such a public place he would have pulled her to his heart and held her there.

He wanted to kiss her until she forgot all her worries but knew that was impossible, not only because others might see and judge her, but also because he knew any forgetting would be temporary.

Instead, he settled for brushing his knuckles along her cheeks, then he took her back to the house. "We must trust things will work out. Lock the door. I'll be back in the morning."

She nodded, but her eyes said she didn't entirely believe his words that everything would work out any more than he did.

She slipped inside. He waited until he heard the wooden bar fall into place, then hurried to his horse and rode away. There must be something he could do to prevent the stepfather from getting his hands on these children.

He might return to Wolf Hollow and see if he could uncover any more information, but that meant leaving town and he didn't care to do that.

By the next morning he had not come up with any solution, and as he rode into town, he watched Jesse and Mr. Perrin ride out.

It was going to be a long day waiting for them to return.

He was earlier than usual and went to the door. Sammy let him in.

"How are you all?" Logan asked.

Jeannie was bright eyed and Sammy sober, which was unusual for him. Beth's eyes were filled with darkness as were Sadie's.

"I wish I didn't have to teach today," she said.

"I'll be here. I will make sure the girls are safe. Sammy will be okay with you." He hoped his words reassured her, though he really wanted to suggest she cancel school for the day and the five of them stay together.

"I know." She looked about at the children as if mentally saying goodbye. Tears glistened in her eyes.

Logan groaned. If she started to cry, he would take her in his arms no matter who was looking.

She sniffed and wiped her eyes. "Sammy, it's time to go." She took the boy's hands.

Logan knew she wouldn't let Sammy out of her sight the rest of the day.

The echo of the door as she and Sammy left was the only sound before Jeannie came to Logan. "Beth says we have to go with *him*. Why don't you and Sadie keep us?"

"I wish we could."

"Just do it." She did her best to look imperious, which tickled Logan's funny bone and, laughing, he swung the little girl into the air.

"I tell you what. I am going to do everything I can to make sure you can stay." He set the child on her feet. He had a few things to do on the outside of the building, but it didn't feel right to leave the girls and go about his work. Instead, he unbarred the door to the classroom. Today he would find something to do in there.

The girls followed him, leaving the adjoining door open so they could go back and forth.

He had some shelves to affix, and he set about the task.

Beth brought a book into the classroom and sat on the floor to read while Jeannie ran about the room. After a bit, she went to the kitchen table to draw on some paper Sadie had left.

There seemed little Logan could do to change things…except try to persuade Beth to speak out against her stepfather.

"Sadie went to see the lawyer last night to find out what she could do to keep you."

Beth continued to look at her book, but Logan

knew she wasn't reading. She hadn't turned a page in a long time.

"The lawyer said we would need more than suspicions to convince a judge. More than the scars on Sammy's back. The lawyer said we had no proof Mr. Perrin is responsible."

Her head came up and she regarded him seriously.

Now that he had her attention, he moved closer and sat on the floor facing her. "The lawyer said if you would tell us what has happened and what the man has done, it would make a difference."

The hope fled her eyes and she ducked her head again.

"Beth, why are you so afraid of your stepfather?"

His questions fell to the floor, unanswered. He waited, hoping Beth would change her mind, but she closed the book, rose to her feet and returned to the kitchen without a backward look.

The morning dragged by. He knew Jesse and Mr. Perrin should be back by noon. About eleven he gave up trying to work and sat on the classroom floor thinking and praying.

The sound of horses brought him to his feet, and he looked out the window to see Jesse and Mr. Perrin ride up to the hotel. They shook hands and Mr. Perrin went inside. Jesse crossed the street, leading his horse toward the schoolhouse.

Logan glanced back at the living quarters. Beth watched him. "Wait here while I talk to the sheriff."

She slammed the door shut and the wooden bar banged into place.

He stepped out the front door and waited for Jesse, who looked resigned. That did not bode well for Logan and the children. And certainly not for Sadie, who loved them.

He glanced toward the store. Sadie would be supervising the lunch hour and keeping a close eye on Sammy.

"Well?" He didn't mean to sound so challenging, because he knew Jesse must do his job.

"He has a house."

"One like where we found the children?"

Jesse lifted one shoulder in resigned helplessness. "It's adequate. One of the better ones in Wolf Hollow." He let the information sink in, then added, "He introduced me to a young woman who said she was prepared to be his housekeeper once he has the children."

Logan wished he could believe he'd heard incorrectly. "You spent the morning with him and you're comfortable with letting him take the children?"

Jesse took off his hat and scrubbed at his hair. "My job is to uphold the law."

"I'm not asking you to break the law."

"Good. I told Mr. Perrin he needed to do a little work on the house before the children could go. I said he had three days to get things ready. You have three days to come up with an alternate plan."

Three days! In three days he could be long gone with Sadie and the children. He let that thought fade. Jesse would track him until he found him, and running was no life for children.

"I'll think of something."

Jesse planted his hat back on his head and adjusted it several times. "Hope you do. Those kids deserve better than Wolf Hollow."

Logan wondered what Jesse had seen besides the

dirt and squalor of the little mining town, but Jesse wouldn't say anything until he had solid proof.

They needed solid proof, and all they had—besides the marks on Sammy's back—were suspicions.

Beth needed to say something.

If he'd hoped spending time with her in the afternoon would accomplish anything, he was disappointed. Beth did her best to avoid him and when she couldn't, refused to answer his questions. And he asked many. Was it Mr. Perrin who'd whipped Sammy? He knew the answer but needed her to be willing to give her answer to the authorities. Had he hurt her or Jeannie? Again, he knew her fears must have some basis. What had he done?

Finally, after he'd dogged her the better part of the afternoon, she stood up, crossed her arms over her chest and faced him. "I don't know why you assume Mr. Perrin has done something to me. Did you ever think you might be assuming wrongly? Don't you think it's enough that we lost our parents and thought everyone had forgotten about us? Isn't that enough to make us sad and afraid?" She could hardly catch her breath.

She stared daggers at him, then took Jeannie's hand and marched them into the bedroom.

Speechless, he watched her go. Had he, fed by Sadie's suspicions, wrongly assumed things? Hadn't she started out not trusting families? Had her assumptions been colored by that?

He stared out the front door, anxiously waiting for her and Sammy to return. Perhaps Sammy would admit who had beat him.

They needed to sort out this business.

Chapter Fifteen

Sadie saw Logan waiting for them as she and Sammy hurried across the street. She sent Sammy to the kitchen, pulled the door shut after him and faced Logan in the empty schoolroom. "They came back, didn't they?" He didn't need to answer for her to know. One look at his face and she knew it was the bad news she'd expected.

Logan paced away to stare out the side windows. "Jesse said the house was adequate and there was a woman prepared to be the housekeeper."

Sadie went to join him at the windows and stared out, seeing nothing. Her regret and sorrow licked at her, like a fire consuming everything else in the way. The children shouldn't be returned to that man. They deserved so much more than *adequate* and a housekeeper. They needed and deserved safety and love. "Housekeeper sounds so cold. So the verdict is we have to let them go…unless we can get Beth to say more."

He shifted to study her with such intensity that she couldn't hold his gaze and looked past him to the far corner.

"Maybe Beth isn't saying more because there isn't anything else to say."

Her eyes jerked back to him. "Why do you say that?"

"I spent a lot of time with Beth today and she finally broke down and said they were sad and afraid because both their parents had died. Nothing more."

Each word felt like the blow of a pickax. Nothing more? She knew his decision about the children to be untrue. "I know it's more than that."

"How do you know? You always talk about the disappointment of family. Are you sure you aren't letting your feelings color your perceptions?"

"My *experience* is coloring my observations."

His look clearly said he didn't understand.

She had to convince him the children could not go back to their stepfather. Would he understand her concerns if she told him what had happened to her? A trembling, like a thousand trapped butterflies trying to escape, filled her stomach. She took a deep breath that did nothing to settle her nerves and began.

"When I was sixteen my father's partner came to my room. He forced me to my bed—" Not daring to meet Logan's eyes, she stared past him to a spot on the wall. "Afterward, my mother insisted I must act like nothing happened. I had to sit across the table from him at the next meal." The trembling climbed upward and she rubbed at her breastbone, trying to calm it. "She said I was dirty, soiled, ruined. I must never tell anyone or they'd know that about me." The trembling reached her tongue and her lips. She scrubbed her lips back and forth, trying in vain to stop the trembling. "When I look at Beth I see my feelings reflected in her eyes. If that man hasn't hurt her already, she knows—

as do I—that he is going to." A twitch drew her eyebrows downward.

She knew she must convince him, and she forced herself to look at him, knowing the horror she would see.

His eyes had darkened to midnight blue. His mouth was drawn back in a hard line.

She would not give him a chance to say anything. One word from him would fell her. "I will not stand by and let Beth go back to him. Nor Sammy, whom he beats. Nor Jeannie, who is a victim in waiting."

He didn't say anything, simply fled the room as fast as he could.

She didn't need any word to inform her of his opinion. Now that he knew the truth about her, he would see her as her parents did—soiled, ruined, shameful.

But she had done what she had to do to help the children. And, yes, to a degree, she had done it for her own sake. Her fondness for Logan had grown by leaps and bounds. She couldn't continue to hide the truth about herself. The sooner he knew, the easier it would be to deal with the outcome.

She fell to her knees. There was nothing easy about this. *Lord, God, You who have been my comfort and strength in days past. Please carry me through this.*

But if she thought the mental pain inflicted on her by her parents was hard to bear, it was nothing compared to the anguish she felt at this moment.

Logan had walked away.

No, he'd raced away.

The thunder of pounding horse hooves drew her attention to the window. Logan riding down the street.

Galloping away.

* * *

Logan knew what he must do. Seeing Sadie so hurt, hearing her story, watching her rub at her chest like she could erase the ugliness that she'd endured had driven huge holes through his heart. He wanted to pull her into his arms but feared, in his state, he would crush her.

He couldn't wipe out the events of her past—events in which she was entirely an innocent victim. But he could prevent Mr. Perrin from being able to treat Beth the same way.

His jaw muscles clenched so tightly his teeth hurt at the thought of those sweet children being hurt any more.

He rode hard, slowing only to save his horse. He had three days to get to the nearest judge in Kalispell and convince him to ride back as fast as he could.

If he had thought the hard ride would keep him from thinking, he was sorely mistaken. It gave him far too much time to do nothing else. And never before—even when he'd known he was partly to blame for his mother's death—had his thoughts hurt so profoundly. Several times he leaned over the saddle horn, moaning. He wanted to shout his protests and anger to the sky. And, in fact, he did so several times, startling Brewster into a sideways dance.

He rode through the night. By the next morning, he was exhausted by his emotions and he turned to prayer. He snorted at his foolishness. Shouldn't that have been his first response?

He prayed for the judge to be favorable to his request. He prayed for the safety of Sadie and the children. He prayed even more fervently for Sadie to realize she wasn't ruined. She was a woman with a beautiful spirit worthy of love and tenderness. And he prayed for a chance to tell her that.

He arrived at the judge's house at breakfast time. The man was a friend of Grandfather's and welcomed him immediately.

"What brings you here looking like something the cat drug in?"

"I've ridden through the night to see you."

"Sounds serious, so you better eat before you faint." The judge chuckled. "I know how much food it takes to keep that big body of yours going." The judge was short and stocky and always found the size of the Marshall men amusing, though Logan had never understood why. He led Logan to the kitchen and his wife placed a hot meal before him. When Logan tried to talk, the judge hushed him. "Eat first."

Logan did so quickly, then put down his fork, planted his fists on either side of his plate and looked the judge in the eye. "There's a family that needs your help." Without revealing any information about Sadie, he provided details of the Weiss children.

The judge stroked his chin thoughtfully. "Apart from the marks on the boy's back, this is all supposition."

Logan leaned back, defeat sucking his strength. "Are you saying there's nothing you can do?"

"Not at all. I'm just considering the facts." He pushed to his feet. "There's only one way I can determine the truth and that's to talk to all parties. Are you ready to ride again?"

Logan bolted to his feet, grabbed his hat and hurried after the judge.

If it took riding day and night to save the children, that's what he'd do.

They rode all day. Come dark, he wondered if it was fair to keep the judge riding. The man was not young, but when Logan suggested stopping the judge said, "We'll push on."

Sadie could barely force herself to move, yet she must. Somehow she needed to prepare the children to leave. Somehow she must ignore her own pain.

It had been two days since she'd told Logan her secret. She hadn't seen him since. Perhaps she would never see him again, apart from social occasions he couldn't avoid, though undoubtedly he'd go out of his way to keep his distance.

Pain sliced through her until she couldn't breathe. She'd done what she thought she had to do. Perhaps it was for the best. Better to know his reaction now before she built hopeless dreams. Before she truly began to believe she could outlive her past.

Afraid the children would wonder at her twisted face, she turned to the cupboard where the dishes sat. Five of everything. Enough for her to have pretended for a little while that she could have a family, be accepted. Be loved. She rubbed her eyes with her sleeve and pushed away her pain. Tonight, after the children left, it would be even worse. She would be more alone than ever before.

How would she survive?

She returned to her task of gathering together things to send with the children.

Beth sat on Sammy's bed, Jeannie's arms so tight around Beth's neck that Sadie wondered how the older girl managed to breathe. Sammy crowded next to them.

All three watched her with wide eyes. Their fear palpated throughout the room.

"Do we have to go?" Sammy squeaked.

Sadie cleared her throat and forced the words out. "You heard the sheriff. He sees no reason you shouldn't return to your stepfather." Jesse's voice had been flat, as if he didn't care for the choice he'd made.

"But he ain't our pa," Sammy said.

"I know, but as your stepfather he has the same right."

"You don't understand," Sammy insisted.

"Hush." Beth gave her brother a quelling look.

"He ain't our pa or our step one, either."

Sadie had been arranging the children's things, wanting to send books and pictures and so many other things with them. Her hands stopped. "What did you say?"

"No, Sammy. You know what he'll do."

Sammy scrambled from the bed and faced Sadie across the table. "Don't he have to marry my ma to be my step pa?"

"Are you saying he didn't?"

Sammy nodded.

She sank to the nearest chair. "Why didn't you tell us this before?"

"'Cause." Sammy darted a glance at his sister, then turned back to Sadie, his expression as much pleading as defiant. "He said if we told or tried to leave or run away, he would find us and hurt us." Sammy twitched as if feeling a whip across his back. "He said he'd steal Jeannie and we'd never see her again."

Jeannie sobbed.

Through her tears, Sadie saw the fear in the children's

eyes and a silent plea. They'd risked all to tell her. And she would not disappoint them.

"Stay here. Bar the doors. I have to find the sheriff." She hurried from the house, waiting until Sammy dropped the bar into place before she turned her steps toward the sheriff's office. She threw open the door. Mr. Perrin and Jesse stood inside.

"We were on our way to get the children," Jesse said.

"Time for me to take them home," Mr. Perrin said with a degree of pleasure.

"I think you'd better hear what I have to say first." She was about to close the door behind her when two riders galloped up the street. She paid them little attention until they reined in and jumped down in front of the building where she stood.

Only then did she bring them into focus. Logan and a smaller man.

Why was he here?

Their gazes crashed together. Heat rushed up her neck and burned her cheeks. Did he see her as ruined?

She didn't need to ask. He'd left without a word. She needed no other answer. She jerked away, stepping aside as the pair clattered up the steps.

"I brought the judge," Logan said, shifting his eyes to the sheriff. "He wants to assess the situation for himself."

Mr. Perrin waved the words aside. "The sheriff has already done all that and is satisfied the children belong with me."

In the deep recesses of her brain, Sadie knew she had to pull her thoughts together and tell everyone present what she knew. But seeing Logan had turned her insides to ice, frozen her immobile.

The judge cleared his throat. "I'd like to talk to everyone involved." He made his way to the sheriff's desk, pushed aside Jesse's papers and opened his briefcase. "Mr. Perrin, seeing as you are here, I will begin with you. Please, would you sit?" He indicated the chair opposite him.

Mr. Perrin looked like he would defy the judge, then grunted his displeasure. "This is simply delaying things. I'd like to take the children home and get them settled. They belong with me. I'm their stepfather."

His claim jerked Sadie into action and she sprang forward. "I don't think you are their stepfather."

Mr. Perrin gave her a cold look.

The judge perked up at her words. "What are you saying?"

"The children say he never married their mother. He has no right to take them."

The judge's face grew stern. "Mr. Perrin, do you have any proof of your marriage?"

"Of course not. Who carries a wedding certificate around with them?"

"Can you find it and bring it to me?"

"I have no idea where it is."

Sadie decided the man was either a good liar or believed he could fool them all. She clutched her hands together and prayed God would give the judge needed wisdom.

The judge opened his inkwell and dipped his pen into it. "Please tell me where and when you were married and by whom. That information will enable me to locate the information."

Mr. Perrin stared at the judge and said nothing.

The judge waited. He watched the man across the

desk from him, his look never faltering. After a few tense moments, he put down his pen and folded his hands. "Your inability to provide these details convinces me that you have not married Mrs. Weiss." He closed his book, put his things back in his satchel and pushed to his feet. "I'd like to speak to the children. Logan, Miss?"

Logan sprang into action. "I'm sorry. This is Miss Sadie Young. Sadie, meet Judge Harder." He showed no emotion as he made the introductions, further confirming Sadie's fear that he wanted nothing more to do with her apart from unavoidable situations.

"The children have been living with her," Logan added.

Mr. Perrin jerked to his feet. "I'm taking the children home now."

Although several inches shorter than the other man, the judge faced him with all the authority afforded him by his position. "You are not taking the children anywhere until I say so." He turned his back on the sputtering man. "If you two would be so kind as to take me to them?"

Her nerves so raw she wondered they didn't bleed through her skin, Sadie led the way across the street back to the schoolhouse. Logan walked at her side, making her every movement wooden and jerky.

They stepped into the schoolroom, and Sadie hurried to the adjoining door and knocked. "Children, it's me. You can open the door."

At the sound of the bar being removed, the judge raised his eyebrows.

"They're afraid," Logan explained.

The judge's expression hardened. "I will get to the bottom of this."

Sammy opened the door. His sisters clutched each other and huddled next to the cupboard.

Logan stepped past Sadie. "Children, I'd like you to meet Judge Harder. He's a friend of Grandfather's and he's come to help you."

The judge greeted them all kindly. "I need to talk to you each alone so I can assess the information I have. Who would like to go first?"

"Me," Sammy said.

"Good man." The judge led him into the empty schoolroom.

Logan hurriedly carried in two chairs so they could sit, then returned to the kitchen and closed the door.

His presence crowded Sadie. She wanted to flee outside and hide where no one could see her. For the past four years she had felt dirty. She'd forgotten the feeling for a few weeks but it had returned, stronger for lying dormant. Or perhaps stronger because she'd been free of it for a time. She'd allowed herself to believe her past could be forgotten even though she knew it wasn't possible.

None of them spoke as they waited for Sammy to return. The rumble of the judge's deep voice came to them from the other room, but they couldn't make out any words.

The door opened and Sammy rejoined them, looking pleased with himself despite Beth's warning frown.

"Beth, would you talk to me?" The judge spoke so gently, so kindly that it made Sadie want to cough. Her tears were so close to the surface that a sneeze would have released them.

Beth eyed him. Likely she saw him with the same acceptance she'd accorded Logan's grandfather.

"I have to go alone?" Beth's voice quivered.

"Would you feel better if Miss Young came, too?" Beth nodded.

"Then by all means." He stepped aside to let Sadie and Beth enter the classroom.

Logan followed, carrying another chair to place close to the others.

"Thank you," she murmured, keeping her gaze on the floor, not wanting to see dismissiveness—or worse, so much worse—in his eyes.

They waited until the door clicked closed, then the judge began to talk to Beth.

"Tell me about Mr. Perrin. How did you come to be living with him?"

Beth reached for Sadie's hand and held tight, then began to speak. "My pa got sick and died after Christmas. Mr. Perrin offered to help Ma out. Ma was sick even before Pa died and got worse. First, he chopped wood, then he brought supplies and then he moved right in, saying he could help better if he was there. Ma didn't like it, but she was too weak to do much about it, and maybe she thought he would take care of us after she died."

Beth's voice broke and she had to stop.

A shudder went clear through her to Sadie's hand.

"Take your time," the judge said.

Beth sucked in a deep breath. "Ma died a bit ago." She stopped, struggling with her sorrow.

"When did he marry your ma?" the judge asked.

Beth shook her head. "He didn't. Ma would never marry him."

"I see. And you have no other family?"

Beth pulled her hand from Sadie's and twisted her fingers together. She shook her head.

Sadie recognized Beth's reaction...pulling back, expecting to be pushed aside.

She blinked. Did she do that? Expect others to see her as her mother said? Did they? Would they? It was an unexpected idea that she didn't have time to think about.

"Beth, I need to ask you a few more questions. Is that okay with you?"

"I guess so."

"Did Mr. Perrin threaten to hurt any of you?"

She nodded.

"What did he say?"

"He said he would steal Jeannie." Her whisper was barely audible.

"Did he hurt any of you?"

"He strapped Sammy."

"Why did he do that? Was Sammy misbehaving?"

Beth rolled her head back and forth.

"Would you explain so I can understand?"

Beth's fingers were so tightly twined that the tips were red, the knuckles white. "He beat Sammy because Sammy wouldn't leave me."

"What do you mean?"

Beth stared at the floor and answered in an agonized whisper. "Mr. Perrin liked to touch me. I didn't like it. He wanted Sammy to take Jeannie and go outside so he and I could be alone. Sammy wouldn't do it."

Sadie's mouth had gone so dry her tongue stuck to her teeth.

The judge's voice grated as he again questioned

Beth. "I know you don't want to talk about it, but if that man has done anything to you, he will be punished. Beth, my child, how did he touch you?"

"Here and here." She pointed at her budding breasts and her legs.

"Anything more?"

The question hung in the air between them.

Finally Beth answered. "I told Mama and she said I must never be alone with him. She told Sammy the same thing." She lifted her head. "I never was."

The judge nodded. "Good."

Sadie's lungs released. She understood Beth's message. Mr. Perrin had not hurt her in the way Sadie's father's friend had hurt Sadie. Only for lack of opportunity, but at least the child would never have to think she was ruined.

Sadie's head jerked up. She would never consider Beth as ruined. No, she'd think the child had been hurt. Misused. The only bad person was the man.

Was it the same with her? Were her parents wrong? Was she, Sadie, hurt not ruined? A flicker of hope flashed in her mind.

The judge pushed to his feet. "I believe I have all the information I need." He planted his broad hand on Beth's shoulder. "Child, I can assure you that Mr. Perrin will never again threaten you. You are free of him."

Beth burst into tears and turned into Sadie's arms.

Sadie held her and soothed her. With tear-filled eyes she asked the judge, "Can I promise her she will always have a home with me?"

"I believe that would be a good idea. Shall we tell the others?"

Beth wiped her eyes and smiled so sweetly at Sadie that she had to brush away a few tears of her own.

They returned to the kitchen, but before the judge could say anything, Jeannie stepped forward. "I will talk to you."

"That's a fine idea. Sadie, Beth, would you like to come with me, too?"

So they returned to the other room, and Jeannie perched on a chair across from the judge while Beth and Sadie stood nearby. Sadie hugged Beth.

"I don't like that man," Jeannie said with great conviction. "He isn't nice to us."

The judge nodded solemnly. "I see."

"My mama and papa died and he came." She choked back a sob. "I miss my mama and papa."

"I'm sure you do. Would it help if I tell you that you can live with Miss Young?"

"Really?"

"Really and truly."

Jeannie raced over and wrapped her arms about Sadie's legs. "I'm so happy."

Sadie knelt and hugged the child. "I'm happier."

"Is it true?" Sammy asked.

Sadie looked over her shoulder. She hadn't realized that Sammy and Logan waited there. She opened her arms to Sammy. "It's true."

Sammy ran into her hug.

"Welcome home, all of you."

The judge cleared his throat. "I love happy endings."

"Thank you." Sadie wished she could have one more happy ending, but it wasn't possible.

"Logan," the judge said. "Could you come with me to tell Jesse to run Mr. Perrin out of town?"

Logan hurried after the judge without a backward look. No word of promise to return.

Sadie closed her eyes and let the pain pass. She had the children.

It had to be enough.

Chapter Sixteen

Logan wanted to stay. Wanted to be part of the happy family at the school, but it was more important to make sure Mr. Perrin would never again be a threat to any of them.

He and the judge crossed to the sheriff's office.

Mr. Perrin didn't wait for them to get inside before he spoke. "Guess I can take them home now."

The judge went toe-to-toe with him. "Mr. Perrin, you will never take those children anywhere. And if you so much as show your face in this town, the sheriff is under orders to arrest you and lock you up. If that happens, you will never again walk the streets as a free man. How you have taken advantage of these children is enough to make me want to lock you up right now and throw away the key."

Mr. Perrin grew deathly pale and glanced about as if seeking a means of escape.

The judge continued. "However, I am a firm believer in upholding the law. But be warned, I will tolerate no interference with these children. Do I make myself clear?"

Mr. Perrin nodded.

The judge stepped aside. "Now get out of town." He turned to Jesse. "See that he leaves well and good."

"My pleasure." Jesse donned his hat and followed Mr. Perrin out.

The judge looked Logan up and down. "Well, what are you waiting for?"

"Huh? You want me to go with Jesse?"

"I think Jesse can handle this situation quite fine on his own. But what about Miss Young? Are you going to leave her to manage on her own? A teacher and a mother. Sounds like a big load to me. I expect she could use a hand."

Logan leaned back on his heels and stared at the man.

"Logan, do I need to spell it out for you. Seems to me you both care about the youngsters. I thought you might care about each other, as well. Am I mistaken?"

"You're an interfering old man. Just like my grandfather."

"I know, but aren't you grateful?"

Logan laughed. "Surely you don't expect me to admit it."

The judge chuckled. "No need. Now I'm going to leave you to work out things with that pretty young schoolteacher while I go to visit your grandfather." He left the sheriff's office and rode away.

Logan's chest slowly relaxed, allowing him to breathe deeply for the first time in days. He didn't need the judge to tell him what to do. He had his heart for that. But he had to sort out his feelings first. How was he to convince Sadie that he didn't see her as ruined?

He stared out the window to the schoolhouse. Would

words be enough? What else could he offer? A smile grew in his heart and spread to his face. He had lots more to offer.

As he crossed the street, his smile faltered. Would she accept what he offered or continue to see herself as her parents had taught her to?

He went around to the back entry and knocked, relieved when Sammy opened the door without having to remove the bar. It was good to know they again felt safe. He meant to do everything in his power to see they always were safe and secure.

"It's Logan," Sammy yelled as if everyone couldn't see for themselves.

Logan stood just inside the door, uncertain how to proceed. "Beth, can you take your brother and sister outside so I can talk to Sadie?"

Beth grinned at him. "Come on, you two." She shepherded the children out to the swing.

Logan closed the door. "Sadie, we need to talk. No, what I mean is I have things to say."

She held up a hand. "You don't have to explain. I understand why you want to avoid me. Most people, if they knew the truth about me, would judge me for what happened. Association with me would hurt you and your family. I understand that." She lifted her head and gave him a determined look. "I ask only that you keep my secret. The children deserve that, if nothing else."

He closed the distance between them. He had only to lift a hand to touch her, but he didn't; nor would he until he made himself clear.

"Sadie, I will not reveal your secret. Yes, there are those who would judge you, but they would be wrong.

I don't blame you any more than I blame the children for what Mr. Perrin is."

She watched him, her eyes guarded so he couldn't gauge her reaction.

"Sadie, I regret that your parents turned against you. They were wrong. They should have stood by you and protected you. I will do that, if you let me."

She seemed uncertain of his meaning.

"Sadie, I am sorry for what happened to you, but I in no way blame you."

Tears pooled in her eyes.

He pulled her to his chest.

She clutched at his shirtfront as sob after sob shook her body. He rubbed her back and waited for the emotion to pass, recognizing it as long overdue. Someone should have held and comforted her four years ago. Someone should have assured her she was blameless. He planned to spend the rest of his life doing that if she would let him.

Her sobs lessened and ended except for a shudder or two.

He waited until she rested quietly in his arms. Then he leaned back and tipped her head up so he could see her face. He grabbed the nearby towel and gently wiped her cheeks dry.

"I must be a mess," she protested.

"You're beautiful. Both inside and out." He thrilled to see the pink in her cheeks, and stepped back and took her hands. "Sadie Young, I love you with all my heart. I want to spend the rest of my life with you. Will you marry me?"

He chuckled as her expression went from surprise to uncertainty to disbelieving joy.

"You mean it?" she asked.

"With everything I am and have." He pulled her close, her face tipped up to his. He wanted nothing more than to kiss her, but he must know her answer first, though he thought he could guess it from the gleam in her eyes. Still, he needed the words. "Sadie, say you love me. Say you will marry me."

"Logan Marshall, yes, I will marry you. I love you so much I can hardly keep it in."

He tightened his arms about her and lowered his head. He claimed her lips, breathed in her scent, reveled in her love as her arms tightened about him, and she returned his kiss, silently promising him everything he needed and wanted.

Their kiss ended and she snuggled into his arms.

"Sadie, I want you and the children to come to the ranch for supper so we can share our good news."

She jerked back. "Are you sure?"

He met her gaze with a scolding one of his own, pleased when she looked repentant.

"Sorry, some habits will take time to overcome. We'd be pleased to go to the ranch with you."

"Good." He kissed her again. "Let's tell the children now."

They called them in. Logan kept his arm about Sadie. "Sadie and I love each other and plan to get married."

Beth looked from one to the other, uncertainty clouding her eyes. "That's nice."

He laughed. "It's more than nice. It's wonderful."

"And we are all going to be one happy family," Sadie added.

"You mean we won't have to leave?" Beth asked, holding tightly to her younger brother and sister.

Logan and Sadie reached for the children at the same time. "You will always have a home with us." The children went into their open arms and they hugged and kissed each of them.

Sadie and Logan smiled at each other across the children, then leaned forward and kissed.

"A family of our own," he murmured.

"What I've always wanted," she answered.

Epilogue

Sadie taught the remaining weeks of school. A portion of her heart would miss this job. Other people's children had helped fill an aching loneliness in her heart. But now she had children of her own and wanted to devote her time to them.

Logan finished the schoolhouse just as the school term ended. Sadie regretted she would never teach in it, but it was perfect for the students of the new teacher the town would hire.

Sadie and Logan had decided to live in town for the time being though they spoke often of moving to the ranch.

But today, none of that mattered. Today Sadie would marry Logan. They would become husband and wife and mother and father on the same day. She looked at the two girls, her heart overflowing with joy.

Sadie tucked in a curl on Jeannie's head. She looked at Beth, who glowed with happiness. The older girl had blossomed in the last few weeks.

"You look beautiful," Beth said, touching the pale pink silk fabric of Sadie's wedding gown.

It still felt a little strange to Sadie to wear bright and cheerful clothing rather than her plain dark skirt and white shirtwaist. Strange and freeing. She admired the dark pink dresses the girls wore. Both girls had their hair curled up.

"You're both beautiful, too," she said.

"Today we really become a family." Beth scrubbed her lips together. "Mama and Papa would be so happy."

"No happier than Logan and I."

Kate and Isabelle entered the living quarters of the school together. "Is everyone ready?" Kate asked. Dawson peeked in. "Is it safe for me to come?"

Sadie waved them all in. "Is Logan ready?"

"Champing at the bit." Dawson laughed. "I know the feeling." He bestowed an adoring smile on his wife and Isabelle blushed.

The organ music began and the wedding party lined up at the door. Isabelle went first, then Kate, and then Beth and Jeannie hand in hand.

Dawson crooked his arm toward Sadie and she took it as they stepped into the finished classroom. There had been lots of discussion and advice about when and where she and Logan would marry, but they decided to marry in the school.

"A great way to officially open it, don't you think?" Logan asked.

"I love the idea." After all, most of their courting had been done there.

She looked about the crowd. Many townspeople and all the Marshalls crowded into the room. Sadie had never thought to feel the acceptance she'd found here. Sammy stood between Logan and Conner. Sheriff Jesse beside Conner.

Finally she brought her gaze to Logan. Tall and blond, wearing a white shirt and black suit jacket. Handsome beyond a woman's dreams and—more than that—gentle and good and kind. She missed a step.

Dawson held her firmly. "Are you okay?" he whispered.

"More than okay," she whispered back. "Wonderful."

They reached the front and she took Logan's hand. Preacher Hugh led them in exchanging their vows, then had them sign the register.

Judge Harder took the preacher's place and had them sign further documents. He blotted the ink and folded the papers. "This makes you officially the parents of three children."

Sadie smiled at the children, who all knew what was happening. They smiled back.

Logan put the papers in his suit coat and signaled the children to join them.

Preacher Hugh spoke. "Friends and neighbors, let me introduce Mr. and Mrs. Logan Marshall and their children, Beth, Sammy and Jeannie."

Amid clapping and cheering and tossed rice, they made their way outside.

Sadie hugged Logan and gave him a kiss. She hugged each of the children. She couldn't stop hugging. They were a family. Bound together by love and trust. "I love you all so much," she said.

"You're now our mama and papa, aren't you?" Jeannie asked.

"Yes, we are but you don't have to call us that," she assured the children. She understood that they would never forget their own parents.

"Can we?" Sammy asked.

"If you like."

"Good."

"I love you, Mama. I love you, Papa," Jeannie said. Sammy said the same.

But when Beth did, Sadie couldn't stop the happy tears from running down her face.

Logan hugged each of them. "I love you, too."

And if people wondered at the tears on everyone's faces, Sadie didn't care. One thing she had learned was it didn't matter all that much what other people thought. All she cared about was what Logan and the children thought.

They were her family now and her heart filled with joy.

* * * * *

Dear Reader,

I once had someone look about at all the happy people surrounding him and comment that they must surely not have the same degree of sadness, problems and disappointments that his life had. But it isn't so. Everyone has their share of problems and pain. It might be the death of a loved one or a crippling injury. In Sadie and Logan's story, there are a number of hurtful, damaging events to deal with. I like to think they faced these things with honor, courage and dignity. I like to think they found God's grace to be sufficient. I pray the same for those of you who have dreadful things to deal with.

You can learn more about my upcoming books and how to contact me at www.lindaford.org. I love to hear from my readers.

Blessings,

Linda Ford

REQUEST YOUR FREE BOOKS!

2 FREE INSPIRATIONAL NOVELS
PLUS 2 *FREE* MYSTERY GIFTS

Love Inspired HISTORICAL

LIH15

Gatlinburg, Tennessee
July 1887

As a holiday, Independence Day left a lot to be desired. Independence was a dream Caroline Turner wasn't likely to ever attain.

The fireworks' blue-green light flickered over the sea of faces, followed by red, white and gold. She schooled her features and made her way along the edge of the field to where the musicians were playing patriotic tunes.

"Caroline, we're running low on lemonade."

"Then make more," she snapped at eighteen-year-old Wanda Smith.

"We've misplaced the lemon crates."

At the distress in the younger girl's countenance, Caroline relented. "Fine. I'll look for them. You may return to your station."

It took her a quarter of an hour to locate the missing lemons. By then, the last of the fireworks had been shot off and attendees were ready for more food and drink.

The celebration was far from over, yet she wished she could return home to her bedroom and solitude.

A trio of young women approached and engaged her in conversation. As usual, they wanted to know about her outfit, whether she'd had it made by a local seamstress or her mother had had it shipped from New York. Before they'd exhausted their talk of fashion, a stranger inserted himself into their group.

"Excuse me."

Caroline didn't recognize the hulking figure. Well over six feet tall, he was as broad and solid as an oak tree and looked as if he hadn't seen civilization in months. He was dressed in common clothing, and his shirt and pants were clean but wrinkled. Dirt caked the heels of his sturdy brown boots. His thick reddish-brown hair was tied back with a strip of leather. While he appeared to have a strong facial structure, his mustache and beard obscured the lower half of his face. His mouth was wide and generous. Sparkling blue eyes assessed her.

"Would you care to dance?" He spoke in a rolling brogue that identified him as a foreigner.

Don't miss
WED BY NECESSITY by Karen Kirst,
available wherever Love Inspired® Historical books
and ebooks are sold.

www.LoveInspired.com

Wyatt glanced at Carolina, but she wouldn't meet his eyes.

Was she feeling guilty over all Matty's firsts that she'd denied Wyatt? First breath, first word, the first step Matty took?

He couldn't say he felt sorry for her. She should be feeling guilty. She'd made the decision to walk away. She'd created these consequences for herself, and for Wyatt, and most of all, for Matty.

But today wasn't a day for anger. Today was about spending time with his son.

"What do you say, little man?" he asked, scooping Matty into his arms and leading Carolina to his truck. "Do you want to play ball?"

Not knowing what Matty would like, he'd pretty much loaded up every kind of sports ball imaginable—a football, a baseball, a soccer ball and a basketball.

Carolina flashed him half a smile and shrugged apologetically. "I'm afraid I don't know much about these games beyond being able to identify which ball goes with which sport."

"That's what Matty's got a dad for."

He didn't really think about what he was saying until the words had already left his lips.

Their gazes met and locked. She was silently challenging him, but he didn't know about what. Still, he kept his gaze firmly on hers. His words might not have been premeditated, but that didn't make them any less true. He was sorry if he'd hurt her feelings, though. He wanted to keep things friendly between them.

"There's plenty of room on the green for three. What do you say? Do you want to play soccer with us?"

Shock registered in her face, but it was no more than what he was feeling. This was all so new. Untested waters.

Somehow, they had to work things out, but kicking a ball around together at the park?

Why, that almost felt as if they were a family.

And although in a sense that was technically true, Wyatt didn't even want to go down that road.

He had every intention of being the best father he could to Matty. And in so doing, he would establish some sort of a working relationship with Carolina, some way they could both be comfortable without it getting awkward. He just couldn't bring himself to think about that right now.

Or maybe he just didn't want to.

Don't miss
THE DOCTOR'S TEXAS BABY
by Deb Kastner, available February 2017
wherever Love Inspired® books and ebooks are sold.

www.LoveInspired.com